Desert Kill

Also by Philip Gerard

NOVELS

Hatteras Light
Cape Fear Rising

NONFICTION

Brilliant Passage

Desert Kill

Philip Gerard

A NOVEL

WILLIAM MORROW AND COMPANY, INC.
NEW YORK

It is the policy of William Morrow and Company, Inc., and its imprints and affiliates, recognizing the importance of preserving what has been written, to print the books we publish on acid-free paper, and we exert our best efforts to that end.

Library of Congress Cataloging-in-Publication Data

Gerard, Philip.
    Desert kill / by Philip Gerard.
        p.   cm.
    ISBN 0-688-12641-3
    1. Serial murders—Arizona—Fiction.   I. Title.
PS3557.E635D47   1994
813′.54—dc20   93-42554
                                                        CIP

Printed in the United States of America

First Edition

1 2 3 4 5 6 7 8 9 10

BOOK DESIGN BY CLAIRE NAYLON VACCARO

FOR RICHARD SHELTON,
WHO TAUGHT ME TO LOVE THE DESERT

*... the confused mind
may substitute, by
some terrible alchemy,
cruelty for love.*

—LOREN EISELEY
"The Real Secret of
Piltdown"

Day One

"Take a ride with me, nephew," Detective Paul Pope said, leaning against the doorjamb of the seminar room.

"Right now?" Professor Roy Pope had watched his students file out and was now gathering up his papers. "Is something wrong? Is Eileen okay?"

"She's fine. But it's something that can't wait."

Roy nodded—he was used to doing what his uncle told him. But he hadn't seen Paul in weeks. He'd missed Roy and Eileen's third-anniversary barbecue the previous Saturday without even a phone call. Now here he was at the university—he'd never come to see Roy on campus before. And he had that no-nonsense tone to his voice. Something was wrong. Roy stuffed his papers into a leather book bag. "Let me cancel my office hours."

They walked down the hall to Roy's office, where the professor dropped off the book bag and tacked a hastily scrawled note to his door. They took the outdoor concrete staircase at the end of the corridor. The sere desert breeze was a relief from the over-refrigerated building. It was midmorning, April, but the temperature was already above a hundred degrees. Roy could feel the heat through the soles of his desert boots. Paul's white Thunderbird was parked at the curb across the avenue, on College Street.

Lieutenant Paul Pope was chief of the homicide bureau, Arizona Department of Public Safety. Never wore a uniform except at police funerals. Drove his own T-bird, in which he had installed a shortwave radio. "I need a car has room for my belly," he always said. He wore light-blue slacks and a gray golf shirt and a two-inch .38 clipped to his belt.

Paul cranked the air conditioning to high and in a few minutes they were on the freeway and had crossed the dry Salt River bed into Phoenix proper. Twenty minutes more in traffic and Paul swung the car onto Grand Avenue, an industrial corridor that cut slantwise across the metropolitan area, and followed the railroad tracks for a dozen long blocks. The traffic was a jam of flatbed tractor-trailers and material haulers grinding gears across complicated intersections.

Paul drove without talking.

Roy aimed the air conditioner vent so that it blew onto his face and neck. "You're going to tell me what this is all about sooner or later," Roy said, looking out the window.

"Oh, I imagine so." Paul lit a Pall Mall off the dashboard lighter and smoked it hard, holding it tight in his lips. Sixty-two years old, his crew cut gone gray. He'd threatened to retire from the cops twice already, but he'd always come back. He was entitled to a disability pension for a beating he'd taken fifteen years earlier, but he'd talked the department out of it. Now in three more years he'd get his gold watch whether he wanted it or not.

Paul smoked a minute, slowed the car, and turned into a factory yard. "Now pay attention here. I'm going to show you a body. You're going to have to look at it. Can you do that?"

Roy sat up straight. "Me? Why?"

"Son, there's only one reason anybody ever asks you to look at a body. Can you do it?"

"Sure, I can do that." Roy's throat turned sour.

Behind the whitewashed cinderblock walls of the factory, along the railroad tracks, teams of uniformed police were searching an area staked out in a carefully laid grid. On a second track was parked a string of Union Pacific boxcars, their doors open. The coroner's wagon was backed up to the tracks. A TV-news action-cam was already rolling tape. Paul and Roy got out and walked past the news crew, ignoring the shouted questions. Then Roy saw the body, covered by a blanket, lying across the tracks. Two men were bent over the body, one with a camera—the police photographer, Frank Stein. The other cops called him "Frankenstein" because he seemed to get such a kick out of his macabre work.

"Got what you need, Frank?"

"A couple beauties. Take a look later." He winked.

The detective without the camera, Wade Billings, lifted the blanket and Roy examined the face. Bruised and dirty. Brown eyes, open. Delicate nose. Skin white as a fishbelly. Hair dark and long and matted. The body was dressed in a cutaway sequined cowgirl outfit.

The head was nearly severed from the slender neck.

The hands were black.

"Know her?"

Roy stared. He had seen that outfit before, a club downtown where one of his students worked. He felt a cold stab in his stomach. He took a deep breath.

"Working clothes," Paul said. "The Club Rodeo on Van Buren. Her handbag was with the body."

Still Roy said nothing. He shifted from foot to foot, as if the ground were too hot. With one hand he brushed lank brown hair out of his eyes.

A uniformed officer approached Paul and handed him a book in a plastic bag. Roy recognized it. "The anthology of short stories? How—"

Paul unsealed the bag and, using the end of a ballpoint pen, flipped open the book to the flyleaf. "Her name," he said quietly. "Cynthia Callison. Your name is in here, too."

Roy did not speak and he could not take his eyes off the body, the cuts, the black hands.

"Must be rough, I know, one of your own students. Just say the word—we can't find any family. We need an eyewitness I.D. for the report."

Roy turned to Paul. "It's not her."

The TV crew tried to shove in closer, but a squad of uniforms moved it back. Another TV news van was already setting up.

"What? Come on, I know it's a shock . . ."

"It's not Cindy Callison."

"Okay." Paul exhaled. "Whatever you say. Wade, Frank? Let's get her out of this sun."

Roy felt his breakfast pushing at the back of his throat: the girl had been cut in half at the waist. Her torso, bloused in a gold lamé halter under a white vinyl vest, lay on the roadbed. Between the ties, her bare legs twisted out of a white vinyl skirt. One white boot had come off and a crushed white hat lay nearby. There was little blood. He stood with his hands on his knees, expecting to vomit, but the nausea passed. He breathed, consciously, counting off seconds. Finally he said, "Run over by a train?"

Paul lit up another Pall Mall as the coroner's people taped paper bags over her hands, then lifted the two portions of the body onto the stretcher. As they did so, the head came loose and rolled off. One of them retrieved it; they lifted the three parts of the body into the wagon and drove off. "Nope, don't think so. Not enough blood. Too neat. Happened somewheres else."

Roy struggled to control his breathing. Of all of his students, why did it have to be Cindy Callison who was mixed up in this?

"Plus," Paul went on with professional detachment, "I checked the schedule with the yard boss downtown. Nothing's been through on this track since five-twenty-two last night, a switcher engine. And she wasn't here then. They're guessing she was dumped this morning."

Roy felt his ears buzzing. The odor of creosote and oil stifled him—he could not draw a clear breath. The heat was overpowering. "Can we go somewhere else and do this?"

Paul nodded. "Of course. I was forgetting myself."

Again they ran the media gauntlet. Paul held up a hand and ducked his head as if to ward off blows. If the TV people were on to it this fast, it was going to be hard to get any peace. To work a case right, you needed a little quiet space to think, to figure. They got back in the T-bird and headed downtown. "I'll be wanting a statement from you, you understand."

"Why? It's not her."

"Well it sure as hell is somebody, and she's wearing the Callison girl's clothes."

"There must be other—"

"She never showed up for work last night. So says the bartender at the Club Rodeo."

"Jesus."

Paul stubbed out his Pall Mall in the overflowing ashtray and coughed. He was smoking way too much these days. The job. "I wanted you to hear it from me first. It's a hell of a thing to find out on the six o'clock news."

"But that doesn't necessarily mean—"

"Roy. Think about it."

Roy felt a fluttering in his chest. "You mean, he's got her."

Paul nodded to the windshield. "May as well face it. You saw the girl on the tracks."

"Just say it, Uncle Paul."

"We have to figure she's no longer among the living."

Roy got control over his voice. "You figure whatever the hell you want."

"If there's something you want to tell me," Paul said quietly, and waited.

Roy stared at the traffic. There were so goddamned many cars in this city. You never saw anybody on foot, except back across the river in Tempe at the university. He almost brought himself to speak, but Paul was already talking again.

"You can help me here. We'll pull the Callison girl's driver's license picture out of the file, but the faster we get the description on the radio, the better the chances."

"Five foot six or seven, tanned. Dark eyes, brown, I think. Black hair, she wore it long." Roy saw her in his mind's eye standing in the doorway of his office, hip cocked, sassy, comfortable with her body, like a woman about to enter a bedroom.

Paul scribbled it all down in a notebook. "That's it? Was she good-looking?"

"Sure—she's pretty."

"A little, or a lot? Come on—help me out here."

"She was gorgeous. Is. Like a model." He was thinking about the clean definition of her face, the delicate high cheekbones. The way her right eye squinted a little when she laughed.

"Lots of makeup?"

"No, not like that." He pictured her two days earlier, the last day he'd seen her in class. "Very natural. Very clean."

"Any disfigurements, any scars?"

"Now how the hell would I know that?"

Paul let it be for a while. Then he said, "She was taking only one course, yours. I checked." He stared at Roy a second as if waiting for him to admit something.

"Oh, I get it. What do you want me to say?"

"Whatever needs to be said here. This is a murder investigation. Your private life has suddenly become my business."

"Look, Uncle Paul—Eileen and I are doing just great." He and his wife were having their problems, but they had been seeing a counselor. He had nothing to do with this. He loved his wife.

"Fine. No need to get your back up. I had to ask."

"Not all us professors sleep with our students."

"Glad to hear it. Then you can help me. I'm clueless as to the habits of university coeds." Paul had married a coed, Linda. His first and only love. How many years ago? He stopped himself from thinking about it. No use to dwell on that now—the way she died had nearly destroyed him. He'd been all these years getting over it.

"They don't call them coeds anymore." Roy was no longer angry. Paul had always been his favorite uncle. He was angry at himself. Eventually, he knew, he'd tell Paul everything.

"The registrar gave us a class list, but I want faces."

"Tell me when. I'll line them up."

"Next class meeting. We'll see who's absent. Somebody knows something—that's the first rule."

"I hardly knew her," Roy said. Which was strictly true. The first time Roy had seen her out of class had been in the parking lot on campus, weeks ago, after the seminar. She wore her street clothes, but he could tell she was going to work. She had that look of purpose, of time running out. He stood by his Jeep and watched her fumble with her car key. She had trouble with the lock—he almost started over to give her a hand.

Instead, he just watched. Her back was to him. Her sleek black hair fell softly across the back of a cream silk blouse. As she leaned over to unlock the car, the weight of her breasts pushed out the blouse. She wore loose-fitting stone-washed jeans, all the more enticing because of the drape of denim between her flexed buttocks and her calves.

He and Eileen had been having trouble, and seeing Cindy like that he had an impulse to step quietly behind her, reach around and cup her breasts, then draw her warm and lovely body into his own. A stupid, dangerous fantasy. He knew that. Yet he looked hard and for as long as he could. It took her forever to open the car door. He watched her step in with one elegant leg, then the other. What would it be like to sit beside her, to stroke that soft denim, the silk over her breasts, to feel her move under his hands? He was feeling horny and reckless, unconnected to anything else.

Just before she drove off, she happened to turn his way and, recognizing him, waved. He lifted a hand in reply.

"Did she hang around campus much?"

"She was what we call a 'nontraditional' student—older than usual, part-time. You know." Roy's throat felt scratchy and raw.

"Twenty-eight, single."

"Right."

They were into the stop-and-go of downtown traffic. The heat radiated off the asphalt in waves. Outside the rolled-up windows of the big car, the motors and horns seemed far away. "Ever see her at the club?"

"What are you trying to say?" He'd gone there, but it had no bearing on anything. It couldn't. Paul would misunderstand for sure. He'd have to figure out how to tell him about it.

"Don't lie to your uncle, Roy."

Roy stared out the window, remembering how she had looked the second time he saw her in the parking lot. He'd finished late and was walking to his car when he spotted her. She turned away suddenly, and Roy felt as if he'd caught her at something naughty. "Once I saw her wearing the boots and all—going to work, I guess. I never went to the club." He realized he'd just told his first out-and-out lie.

Paul nodded, giving nothing away. You never knew what was in his mind while he listened. That's what made him a good cop.

"She was an A student, hardly ever missed class. She even came by the office last week."

"What did you talk about?"

"Class work. It was only a couple of minutes."

Paul nodded. "Good. Start remembering stuff like that."

Roy was still shook up from what he'd seen. "What were the bags for?"

"Bags?"

"On the hands. Paper bags."

"Oh, trace evidence. Blood or skin under the fingernails, soil on the palms, like that. Paper doesn't screw up the chemistry like plastic does. Maybe we'll get lucky and find out who the poor girl was. The fingerprints were burned off."

Roy tried to take it all in. "What you said about the train. You're sure?"

"Right. Some goddamned lunatic cut the poor girl in half himself."

After he gave a brief official statement, Roy walked with Paul to the back door of the stationhouse. The place was a mob scene of cops and reporters. The hot TV lights burned every shabby corner of the briefing room. To Roy it looked like an overexposure, a surreal version of a police station. Paul pushed his way through into the parking garage. "Going to be a noisy investigation," he said shaking his head. To Paul, every distraction was "noise." He hated noise.

A wiry detective appeared at Paul's elbow. "Gino can give you a lift back," Paul said. "He's going that way. I've got to start the process here."

"Fine," Roy said. The detective looked bored. Roy had seen him around the cop shop now and again on visits to Paul. Gino was in his mid-thirties but looked younger. Dark but beardless, wearing a lightweight suit without a tie. He always seemed pulled together, unlike Wade Billings and the other sloppy detectives.

"Hope it's no trouble," Roy said to Gino.

"No prob. Get me out of this madhouse."

Paul and Roy waited until Gino brought his unmarked blue Ford around. "Stick close," Paul said. "If she's alive, we'll find her."

"Right."

Paul looked at him steadily out of his gray eyes. "This hasn't hit you yet, so take it easy. If you need to call, call."

"Right."

"Thattaboy." Paul squeezed his shoulder like he used to do when Roy was a kid. "And Roy? Always tell your Uncle Paul the truth." He slapped him on the back, a little too hard.

Paul Pope lived in an adobe ranch house way out west of town. He had built the house himself—it took him four years. For the first year he lived in an old Airstream trailer. Once he had walls and a roof in place, the trailer became home to Esmeralda, a Mexican woman who appeared one day to keep his house and fix his meals. Paul had known her in the old days, but their connection was vague and he never talked about it with Roy.

Roy reloaded. They were shooting cans and bottles off a fence rail. It was how Paul relaxed, but it made Roy more anxious. What were they doing here, instead of out searching for Cindy Callison? Paul was a man of action—Roy had always envied him that. Yet here they were.

"You can't always stare a thing down," Paul said. "Sometimes you have to look away from it for a spell to see it clear."

Roy still believed they ought to be out doing something. Action—he wanted action. But Paul was the pro. Paul was in charge of this.

Paul at first emptied several loads from his service revolver, then switched to his favorite piece—an old Colt Army .45, the kind you had to cock with your thumb. He fired six times, not hurrying, and popped off six Tecate cans.

Roy fired an old .38 police special Paul had given him as a present while he was still in college. Roy kept it at Paul's. He fired two-handed, the way Paul had taught him years ago. "Every man ought to know how to handle firearms," Paul had said. He believed it took the silly romance out of guns. Paul fired the long-barreled Colt with one loose hand.

"We don't know who she is yet," Paul said, flicking out the empty shells one by one. "The dead girl. They'll keep running it on the news for us."

"She's dead. I don't see the point now."

"I was hoping we could connect her to the Callison girl. Who lived alone. Who was seen by exactly nobody after she left your class. Who never made it to work. Who never even went back to her apartment."

"She's alive, I know it. We should be out there looking."

"Two dozen good men are out looking. They're the legs. We're the head." Blam, blam, blam. "Won't do any good to be running willy-nilly all over Creation."

Paul's portable phone chirruped. He talked into it for a few minutes, giving orders. He made two more calls—one of them a return call to the FBI, agent named Carter. Pain in the ass, him and his partner Hobbes. They wanted in on the kidnapping angle, but it was still Paul's case. He would cooperate, but he wasn't about to give it up to the bureaucrats. He went back to shooting, relaxing hard.

Back at the house they sat in sun-faded rattan chairs on the long porch under the mesquite ramada, and Esmeralda served them scotch on the rocks in heavy tumblers. The porch faced west and they could watch the sun pinking the cloudless sky low over the White Tanks—named for White's Tank, the only watering stop on the old stage road to Carefree. Zack the dog, a white giant of mixed malamute and shepherd blood, sprawled across the warm stone floor looking like he'd been shot running. Roy's shirt was sweated through and cooling him now by evaporation. He was long in the habit of wearing tropical tans in this heat.

When he'd first joined the faculty last year, his colleagues at the university used to rib him about dressing like Ernest Hemingway. Roy was lankier than Hemingway, though. Mildly handsome—not as rugged-looking as Uncle Paul. His wife Eileen said he had thoughtful eyes, whatever that meant.

"Some of these days I'm gonna put me a little corral down there, couple of good roans. Then you and me can ride the hills at sundown."

Roy nodded, imagining what it would be like to ride off into that raddled golden light, feeling it wash over his shoulders and bathe his hot face. It would be soft, coming from far off, carrying the sweet scent of tomorrow's weather. He wanted to be out from under this thing.

Esmeralda was dark, pretty, and painfully shy. She often lingered at Paul's elbow like a daughter, waiting, it seemed to Roy, for permission. For what? She had been around since before Roy went off to graduate school in California, but he could swear she was even now barely out of her teens. It was the smooth skin, he told himself, the coppery pigment that kept the sun from ruining her complexion. Eileen had once calculated that Esmeralda was pushing forty. Amazing, Roy thought. In this dry climate.

Paul never said much about her. Roy did know that for years now Esmeralda had entertained only one suitor, Zapata, named after the revolutionary hero. Zapata traveled extensively in a primer-gray Pontiac and was gone for weeks on end. Roy had heard a rumor Zapata was a *coyote* who smuggled illegals across the border. When he asked his uncle about it, Paul only said, "Live and let live." Zapata's Pontiac was parked outside her trailer now.

Roy's arms and face were flushed with sunburn. He sipped the scotch and felt it go to his head. He had always felt at peace here, from the first time he ever set foot on the place.

Not today, though. Today he could not get Cindy Callison off his mind. She was out there, somewhere, in danger, while he and Paul sat drinking.

He'd watched her watching him in seminar that last afternoon when she disappeared. Could it have been only three days ago? She kept her hands beautifully manicured, and when she raised her hand to ask a question, even across the table, the skin glowed. She never blinked her eyes but looked straight at him. When she was answering a question, she would look at the ceiling, focusing her mind. Before class that day, she came to his office. She wanted to talk, but he didn't know what to say. He should have said something.

"So tell me about this book you're writing, professor," Paul said. "Get our minds off this thing."

"Narrative closure," Roy said. He couldn't quite muster his seminar voice. He loved teaching, but he often heard a hollowness in his voice when he got wound up and started lecturing—as if he were a salesman. For a few months during college, he'd actually sold vacuum cleaners door-to-door, but he was no good at it. He wondered if he were any better at teaching. The book seemed trivial now. "You wouldn't understand."

"Don't be such a snob—try me."

"Stories," Roy said. "How they end. Why so many of them end falsely. Why people crave a happy ending, you know."

"Like the movies."

"Right. But real stories tend to finish badly. No happily ever after."

Paul shook his head. Roy wondered if he was thinking of Linda. "Pretty bleak, nephew. You sure the world needs your point of view?"

"You asked." Roy sipped his drink. Whenever he talked about intellectual stuff with Paul, he felt like a naive kid, like Paul was just humoring him. Try as he might, he could never manage to make the life he'd chosen sound important or exciting—not compared to Paul's world, in which every day was a matter of life and death. This time, somehow, the drama had intersected both their lives. "Was that the coroner on the phone earlier?"

Paul nodded. "The body was stripped after death. He cut her apart with two, three strokes at most."

"An axe?"

"A knife. Machete, maybe. Then washed her. Then dressed her up as Cindy Callison."

"Why?"

Paul rubbed his eyes. He had been at the office since before sunup. If he got in early enough, there was just the police reporter from the newspaper and no TV cameras. "There was a case in Cleveland, in the thirties. The Mad Butcher, they called him. The Torso Killer. Used to switch clothes, too. Hacked up a dozen people for sure, maybe as many as forty. Same style."

"Jesus. How'd they catch him?"

"Never did. Never figured out just what he was trying to prove." Action without motive always troubled Paul—he liked to know what he was up against. The *why*. "You want to put that one in your book? Ezzy, more hooch, *por favor*."

Esmeralda returned immediately, though without seeming to hurry. She left the bottle and a bowl of ice on the low table in front of them. Roy saw her dark eyes watching Paul for approval. Her long silken hair fell across her face when she leaned over. She seemed to move without noise or effort, like a ghost of herself projected into air.

"*Gracias*, dear." She backed away and drifted off on another errand.

"That helps a hell of a lot."

"You don't always catch 'em, Roy. That's the second rule."

They were talking about kidnapping. Murder. "I don't want to hear that."

"It's a good town to be a cop in," Paul mused and took a big gulp. "There's a lot of killing in this town."

Roy didn't want to talk about killing. He wanted to talk about the sky folding up over the White Tanks, and the desert noises coming up around the houses. When he was a kid, he used to roam the desert alone. He didn't have many friends. They'd moved around too much, always in the West, following his father's work as a geological surveyor—Phoenix, Boulder, Sante Fe. Even if he'd had a chance to make lots of friends, Roy was temperamentally inclined to spend time by himself. He had learned to look hard at things—the play of light across the hills, the spiraling glide of a vulture above the rimrock.

Eileen always said he lived too much inside himself, he should talk more about what was on his mind. But if you talked about things out loud, you gave up control. As he got drunker, Roy could trick himself so that Cindy Callison seemed farther removed, like it hadn't really happened. She had walked away, and that was that.

"I get the funny feeling that maybe we're coming in on the second reel, you know?" Paul interrupted himself to take another sip. "The chances of finding somebody who kills only once are not good."

"So you hope he kills again? What—"

"Don't put words in my mouth. That's not what I said. But I'll bet you a million bucks he's killed before and we just don't know it yet."

Roy stared off at the mountains, now barely limned by the dying sun. He was thinking of Cindy Callison's visit to his office the day she disappeared. She had missed seminar the previous week and come to apologize. "I'm having some trouble right now," she said, leaning across his desk. "Personal stuff. But I can do the work." Roy had just had a spat with Eileen, he was distracted. She said something else—did it matter now?

"I have this fantasy, a kind of weird sense, whenever we get a murder. That all of them are connected. That every single one of them is linked together somehow. Without the first one there wouldn't be the second, and so forth."

"One person? One perpetrator? Come on."

Paul coughed again and wiped his mouth with a red kerchief. "No, that's not what I mean. One force, maybe. All the killings everywhere in the world are connected. Down through the years, the centuries, all the way back to Cain. Crazy, huh."

Roy looked at his uncle. Just now such a notion didn't seem so crazy. Whenever he came out here in the evening or early morning, away from the city, things did indeed seem all connected. For such a hardheaded cop, Paul had a mystical streak in him that always caught Roy off guard. It was like in that F. Scott Fitzgerald story—in the middle of an ordinary conversation, Paul would just go glimmering.

Zack raised his head and, ears erect, sniffed the air. Esmeralda returned, hurrying. "I would go inside now," she warned. "The dust is coming."

Roy saw no sign of storm, but Paul was already hoisting himself
out of his deep seat and gathering up the botttle and ice. Zack rose
and shook himself off and nuzzled at Paul's thigh. Esmeralda vanished.

Once inside, they fastened the windows and sat in soft leather
chairs and before long a dust storm swept over the house, blowing
away the last light. Zack coiled under the carved mesquite coffee
table. Evening became suddenly night, and the room cooled. Paul lit
two kerosene lamps. "A softer light," he explained. "Your eyes don't
get cut with the edges of things." With the scotch and the warm light
and Paul's deep slow voice filling the cool room, Roy found it hard to
imagine that out there, somewhere, was a man who had taken Cindy
Callison. Out there, the night was not safe.

Roy said, "What kind of a man could do that?" The question
seemed very spooky in this room at this hour, with the blow going on
outside. He wondered where Esmeralda had got to—was she down
the hill at her trailer, drinking alone from a wine bottle greasy with
fingerprints, trying, like them, to soften the hard edges? Probably not.
She seemed like a woman who had come to terms with the desert.

"Not a man," Paul said. "Something else."

"You have a hell of a job. Why in the world you do it."

Paul stared for a while, and Roy let him. "When Linda died, I was
still in law school." He seemed to think about that for a second, then
went on. "I was studying to be a lawyer. How about that." He seemed
astonished himself that it had ever been so.

"Back then, it was still an honorable profession. The law." He
drank. "When Linda died, there was no point. You see?" It was not
a rhetorical question. He waited until Roy nodded definitely. "I found
I could no longer face the great mysteries. I needed, I needed"—he
drank—"a smaller mystery. Concrete. To focus me." He turned his
loose fist in the air, then lit a cigarette and refilled his glass.

Roy watched first one lamp, then the other, wicking up fuel and
air in a golden flame. Here he goes, glimmering, he thought.

"There's something elemental about it, why one person does great violence to another." Paul heard himself sounding as professorial as Roy and smiled.

"You catch lots of bad guys." Roy had newspaper clippings lauding his uncle for solving important murders over the years. Paul had citations, medals, an award from the mayor.

"That's not what I mean. There's some switch, down in the dark part of the soul. Each of us has it. Buried way down, way down." He tapped his chest, his gut. "Deeper than we ever have to go in ordinary life. Nobody, nothing, ever forces most people down that deep. That's my job, to go down there."

The wind rattled the windows, but the flames in the lamps held steady. "Murder is a crime against imagination. Do you understand?"

Roy didn't quite like the way Paul was looking at him. "To catch a murderer, nephew, to solve a murder? You have to commit the whole deed all over again yourself, up here." He tapped his skull. "And in here." He pointed to his heart.

But Roy couldn't imagine it. What kind of a man could ignore her screams, could hack through flesh and bone, then carry it all, forever after, in his memory?

"You know what killed her, the official cause of death?"

Roy shook his head.

"Decapitation."

Day Three

The apartment was dark—Eileen was gone again. Roy had half-expected that she'd still be away. She would do that every so often now, just go away for two or three days to her sister's. Just pack an overnight bag and leave, then call when she arrived at her sister's and tell him they could work it all out when she got back. It was always the same reason, and they never worked it out. They'd get along fine, as if they'd forgotten what happened in California. Then she'd disappear and call him.

"Then come back right now," he'd say. "Let's talk about it now."

"Don't be silly," she'd say back. "I'm already here," as if "here" were Paris and not Scottsdale, scarcely twenty minutes away. She might go on a Tuesday or a Sunday, but she never stayed away more than three nights and always came back slightly subdued but ready to make up. What had she done for all that time away from him?

Whenever she returned, they didn't talk about it. It had been his fault, the thing in California. He had let his anger get the better of him, and then he had made it worse. But that was over. Even she agreed it was over, but somehow they could not quite get past it. And every day he fell deeper in love with her.

He could list all her good features—her shimmering brown hair, her lively eyes, her lovely softness, the way she had of filling a room with herself. But why he loved her was simpler. He couldn't explain it, exactly. The first time he had ever laid eyes on her, sitting at an outdoor table on the Irvine campus, he'd loved her without choice. He was finishing a Ph.D. in English. She was getting a master's in communications. They loved words together.

And here they were, four years later. He was an assistant professor on the tenure track, and Eileen was a free-lance business consultant. And they couldn't talk about it. Cindy Callison was missing, presumed dead, and Eileen was just plain gone. A hell of a night for that. He poured bourbon into a coffee cup, then added ice. Out here he never drank anything without ice. He knew he ought to slow down—he didn't usually drink this hard. But under the circumstances it calmed him.

Eileen was the extrovert of the family—she loved parties, dressing up, entertaining. She loved to meet strangers and ask them about their lives. She had that knack of making anyone she talked to believe that they were the most important person in the room.

Roy preferred to stay at home with his books and papers, the quiet, dreamy life of the mind. For him a big evening's entertainment was renting a classic movie and running it on the VCR. Going out meant going out alone—to hike in the desert, to sail on one of the nearby lakes, to hear a lecture at the university. He wore suntans so he didn't have to fuss with clothes. Habits protected you from having constantly to make choices.

Eileen never nagged him about his drab appearance. She never minded the books piled in odd corners all over the apartment, foolscap markers sticking out raggedly between pages. He loved talking to her in those quiet, secret moments in bed, or over supper, or driving together on a long trip at night. But it hadn't been like that lately. Lately, he was lonely, even when he was with her. He figured it must be worse for her.

Maybe he should get a dog, something big and shaggy like Uncle Paul's Zack, a pal for nights like this. He wanted just to sink his head into something soft and feel a blood warmth.

Roy sat on the couch and laid the revolver next to him. He'd carried it home without paying attention—he'd have to take it back out to Paul's. He didn't like keeping it in the apartment. It belonged out in the desert, not in a quiet university town. He turned on the television to an old gangster movie.

*   *   *

He woke at ten o'clock to a gravelike quiet. The videotaped late news was on, without sound. There was the familiar factory siding and the coroner's wagon and the blanket-covered body of the woman. There was Paul's T-bird pulling up, the two of them getting out. Roy leaning over the body and nodding, dumbly, then backing off and lowering his head to almost retch. The camera zoomed in on him and he watched the anguished expression on his own face. His eyes widened and squinted, his mouth moved without forming words.

The camera cut to the coroner's wagon, back to two men carefully tying paper bags over the dead woman's hands, and then a photo of Cindy Callison was superimposed onto the screen. Her driver's license picture—they must have pulled it out of the file.

They were putting out the word—might as well print it on a milk carton.

They did not show the part when the woman's head rolled off the stretcher.

Roy got up to make himself another drink. That time at his office. Did it matter? Maybe—maybe it was a clue to where she was, how to get her back, how to keep her alive. Unthinking, he carried the gun out to the kitchen with him.

The door swung open. "Jesus, don't shoot!" Eileen said.

They lay in bed with the light on. Roy could not have put into words what he needed. "Must have been awful." Eileen stroked his forehead. "I saw it on the late news and came right back."

"Never seen anything like it."

"If anybody can catch him, Paul will. You know that."

Roy knew the odds: Cindy Callison had probably been dead for days.

"Don't think about her," she said. "Lie still. Put it out of your mind."

"How can I?"

"Hey," she said in a different tone. "She's just your student—right?"

"So she's just my student—isn't that enough?" Roy lay with his head pillowed on her breasts and the air conditioner humming, his arms tight around his wife, his eyes open.

Roy and Eileen were on their second bottle of champagne in the revolving Compass Room at the top of the Phoenix Hyatt. Eileen's idea—she loved restaurants. Among the white linen tablecloths and the glittering crystal, it was hard not to feel cheery. They had begun facing east, toward Scottsdale far across the low drab buildings of the old downtown, then gradually turned southeast, toward Tempe and the Salt River, then southwest, facing the factory district and the railroad, and at last west, Uncle Paul's domain of mountains and wide-open desert.

They watched the silver planes float out of the painted blue en route to Sky Harbor Airport. Hanging in the void like that, the planes always seemed impossible. Tricks of the eye. Both his parents had been killed together in a plane crash in Dallas nine years earlier. Still, he couldn't take his eyes off the planes. They were strangely comforting, suspended far away in the soft sky.

He watched, too, the light traffic far below on the crosshatch of streets fanning out from Central Avenue and Van Buren, the city center. He picked out the railroad, cutting like a suture across town.

When you don't know where to start, Uncle Paul always said, then start somewhere. Cindy Callison was down there, somewhere.

Eileen was wolfing down large portions of eggs Benedict and rattlesnake meat on the side. She ate ravenously. The more exotic the food, the better.

"How you can eat that stuff," Roy said, smiling. He liked being up high.

A new waitress came over to refill their water glasses. Julie Kraus, from the seminar. "Hi, professor. Saw you on the news," she said, filling the glasses deftly. "Pretty horrible, wasn't it?"

"It's a bad time for everybody," Roy said. He really didn't want to get into it—they'd come here to forget it for a while.

Julie shifted from foot to foot, as if she were about to say something. "What is it?" Eileen said. "Sit." She patted the seat of an empty chair.

"Not allowed to sit with customers, Mrs. Pope. But like, I just wanted to talk about it with someone. You know?"

"The detectives talked to you." Roy had lined them up for Paul, as promised, and they'd been no help. Nobody knew Cindy Callison outside of class, nobody had seen where she went afterward.

"She met someone new, that's all I know," Julie said. "She'd left her old boyfriend—he was a creep anyhow. Really fucked up. Sorry."

"Never mind," Eileen said. She drank all of her water, then took Roy's glass. She dipped a napkin into it and dabbed at a spot on her blouse. Roy watched the water darken the sheer fabric above her nipple.

"Did you know her old boyfriend?" Roy knew Paul was looking for him.

"Nope."

"So how do you know he was a creep?"

"She told me. We'd talk, you know."

"I didn't realize you two were friends." Julie had never, to Roy's best recollection, even sat near Cindy Callison. Nor had he ever seen the two talking together before or after class. Was she just trying to get in on the drama?

"We weren't friends, exactly."

"When did she meet this new fellow?"

"I don't know. She told me about him two weeks ago, at Wednesday seminar."

"What did she tell you?"

"He was a nice guy. That's all—that she finally found a nice guy. How about that."

Is that what I am, Roy wondered—a nice guy?

"That's all?"

She nodded and bit her lip. "He was a genius, that's what she called him. A real genius. He was going to make everything all right, you know?"

"You told the detectives?"

Again she nodded.

"You never saw this guy?"

"Nope."

"Not even once? He never picked her up after class?"

"I just feel bad, professor. She's going to end up like the girl on the railroad tracks, I just know it. It's fucked up." Her eyes were brimming and she turned away.

Roy sipped his champagne, but the bubbles went up his nose. He had suddenly lost his appetite and the room was spinning, he could feel the motion. He sipped water and took a deep breath and waved for the check. A third waitress brought it in slow motion and he flipped bills onto the tablecloth to cover it.

"Let's go," he said. He grabbed Eileen's hand and held it all the way down the speedy glass elevator and out onto the baking sidewalk.

"Don't know what got into me," Roy said, standing bent over, his palms on his knees. "All of a sudden I couldn't breathe."

Eileen said, "Maybe you'd better tell me about it."

"Nothing to tell," Roy said.

They crossed the street to the car-park booth—it worked on the honor system—and Eileen put two dollars in an envelope. "I'm not blaming you for anything. But after all I went through," she said, jamming the envelope into the slot, "you'd better tell me."

"Like I said, nothing to tell." He took her hand.

"Right," she said. "Whatever you say."

Good morning, Mr. and Mrs. America and all the ships at sea.

Do you read me?

Here's where I am and here's where all the nasties don't follow, over.

Here's a hole in the fucking world.

Been a busy nut-rocking kind of night, Mouseketeers, but I got the goods. Takes a macho camacho to do what I did, lean and mean with a love bone for a heart.

Copy?

My voice is riding the air, man. I'm shooting it out there to all you red-eyed dudes and dudesses. I'm the badass jock with the permanent wakeup call. I'm the all-night diner and the motorman's friend and the light at the end of the fucking tunnel.

I'm the last thing you see before you fall asleep at night.

I'm eyeing you with the eye and talking you the talk, I'm whispering into your dreams, amigo. I'm the U in fuck.

I'm the one you see out of the corner of your eye. I'm the lights in your rearview mirror, gaining on you. I only come out at night.

Static, bro, white noise, rapping the rap and jamming the jam and squealing at the high hertz.

Stay tuned, amigos.

Day Five, Morning

Roy walked from his office across the street, past the church, the deli, and the Greyhound station, and met Paul in the shimmering parking lot of the athletic complex. Paul said, "That Julie girl said Cindy Callison wrote everything down in her notebook. Never let it out of her sight. Maybe we'll get lucky." They had already searched one locker—Paul had thought of that right away, as soon as Roy had said she used to bring a gym bag to class. Empty. But then the athletics people called and said it was the wrong locker—they got the student numbers mixed up.

Wade Billings stood by with all the paperwork. Stein had his cameras. Gino hefted the bolt cutters. "You ready to do it?"

The campus guard at the locker demanded all sorts of I.D. He wanted driver's licenses and badges and confirmatory phone calls. Finally Paul said, "Stand back, Jethro—we've already danced this tune once."

Gino snapped the lock with the bolt cutters, cleared it from the catch, then opened the door. He stood back. "See for yourself, lieutenant."

There was no notebook.

"Get out of my light," Paul told the campus guard. There was a lavender Danskin leotard looped on the right hook. Black satin athletic shorts hung from the left hook. White Reeboks were neatly placed on the floor, and on top of them soiled black slipper socks. Paul sniffed the Danskin in a gesture that was entirely dignified. "Hasn't been washed lately," he declared. Gino took the Danskin, then slipped it into a plastic bag.

There was a black plastic Sony Walkman with a Smokey Robinson and the Miracles tape inside.

Gino dusted for latent prints and then held open plastic evidence bags into which Paul deposited the broken lock and each separate item of clothing. Both men wore disposable latex gloves. Stein shot pictures of everything, just in case. Billings hooked his thumbs into his belt and rocked on his heels. Roy stood and watched. The campus cop crossed his arms and nodded as they worked. With a penlight, Paul probed every crevice of the locker for clues, even getting down on his knees on the painted concrete floor.

"Bingo," Paul said, and held up a single bright sequin with his tweezers.

"She was here," Gino said. "The outfit was. But when?"

"Canvass the whole complex," Paul said. "You know the drill. Dial up some uniforms. Call me with whatever you get."

Wade Billings rubbed his palms together. "Let me at some spandex bunnies." He and Stein left with Gino.

"I can help," the security guard ventured.

"No, you can't," Paul explained. "Roy, let's take a walk."

Roy carried the evidence bags for Paul as they ascended the stairs into the circular corridor. "Okay. What's missing?" Paul lit a cigarette.

A big woman with a whistle said, "Hey, you can't smoke in here."

Paul coughed and patted the badge clipped to his waistband.

Outside, Roy stood by the trunk of the T-bird, waiting for Paul to open it. "Not in there," Paul said. "Backseat. Let's keep the stuff from melting." They stood in the sun, Roy feeling the heat rise off the asphalt. He leaned against the hot metal fender.

"Let's just say she was here," Roy said.

"She didn't get dressed for work here, or did she?"

"Could have worn either her street clothes or the cowgirl outfit. Carried the other."

"Maybe somebody went through the locker ahead of us."

"Maybe anything." Roy wanted to get into the car, out of the heat.

"She met someone. Maybe she planned it, the party went wrong.

Girl like that, her line of work. Only had two hours between the end of your class and the beginning of her shift."

"Not much time."

Paul shrugged. "Say she works out for an hour. It's a twenty-minute drive to the club. That leaves forty minutes." They'd picked up her car right away—impound had it now. A rusty Datsun with a hundred thousand miles on the odometer. They'd dusted it and vacuumed it and pulled off the rocker panels—nothing but a dead battery.

"Her car was here. She had forty minutes to leave, do whatever it was she did, and get back here. Say thirty-five—she was always early to class. She'd get to work early, too."

"Only she didn't come back, did she. Never punched in."

"What are you asking me for?"

"Go on."

"Two possibilities. One, she left on foot herself, two, she left on foot with someone else. She didn't go far. Mill Avenue."

As he spoke, a string of empty hopper cars clattered by on the tracks behind the lot, headed west. Half an hour, Roy thought, a bad half an hour, and her life was in the hands of a maniac.

Paul said, "Three, she got into somebody's car. Maybe she was picking up some cash on the side?"

"Come on. Not her style."

Paul squinted at him, as if to say, So how come you're all of a sudden an expert on her style? But he said instead, "Four, she got on a bus."

"And left her car?"

"Right. She didn't go anywhere without her clothes. Five, she was carried out dead or unconscious—"

"Somebody'd notice." Would he have? What had he noticed that afternoon, when he'd been too busy feeling sorry for himself? What Cindy Callison had said to him at the office? Her expression when she read the note he passed her at the end of class? Eileen's voice on the telephone?

"A bag of baseball gear? Bats and bases, a canvas sack with all those lumps? Wrestling mats? Team laundry? Don't be such a baby. If you really want to move a body around, you can do it. Who expects to see a corpse being toted around in this Disneyland?"

They drove for a while, Paul gazing straight ahead from behind massive black-framed sunglasses. Roy had no idea where they were going. He'd lived in Phoenix on and off his whole life—when he wasn't in Denver or Rock Springs or Bisbee. His father worked for the big copper outfits. In the old days, when Roy had visited Paul on vacations, Paul would sometimes get a certain look in his eye, vacant and preoccupied. "Let's go for a ride," he'd say, and Roy would eagerly slide into the front seat of whatever big car Paul had. Paul always ran big cars—Buicks, Oldsmobiles, Lincolns. He always had a dog and always ran big cars.

Then he'd drive for hours, winding out the powerful engine on the open desert roads for a hundred miles without saying a word. They might wind up in South Tucson looking for three-alarm Tex-Mex chili, or they might find themselves in a nowhere of bare mountains and bleak horizons scraped clean of people—Quartzite, Ajo, Why.

Paul would sigh like a man conceding an argument and skid the car to a halt in the middle of cactus, sand, and rock. He'd heave himself out of the car and Roy would follow, and Paul would stand there staring off into the distance. At what, Roy never knew.

Sometimes Paul would stride off into the rough country looking for cactus, with Roy tagging along as best he could. Roy recalled the first time, out west of Tucson, how Paul climbed a rugged saddle and found the giant saguaro with its two enormous arms bowed down and around. How Paul ducked under carefully and came up inside the arms and stood there for long minutes, till tears welled in his gray eyes.

Roy tried it after him, but felt nothing special.

"What does it do?" he asked his uncle later, in the car, speeding around blind curves with the dry wind burning past his ear.

A few miles later, Paul said, "There is a peace."

"I didn't feel anything."

"You're too young. You don't require that kind of peace yet."

When Roy pressed him, Paul went wandering: "A saguaro is just a bundle of tubes filled with water . . . standing under the moon . . . soaking up the lightning charge of the sky like . . . like a big battery. And a good one that has those special arms can circle a man who needs it. You can feel it tingle, charge you." Paul's fingers flexed slowly as he said it, and his dreamy eyes held the fast contours of the white road.

Those times were spooky, but Paul would act as if something important had been settled. Those times Roy would feel closer to his uncle than seemed possible any other time.

He felt that closeness now.

"Listen to me," Paul said after a few minutes. "Cino, the captain, Billings, Stein, even the FBI, they think this joker has vamoosed."

"What do you think?"

"They think, Eliot Ness never got his torso killer, so why should we get ours?"

"Hasn't even been a week."

"A week is a long time for a psycho. Maybe he's gone underground. Maybe he just split."

"You think so?" Roy found it hard to control his emotions.

Paul shook his head. "Nah. He'll crawl up out of some hole we're not watching."

"Good," Roy said quietly. "I want you to get him. I want you to find her."

Paul punched him lightly in the shoulder. "You're more like me than your old man would want to admit."

"You didn't like him much." They were headed downtown along Van Buren, a strip of motels, bars, rundown shopping centers, and pawnshops. They passed the Club Rodeo and for a moment Roy panicked, thinking Paul was going to stop and haul him inside to confront the bartender. "This the guy?" Paul would say, and the bartender would answer, "Yeah, that's the creep I seen." But they passed by fast.

"I liked him fine. I even lent him money from time to time."

"I never knew that."

"Add it to your list. No reason he'd brag on it. He just didn't trust me, not altogether." Paul coughed. "Always worried I'd leave you in a cathouse on Revolution Street, kill you with mescal, teach you the bad habits."

"He was a straight arrow."

Paul seemed to be remembering something specific. "He did his share of lone-wolf prowling."

"You got to be kidding. Dear ol' Dad?"

"I ain't saying he was a bad man. He was as good a man as any."

Paul stopped in front of Junior's Pawn & Gun and left the engine running. "Don't go anywhere—you're the weak link in the chain of custody."

In a minute Paul returned to the car with a cardboard box. He opened the lid and lifted out a Colt revolver identical to the one Roy had watched Paul shoot. "Had it repaired?"

Paul was smiling broadly. "Not hardly," he said. "Look at the serial number."

Roy looked. "So?"

"One digit off from mine. See—1898. They're in sequence."

"Some luck."

"Luck, hell. Fate."

They logged in the evidence at the stationhouse and Paul drove Roy home. At the curb, Paul said, "Come visiting one of these days and we'll try her out."

Eileen held the door open for him. "What are you doing home in the middle of the day?"

"That's a hell of a note to walk in the door on."

She pushed back her hair and put a hand on her hip.

"You want to know what we found?"

She bussed him on the cheek. "I want to go out to lunch. Then I want frozen yogurt."

He grinned. She could always do that to him—jar him out of a serious mood with just a look and a quick kiss. Still, at lunch Roy became pensive again. The booths were molded plastic, like in an airport departure lounge. He didn't think often about his parents—Roy was deliberate about when and where he would let himself remember them. Right after the accident, he'd thought of nothing else, dreamed of no one else. He'd wake in panic, in the dark, and know, really know in the cold pit of his stomach, that he would be alone for the rest of his life. He wished he could have seen the bodies, because, failing that, he realized a part of him would never quite believe they were dead.

Only on TV had they seemed really dead.

Identification of the remains had been problematic, mostly based on wedding rings. But could not another couple have worn the same golden bands? Had the same first names? It was illogical and impossible, according to the passenger list, but then again they had originally been scheduled for a different flight. But their cab had a flat and they missed the earlier plane—which arrived safely. Then the plane they were on crashed. What was logical and possible about that?

"Is the club sandwich okay?" Eileen said. "The Reuben is terrif."

Roy nodded and gulped his iced tea.

"I had to get out. You don't take me out anymore. You never take me anywhere." Her voice was playful, making fun of the cliché, but he knew there was some truth in it, too.

"Where do you want to go?"

"It doesn't especially matter—the point is to get out in the world once in a while. You spend all your time with your nose in books. Now you're chasing around with the cops. Either way, I don't get to see you."

Roy said something sweet, but his mind was still brooding on his parents. The cause of the crash, it was determined eight months later, was wind shear. There had been no negligence, it was nobody's fault. No terrorist plot, no bomb, just local bad weather. Turbulence. The airline paid for Roy's doctorate.

A little later Roy and Eileen sat on white patio chairs and ate their frozen yogurt off a round white table. Eileen watched him for a bit, then touched his arm and said, "It's nice being out together. What's bothering you?"

"I'm okay. I just think about them sometimes."

"We could talk about it, if you want."

"Too pretty a day for that."

"Professor." It was a blonde wearing a white apron. "I didn't see you come in at first—I was in the back." He recognized her now as a student from his Intro to Lit course. Many of Roy's students worked in shops and restaurants in Tempe, a small college town in the middle of greater Phoenix. He ran into them everywhere. "This had your name and course in the front, so you may as well take it. There's no other name. I found it when I was cleaning under the tables."

She laid a slim red notebook on the white table.

"Thanks." He looked at it, took his hand away from Eileen's, and opened the cover of the notebook. The handwriting was a neat cursive, done in fountain pen. He recognized the penmanship—Cindy Callison's. She always wrote in fountain pen. His stomach dropped. Had she written about him? It wouldn't matter to the case, but it would matter a hell of a lot to his marriage. He had to get somewhere and read it fast, before Paul got hold of it.

"What is it?"

"Her notebook. Shit! So this is where she came that day."

"You've got to call Paul. Come on, there's a phone over there."

"Wait a minute. I'll call him from the house—I want to look at it first."

"You sure you know what you're doing? What's in the notebook?"

"I'll know after I read it."

"What is it—love letters? Roy . . ."

"Take it easy."

"This is a bad idea. You're messing around in something you don't understand."

"I'll make sure the detectives get it soon. It's been almost a week—what's another few hours?"

"How can you say that? Who knows what another few hours means! What if she's alive?" Roy didn't have an answer and he could argue best by silence.

"Okay. That's how you want it. But if Paul asks, I'm going to tell him. I won't lie for you. Not to Paul, not about this."

Day Five, Afternoon

Paul was waiting for them in the parking lot of their apartment cluster. He sat in the T-bird, motor running, air on high, smoking his fourth Pall Mall. He powered down his window and waved. "Can I borrow your husband for a few hours?" Eileen nodded. Roy kept hold of the red notebook and got into the car.

"What's that—notes for your book on happy endings? You can leave it inside, if you want."

"That's okay. I don't feel like getting out again."

"Suit yourself." Paul put the car in gear.

Down at police headquarters, Paul ushered Roy into a windowless interrogation room and sat him down behind a scarred Formica table. "Coffee and soft drinks in the lounge next door," he said. "Give me a few."

The door was shut tight. He was alone. He would read it, one page at a time, until Paul returned from his interrogation. With the air conditioner humming over his left shoulder, Roy opened the red notebook and read:

I've got no notes for the first week of class. I just listened, nobody listens anymore. I'm no genius, but I can spot a bullshitter. Too many fakers and fuckers in this world—got to take the good ones where you find them.

Come on, Dr. Roy—teach me something I don't know.

Roy had a funny feeling in his stomach. He didn't know if he should, if he could, turn the page. All along he'd been asking, Who was she? Confident that knowing exactly who Cindy Callison was, how she had thought and felt about things, could give him the crucial clue to find her. But did he really want to know? Was he prepared to find out?

After all this time, finally he had met a student who could inspire passion. He had expected class notes, the odd clue or two, not a diary. Not confessions. Not epiphany.

Paul and his team of detectives would be a long time with the boyfriend, playing good cop/bad cop. Hours, probably. He would read.

Out here, nobody cares where you come from. The clock starts when you get off the bus. Day one. Forget what happened yesterday. You are who you say you are—nobody hassles you about it.

Phoenix was as far as I could get before I ran out of money. There are plenty here like that, the underground people—I meet them every night.

Then followed pages of notes outlining assignments due, long papers about narration, plot, theme. Roy saw his lectures quoted lucidly and in great detail. Had he been so articulate in class? He wanted to think so but couldn't quite believe it.

There were his old friends from Stephen Crane's Blue Hotel—the cowboy, the Easterner, old Scully the hotel keeper, his mean son Johnnie, the gambler, and the ill-starred Swede. She'd written, *The rest of the class don't seem to understand how people can get caught up in things, how life carries its own momentum. I could tell some stories myself. How you get on the outside looking in at your own life sometimes, you watch yourself doing stuff you could never imagine doing in your wildest dreams, crazy stuff.*

How you make things happen to yourself.

Like this: I slept with a woman once. I mean, actually made love to her. Shocking, right? Crazy stuff. But it wasn't bad, really. It was really very tender, a one-time thing. That night it was something that just had to happen—it was going to happen no matter what. Like it needed to happen. You just get caught up.

Roy's mouth was cottony. He wanted a Coke from next door, but he dared not stop now. Here was every literature professor's dream: a student who had taken the stories to heart, thought hard about them, informed them with her own life, and let the stories, in turn, inform her life.

And, he thought, We saw how that turned out. He read on.

The stories haunt me. "A Rose for Emily," what a creepy deal. Sleeping with a corpse—though I've had a few cold ones myself, ha ha. What was weird was, that night I had a long nightmare of climbing stairs, sure of what I'd find up in that old locked bedroom, yet climbing all the same. Like a ditzy bimbo in some bad slasher flick, nightie and all. There were men out in the yard spreading quicklime, just like in the story.

What I always wondered in that story was, what happened to her servant Tobe? The old black man who waited on her and was loyal when the rest of the town turned against her? When she died, he went out the back door and was never seen again—where did he go? They never tell you what happens to the little characters, the people on the edges of the action. You get the feeling the stories are all written by the fuckers in charge. But the little characters have lives, too, even in stories.

He must've known she'd killed her lover—he could've smelled the poor guy rotting away upstairs. Even the townspeople complained. Why didn't he ever tell? Why did he stay until the end?

Roy had never considered Tobe's predicament: he wasn't the star of the story. So the stories had gotten into her dreams.

Roy heard voices in the hall, then the door opened.

Paul came in with a stranger and they both sat down. Gino and Wade Billings stood flanking the door, arms akimbo, like palace guards. Some kind of cop routine. Roy closed the notebook quickly and covered it with his hand. "Meet our mystery man, Peter Loomis."

"Pete," the stranger said, "just plain Pete."

Roy shook his hand. "Hi, Pete, what do you know."

"Apparently, not much." Paul paced the room and Loomis's eyes followed him. Loomis was tall, even seated. The reason, Roy supposed, that his uncle preferred to stand—some psychological-advantage technique learned in cop school. Loomis wore a starched oxford shirt with the collar unbuttoned. He was well-built, muscular and tanned. A bodybuilder, too big for the chair.

"He's already made his so-called statement."

Roy couldn't help feeling sympathy for this Loomis fellow, with his tired gray eyes and knotted fingers, sitting as if in study hall. What did Paul expect Roy to do, what did he want? What was he supposed to say? Roy didn't say anything. They all stared at one another. Then Paul said, "Come on, Loomis, let's get you squared away for the night."

Loomis looked up in surprise and unclasped his hands. "I'm under arrest?"

"Not quite, but we're holding on to you overnight anyway."

"Can I call someone? Don't I have a right to—"

"You got all sorts of rights, pardner, starting tomorrow morning. Get used to the idea."

"I didn't do it."

"Do what? What didn't you do?" Paul said.

"I don't know where she is. I wish to God I did."

"Where do you think she is?" Billings asked, trying to sound casual. But his face was pink from exertion and his underarms were sweated through.

"You tell me," Loomis said, and put his face in his hands.

"Cut the crap. Give me a name. A place."

Loomis spoke through his fingers. "I didn't kill her. I swear."

"Who says she's dead?" Billings asked, finger-combing his thinning brown hair.

"That's what you believe . . ."

Paul said, as if baffled, "I didn't say she's dead—did I say that? Nobody said that. Is she dead?"

"But you believe—"

"Were you pimping her?"

"I would never do that, I swear."

"I bet you were pimping her. Tell us now or tell us later."

"That's not how it was . . ."

"I can't stand any more of this shit." Paul hustled Loomis out and returned quickly enough that Roy didn't have time to read further. He said, "You keep any scotch at your place?"

On the way to Roy's apartment, Paul said, "You think he did it?"

Roy thought about that. "Loomis doesn't have the eyes for it."

Paul lit a Pall Mall and had a coughing fit. "Claims they'd had a fight weeks before and weren't even seeing each other. So that makes him the first boyfriend. Ballplayer in college. Used to be. Now he parks cars. He sure ain't no fucking genius."

"Why would he have done it?"

"Ask his priest. But even he admitted he has a hell of a temper. Smacked her around a couple times, that's why she split."

Roy shook his head. "Whoever did this didn't do it out of passion. It wasn't a temper tantrum. You said so yourself."

"Why didn't he come forward right away?"

"Maybe he was just waiting for you to catch the right guy."

"Look: when a person gets murdered, nine times out of ten the killer is someone they knew well. If it's a woman, more than half the time it's the husband or boyfriend."

"Statistics don't make a person guilty."

"Don't jump to conclusions. This Loomis is wrong."

"Says you."

"Says twenty-five years on the job. I can pick a wrong guy out of a crowd every time. When somebody doesn't come forward, it ain't cause they're busy spreading good news."

"That's pretty thin, even for you. Where I come from, we prefer a logical argument."

"Where you come from wouldn't know logic if it jumped up and bit you in the ass."

"See what I mean."

"Okay, try this on for size. Guess what Loomis was before he showed up here."

"A butcher."

"Better. A med student. Father's a hotshot thoracic surgeon. Junior flunked out after a year at Jefferson in Philly. A year of gross anatomy—cutting up dead bodies."

"How about that."

"So we keep a close eye on Mr. Loomis in case he does any operating without a license."

"You really think the guy we just met is capable of it?"

"Anybody is capable of anything, that's the second rule." He lit a second cigarette from the first and coughed again.

"You're getting your rules mixed up."

"Name me someone we both know who isn't capable of murder."

"Just about everybody. Me. My father."

"There's no harm in telling you now. Your Dad once shot a fellow in Nogales. See what I mean?"

"What are you talking about?" Roy remembered him as a timid man who studied rocks.

"Some day when we're both drunk enough, I'll tell you all about it."

Later in the afternoon, at Roy's apartment, Paul sequestered himself in the back room, Eileen's office, to make phone calls. Roy sat in the living room and read page after page of Cindy Callison's life from the inside out.

It was in there, about his first visit to the club. How he'd watched her dance: *Didn't think I could see him back there in the shadows, but I did. The lights cut people into silhouettes, but I could tell by how he moved. My goddamn teacher, under the red lights. Our little secret.*

And Roy was keeping it a secret from Paul. It was no big deal, but it would look like something else. A few nights after he'd seen her in the parking lot wearing her working clothes, he was driving around the way he sometimes did, just to be out of the house. He found himself passing the Club Rodeo. No accident. He knew she worked there—she'd told the whole class by way of introduction during their very first meeting.

Roy parked and went inside.

Inside, the Club Rodeo had been dark and cavelike—red lanterns fixed along the walls, lariats, steer horns, saddles. He slid into a booth at the back, away from the bar, and leaned an elbow on the ersatz corral fence. The place was full of men—guys in sports shirts, western-style suits, biker vests, salesmen and lawyers and concrete finishers.

The bartender was a big brutish guy with a handlebar mustache and a black Stetson and a black snap-button shirt, all pumped up with muscle—a steroid freak, Roy decided, a lifter or a boxer.

From a waitress dressed in a gold lamé vest and a short white skirt he got a watery scotch for four bucks. The waitress looked like a kid, eighteen or nineteen, underage. He sipped the drink and watched the show.

On stage in the broken light, a curvy blonde danced to country rock piped through monster black speakers flanking the stage. She was topless, clad in a gold G-string, toy six-shooters riding her slim hips. From time to time she drew the guns and fired caps, then blew imaginary smoke off the ends of the barrels.

The song was called "My Forty-Five-Caliber Man," and when it got to the bridge she drew her right-hand pistol and began to suck the shiny barrel, taking more and more of it into her mouth. Scattered applause broke out. Men hooted and whistled and cheered. The dancer bent over the first row of tables and let the men stuff bills into her G-string. She leered at them and licked the gun barrel, swaying her tits, and they went crazy for her.

Her head came up, her big brown eyes searching the room as if looking for somebody in particular. Roy leaned back into the shadows of the booth. There was no mistake: under the blond wig, it was Cindy Callison.

After the first show, he'd stuck around, sipping his watery scotch and trying to decide what to do next. Meanwhile, by turns, each of the cocktail waitresses climbed onto the stage and, to loud country rock, stripped off their gold lamé vests and their white cowgirl skirts, their white gloves and hats, their sheer blouses, their gold brassieres.

He watched, aroused and somewhat bored at the same time. Then it was his waitress's turn. She ascended the stage and then mounted a mechanical bull. Roy was amazed at how she could flex her body. Suddenly there was a husky voice in his ear—Cindy Callison, dressed.

"Thought that was you, professor." She licked her glossy lips.

"I don't usually—"

"Hush. I don't usually, either."

"I better get going."

"Don't rush off. I got another routine at eleven-thirty, if you can wait around."

"My wife will wonder."

Cindy looked at him with a kind of honesty and even sympathy. "No, she won't. We can talk after, if you want."

So Roy stayed for the second show but finally lost his nerve, slipped out before she was back from her dressing room. What in the world would he have to say to her?

Roy kept reading about himself. *He split, though—couldn't handle it. Must have spooked the shit out of him, to land up in the middle of a real story. Wish he'd have stuck around. Guess I came on too strong—all that bogus slinky crap you pick up from the other girls. You can't pull that stuff on a real person.*

Been around the hard people too long. But I don't feel hard.

Trouble was, Roy went back.

She had sat across the table at that last seminar, watching him. Waiting for a word, a sign? Just an hour earlier, they'd talked in his office. He could keep her after class, they could go somewhere. He could tell her about Eileen—she would understand. When he handed back her paper at the end of that last seminar, he slipped her a note with it: see you in the parking lot, one hour.

He worked in his office for an hour, distracted, putting it off, regretting it already. The note was a foolish idea. What if he had read her wrong? His job could be on the line. She might be furious with him. But he wanted to see her. He didn't know what it would lead to, didn't know if he wanted it to lead to anything. Finally he arranged his papers and books for the last time, stuffed them into his book bag, and started out.

Just then, the telephone rang. Eileen. She called him so rarely at work these days that he immediately felt discovered, ashamed. "I'll be home soon," he assured her, then went out to meet Cindy Callison.

He got out to the parking lot fifteen minutes late and waited an hour for her, but she never came. He felt guilty. But, really, he hadn't done anything, not yet, he told himself over and over. All he wanted to do was talk. Right. He relaxed and waited, but she never showed. Or she had been here and, tired of waiting, had left. Gone, for good?

If his life depended on it, could Roy prove where he went after class? That he did not see Cindy Callison after she left the seminar? As far as anybody knew, he was still one of the last people to see her safe. Except for the killer, perhaps the last. No, he couldn't. What could anybody, after the fact, prove to be absolutely true about his own life?

He began, really for the first time, to understand what he and Paul were up against. How in hell could they ever find out what had really happened? Would they ever do better than an approximate guess?

And, sooner or later, would suspicion fall on him? Did Paul suspect already that he had lied, or at least skirted the truth?

He tore out the page about him. What he was doing was wrong, and he knew it. He told himself it didn't matter to the case, it wouldn't hurt anybody. He folded the page and jammed it into his pocket.

Then he read more: *Hawthorne traveled on dark roads, that's how Professor Roy put it. Who by the way has a couple of dark places in his own head, so maybe he knows. He wrote about the world that shadows our own, and his characters were too pure for this life. Pure action is always fatal. Absolute values are always fatal.*

Roy rubbed his eyes. Come on, he thought, tell me where you are. Give me a clue.

A dozen pages later, Cindy Callison had written, *The hardest time of the day is after I get off work. I drive home alone, always afraid of who's out and about on those dirty dark streets—the creeps and hustlers and crackheads and just plain fuckers. Then I get home to my apartment, where all the lights have been left on. This dates back to fourth grade. I came home from school one winter day. A real chiller of a day—what is it they say: the first day of the rest of my life. Like, what was yesterday? I'd stayed after school for piano lessons, as usual on Fridays.*

It was already dark, the streetlights were buttery and the sidewalk was gray and the grass was black. All the houses on the block were lit up—you could see through the windows people sitting around the supper table or reading newspapers or watching TV. You could see their faces, in the glow.

Our house was dark. I remember to this day that I stopped right there on the sidewalk under the streetlamp, wouldn't even go on the driveway. Not a single light was on, which about made me freak.

I stook there in the cold for a few minutes and then I walked over the frozen grass up to the front door—locked. Now I was really scared. I didn't have a key—never needed one—so I went next door to Mrs. Whitlock's house and she and her husband went back over with me.

I squeezed my schoolbooks. Mr. Whitlock cupped his hands around his face and looked through the living room window, then shook his head. We went around back, and that door was unlocked. They knocked—ridiculous, right? This was life and death. I wanted to scream.

They went first into the kitchen. Then we turned on all the lights and went through every room in the house. Nobody. Mr. Whitlock looked in the basement—nothing. We went upstairs—the beds were all made, nobody was there. Creepy.

Roy could see it coming, an old story.

We found them in the garage. The motor wasn't running any-more—the car had run out of gas. They must have done it right after I left for school, didn't leave a note. They were sitting in the front seat, arms around one another. Mrs. Whitlock told me not to look, but I did. Who wouldn't? I even touched them. Their faces had turned bright red.

I never set foot in that house again. My aunt gathered my stuff without saying a word and I lived with her from then on. And we never spoke about it, and no one ever worried out loud about why.

I'll never go into a dark house again. Once I'm home, I usually have a nightcap, Amaretto, then try to read myself to sleep. But I don't. Many nights I sit there in bed feeling soft and pretty and lonely, and I get distracted from my book. I sit and think, just think. Which is the hardest thing of all.

Remarkable, Roy thought. He stopped reading and listened to Paul murmuring into the telephone from time to time. He heard the clink of ice. The kitchen clock ticked. Light poured onto the table through the window. He read on.

Class is starting now, got to listen. Prof. Roy is a good man, sometimes troubled—you can see it in his eyes, the way he looks past me, past all of us. When he talks he carries me away. Someday I'd like to talk with him alone, without the noise of the other students—their endless squirming and shuffling and gathering of books.

They're so—young. Sometimes I feel about a thousand years old.

About how Roy felt, at that moment. He flipped the page to a new entry.

Fuckers think cause you hustle drinks, shake your boobs for a buck, that you're some kind of whore. But I'm safer on stage than when I walk down Central Ave. in broad daylight. It feels kind of pure, and kind of hokey, too. Fun. Anyway, I'm getting out. I don't know how, but I am. Don't want to hide in the dark anymore. Want to go to work in the morning, like real people.

Sick and tired of the fuckers judging me. Discounting me. Prof. Roy takes me seriously. When I look into his eyes, he looks back, doesn't judge me. I can imagine sitting with him, alone.

We'd speak about literature, about stories, think out loud together, share our minds. And I'd find out about his life. Somewhere in between his words, like in class sometimes, I'd learn something I need to know. He would be looking at me the whole time. Not past me but straight into my eyes. It wouldn't be in the classroom but in a new place, and nobody would interrupt. We'd talk as long as we both felt like it.

Him and me, just like that.

Now and then he'd touch my arm gently and say, "Do you understand?" I'd nod, and our heads would draw closer, our voices would get softer.

I'd find out what's in his heart.

He could just picture her there, seated in the cool seminar room twenty minutes before class, savoring the quiet and writing carefully, in no hurry. He tore out that page, too.

That Hemingway, now there's a man who can write. Why did he have to be such a braggart and blowhard? I bet he paid attention to other people, to what he saw and heard.

And just what was he so afraid of all his life?

Hemingway didn't go over well in class. I think the time when people had real emotions about courage are long gone. Lot of sniveling pukes we are—living in a world in which courage is beside the point. Courage nowadays would only get you arrested.

A few pages later: *Pete and I are through. He's turned into a bully, and I can't stand a bully. I spoke to Julie about it and she agrees. She's a sweet thing but doesn't know much about the world. Told her I had met someone new and terrific, but not who. Nobody wants to hear the truth all the time.*

Pete calls almost every day and I just hang up. You can never go back without losing self-respect. Pete fucks boys. I know this, and I know who. I don't judge him for it, but it confuses me and I need straight answers these days.

So Pete Loomis did have his secrets to keep.

Everything I've ever done, I have had to learn all by myself.

Prof. Roy is another matter. Sometimes sex unacted upon can be a kind of electricity between people, makes you tingle just to be close. You can feel it crackling along your arms and hear it in your voices. How long can it go on?

He was nearing the end.

"A Good Man Is Hard to Find." The Flannery O'Connor tale of the dotty grandmother and the homicidal Misfit. So true. Pete has stopped calling, but I wonder what he'll do next? And is there really a moment of grace before death, like in the story? At that last second, staring oblivion in the face, would you have faith and forgive, as the grandmother does in the story, after the Misfit has slaughtered her whole family? Or is that a load of crap, too?

The scene, as always, made Roy shudder. On their way to Florida, the family finally runs into the homicidal maniac prophesied in the first paragraph of the story—the killer Misfit. His gang leads the members of the family, one by one, off into the woods and shoots them like steers: father and son, mother and daughter, leaving at last only the grandmother, who got them into the mess in the first place. The Misfit saves the grandmother for last so she can hear all the others die and have a long moment of knowing she is utterly alone without hope of rescue, facing her own murderer, facing an eternal test of her faith—free to choose ignominy or grace.

She chooses a crazy kind of grace: Pray to Jesus! she admonishes the Misfit in an ecstasy of martyrdom, and reaches out her hand—the Misfit recoils, snakebit, and shoots her three times in the chest. For the grandmother, as for the others, there is just no mercy to spare. So much for happy endings.

Did my parents have a moment of grace? They had their arms around each other and knew, as they breathed in the exhaust fumes, that they'd never be parted in this life. Maybe that's all there is.

Roy paused in his reading, recalling wreckage strewn over parched miles of Texas plain, a phone call in the middle of the night, the time such phone calls always come. Both his parents, too, taken at once.

I think that moment of grace is what I have in class sometimes, just before the others arrive, in that minute or so after I have written down honestly what is on my mind. The room is quiet and cool and the reading for the day has settled deep in my memory and I feel ready. Then he walks through the door with all that confidence and passion for the stories, and begins to speak . . .

But then it goes away—I think as soon as I become aware that other people are in the room with us. All those kids. The energy is drawn off and wasted. The stories lose the deep-etched quality they had, and I start to wonder if I have understood them at all.

But she was wrong, Roy told himself, to think it was always that way: once in a great while there were golden moments when his voice caught and held them, and the energy coursed back to him in a dizzying, ever-accelerating loop, and something important was discovered. Those times left him breathless, high, feeling invincible.

I just came from his office. I wanted him to close the door and invite me to sit down and talk to me in low, soothing tones and smile, as if something of value were understood between us, and reassure me with his wisdom.

Christ, Roy thought: wisdom—who has that?

Then, after the seminar, I wanted to make love to him all after-noon. Not fuck—make love. The real thing.

He didn't do anything and he should have done something.

But I knew when I walked in I could never expect that, not under fluorescent lights and him in his professor's chair sitting behind his professor's desk seeing me like I was next in line at the free clinic.

I should never have said all that. Thought it, but not said it out loud. Even though I had to. Fuck romance, right?

So she had written this after coming to his office, before the seminar. Then she had left the notebook behind at the yogurt shop.

If I could have kept myself under better control, if I could have, I'd have told him that the stories matter. That his voice follows me through my day and that I've come to rely on it for courage. That courage isn't irrelevant to my life. That I understand what he's trying to teach us.

If only Roy knew what he was trying to teach them.

Last night, I dreamed of my parents, embracing in the front seat of that old Pontiac in our garage in Columbus. The engine was running and I was in the back seat. My hands were bright red and I was crying hard.

And I knew why they did it.

When I woke up, my pillow was wet. The dark was soft and comforting, a large airy cushion, and I knew from now on everything was going to be all right. That's what I was going to tell him. That's why I touched him. After class today . . .

That was the end of it. He carefully tore out all the pages about him.

Over his shoulder, Paul said, "Just what in the hell are you doing?"

Roy slapped the notebook closed and turned around in his chair. "Reading."

"Like hell! Tampering with evidence!" Paul grabbed up the note-book and flipped through it.

"I can explain—"

"I ought to explain your ass right into the lockup." Paul walked to the sink and ran water into a glass.

"I'm sorry. I was afraid, if I showed you, you'd take it away from me."

"Damn right I would. Where'd you get it?"

"The yogurt place on Mill. But listen—she wrote this before class . . ."

"How long have you had it?"

"Since lunch."

"Jesus Christ, you can be dumb." Paul drank his water, then made a call from the kitchen telephone and gave some orders. He hung up the phone and sat on the edge of the table, breathing hard. "Just when were you gonna let me read it?"

Roy handed him the notebook. Paul held out his other hand. Roy fished the wadded-up pages out of his pocket and handed them over. Paul uncrumpled them and read them. "So she had a crush. Jesus Christ. What else you holding out on me?"

"Come on, Paul. You know me better than that." But his voice sounded thin and false even to himself.

"Tell me now, tell me later."

"Nothing to tell. I swear."

Paul glared at him a moment longer, then settled into an over-stuffed chair in the living room to read the whole notebook. With chalky hands, Roy poured himself a double shot of scotch and drank it down, and then another.

When Eileen returned home half an hour later, she found him sitting at the kitchen table, head on his crossed arms. "What's wrong now?" she kept saying. "For God's sake, what's wrong?"

The next day Roy was back at the cop shop. Paul kept telling him to stick around, give him ideas. The TV people had gotten bored and, for the moment, had left Paul in peace. The FBI was hanging back, waiting for a break. If it was a loser case, they didn't want it.

"We've checked all the hospitals, the morgue, she hasn't turned up. Gino's running down motels. Got a team staking out the Club Rodeo, but I think they're wasiting their time."

"Any more on the old boyfriend?"

"Nada. Maybe he's our guy, maybe not. I'd sure like to find this new character. This genius."

"The kids are all spooked," Roy said. "They keep on waiting for her to show up for class."

"They're just kids, they don't realize." Paul kept looking at him, as if urging him to disclose something private, but Roy resisted. On the back porch with two tall scotches in his belly and the sun dousing itself into the mountains maybe, but not here, under fluorescent lights. Why were police stations so goddamned ugly?

"Murder's a funny crime. Just when you think you've seen it all, something new comes along."

Roy recalled the late-news videotape, the bags on the woman's hands. "Did the bags help?"

"The bags? Nothing yet. We sent the hands out to the FBI lab."

"You what?"

"S.O.P. in a case like this. The hands were amputated at the morgue and sent off registered mail."

"Christ, you guys are something else."

"How the hell else we going to get prints? Sonofabitch must have used a blowtorch."

Roy shook his head. "You got any coffee?"

"Help yourself over there. It's all according to the theory of transfer and exchange. The perp brings something to his victim, or to the scene of the crime, or takes something away. Or the victim takes something—hair, skin, clothing fibers. Physical evidence. What came from where and from whom. You connect it all up."

"Right." So there was a science to it—or they pretended there was. The coffee was bitter and too hot.

"It goes without saying, nephew, that all of this is in strictest confidence. Don't let me be reading this in the paper. You are a consultant on this case."

"What do you want from me?" Roy wanted to be out of it, a safe distance away. He also wanted to be right there when they found her. *If.*

"Who knows. I need somebody to ask me the right questions. My gut rumbles one way and I got to go with it. It's got me this far."

Gino, wearing a snug tan suit, came into the office and handed over another folder. "The final report on the car," he said. "Big help."

Paul read the folder. "No tickets. Valid permit. A vapor trail."

"Just like her apartment," Gino said. "We went through everything. Took us hours." He gave Roy a look that said, What are you doing here? But he didn't say anything else.

Just then the phone rang. Paul picked it up and listened for a moment, then tucked the folder under his arm. "Gino, round up Billings and Stein."

"You got it."

"Roy, take a ride with me."

As Paul steered his T-bird out of the police garage, fighting traffic that didn't want to yield to his flashing dashboard light, Roy asked, "What's up?"

"You'll see, directly."

"You're about as talkative as Gino."

Paul gunned the car in front of a jacked-up four-by-four and squealed tires. "Gino talks plenty when he has something to say."

"When's that?" The sudden acceleration pushed Roy against his seat back. "Jesus, Uncle Paul—who are we chasing?"

Paul was doing fifty down the short block like it was no big deal. "That kid's smart as they come—you'd be surprised at the stuff he knows. What he can carry around inside his nut." Paul tapped his skull and veered around a truck in a loading zone and braked for the red light before running it. "You want a guy working for you who'll listen instead of talk all the time."

"I can see what you mean." Roy did his best to ignore the high-speed, lurching stop-start.

"A gypsy or something, good instincts about the bad guys. Memory that won't quit. It's the culture, nothing's written down."

"The oral tradition."

"Right. Soaks it up like a sponge, saves on paperwork."

"You like working with him."

"Yeah, I like it fine. He came out from Jersey, the state police. We've had him, what's it been, five years maybe?" Paul remembered how Gino had impressed him at their first meeting by turning the interview around—Paul did all the talking. Gino had all the right answers but nothing extra. Paul liked that—a cop who could keep his mouth shut. No big talk, just results.

"But you don't ride together."

"Some days yes, other days got too much ground to cover. You know how short we are on manpower. But he's my man. I show him things. When I'm gone, he'll be chief investigator."

"Not soon, I hope."

"Oh, sooner than you think. It's creeping up."

Paul slung the T-bird around the corner onto Central and opened her up. They sped north up Central at an alarming speed, dodging in and out of the heavy traffic. Roy could not help imagining how the white T-bird would look from the revolving restaurant at the top of the city's skyline: heading north in a straight line, intersecting other straight lines of stopped traffic. At night, the endless cars would move along like yellow bubbles in a glass tube.

At a vacant lot near Indian School Road, they pulled in among the flashing lights of police cars. Paul clipped his police I.D. badge on his shirt pocket and handed Roy a spare. "Just put it on and don't do anything really stupid," Paul said. "At least the six o'clock news isn't here yet."

The lot was full of junk—tires and rotten boards and an old washing machine on its side. Two uniforms had a Mexican kid between them.

"Chico and his buddies there were playing hide-and-seek. Guess what they found in that old Whirlpool."

Sticking out from a bundle of newspaper were two feet. Another newspaper bundle, partially unwrapped, held a female torso with the breasts removed.

No arms, no hands.

Her head was in a shopping bag. The eyes were gone.

This time Roy did throw up.

"Christ, don't fuck up the crime scene!" Paul said. "Anybody see who put her in there?"

"No, lieutenant. Nobody out here but traffic," Wade Billings said. Cars sped by in a ceaseless stream scarcely fifty feet away on Central. Some of the drivers slowed down to gape from behind closed windows.

Paul nodded. To Frank Stein, he said, "Get plenty of good pictures. Get the face. Close up. As often as you have to to get it right."

Stein said, "This here is Hollywood stuff today," and grinned

"He cut her all up," Roy said, trying to fathom what he was seeing.

"Yeah. Look how white she is. Shit."

"It isn't her," Roy said quietly. "It isn't Cindy Callison."

"Look harder."

"Christ, Paul—this girl can't be more than fifteen years old!"

Paul nodded. "Okay. Wade, anything been touched?"

Billings read off his notebook. "No. The first officer secured the scene and his partner called it in."

"Good. Consider this whole lot the crime scene."

To Roy, Paul said, "Stand there. Don't move. Don't pick up

nothing. Don't spit or whistle or fart. We've got a hot scene here."

Roy did as he was told. He breathed slowly and deliberately, but his heart was clamoring. He thought of Cindy Callison's soft troubled face, then of the face of his wife. Then he counted the cars along Central Avenue. He did not look again at the body parts.

At last Hoff, the coroner, arrived and made a preliminary examination of the remains. He went from one package to the next, humming show tunes. He looked into the shopping bag, then carefully lifted out the head and stopped humming in mid-bar. "Christ Almighty, Paul—look at this!"

Paul looked at the head in Hoff's hand. Roy looked, too. It was true: she was smiling.

"That's not natural, is it?"

Hoff said, "I'll say it's not—he's sewn a goddamned prosthesis in her mouth."

Roy spent the afternoon holding office hours and conducting his literature seminar, talking about the stories. After what he had seen this morning, it was hard to concentrate. But as always the stories soothed him. The stories always made sense. You could analyze them and come out with meaning. That would be in his book.

It was the stories he had always loved. What they did to him in his chest as he read them. How the words stirred him to joy—imaginary people created out of memory and hope, moving urgently through a dream of action, choice, resolution. Making sense out of the world's chaos.

That would be in his book, too—the magical parts of the stories, the stuff you couldn't explain away. The stuff that, even after a perfect ending, you couldn't account for. Right now he needed a story better than the one they had seen this morning.

Today they discussed Shirley Jackson's story "The Lottery," in which ordinary town folk end up stoning to death one of their own to assure a prosperous year ahead. The students didn't get it. "There's no lottery like that," one of them said. "Nobody would agree to allow some people to die just so the rest of us could have a better life."

He wanted to explain it. He had a hold on the idea, but he could not make his words behave in sentences. "Right," he said quietly. "Class dismissed."

The moon is down, the sun sleeps in the cradle of the hills. There are no clouds inside this snakish rampart of mine. Serpent coiled in egg, over. My heart is a hot stone balloon. She lives in my stomach now.

Sulfur in the belly, wine in the head, love coming in at the eye.

You could shovel out this black air like coal, but what have you got? I glow from the soft ember of my heart, incinerating to ash. You could hose me right down the fucking chute, couldn't you?

Come close to the bars and watch this, my little baboon. Don't be a-scared of me. She's on the table, all the flowers around her—red roses for a blue lady.

Let me prop the book up in the kerosene light. Soft yellow damp. Feel it? A razor will do. Let me hold the wrist just so, how do you do. Let me slice an even circle just so deep and no more. Stay on the blue line, page forty-two.

Copy this:

Slide the tips of index fingers under the epidermis and lift until you feel a slight tear. Wax, soapy stuff, rubber.

Gently tug upward on the epidermis until you have lifted it clear of the soft tissue and points of attachment over the muscle. Turn inside out, then peel down evenly. Be careful not to tear the thin membrane.

When you have freed the complete segment, soak in a mild saline solution for fifteen minutes. Air-dry but avoid desiccation. Turn outside out again, gently. Application of dermal prints is now possible.

Look—I can stretch my fingers inside your hand!

Lubricate daily with glycerine to preserve elasticity.

I wiggle my fingers, stretch my fingers in their new skin.

Over and out.

It was Friday afternoon before Roy saw Paul again. After his late seminar, he drove Eileen out in the Jeep to the desert house in time to beat the rush of traffic leaving the city, and the three of them and a psychologist named Jane Featherbead held a very serious happy hour. She'd been around for years, since before Roy had left for graduate school, but Roy had never really gotten to know her. Now she had bought land near Paul and saw clients in her home. She was an amateur potter and had developed a fashionable therapy out of her hobby. Sometimes Paul used her on cases. They were old friends, and she made herself at home.

Jane was part Navajo and almost as dark as Esmeralda. Her body was long and sinuous and strong. The bones of her naked shoulder blades were brown above the bright floral needlepoint of her Mexican sundress. A striking woman, not pretty. Roy was intrigued at how Paul always managed to surround himself with interesting women. On this case it was almost as though he were gathering the people around him whom he most trusted. Jane was a professional, but Paul could easily have found a better-qualified psychologist, one who specialized in criminal justice. Just as he could have easily found a more useful sidekick than Roy. It was almost, Roy realized, turning into a family matter.

They sat on the long porch with the bowl of ice and the bottle of Cutty Sark and watched the sun smear the White Tanks in pinks and golds. Esmeralda silently brought baskets of fresh-baked tortilla chips and bowls of thick hot salsa. Zack lay in his usual position. From time to time in his sleep he farted and growled.

Jane drank margaritas and after one drink Eileen joined her. Esmeralda brought them in heavy frosted glasses thickly rimmed with salt. Down the hill, Esmeralda's oldest, Paco, was shooting at rabbits with a BB gun.

"Can't you make him stop that?" Eileen said, as the gun snapped again.

"He can't hit anything," Paul said. The boy didn't shoot for a while; for a while, nothing happened at all. Skin tingling from the peppery salsa and from sunburn, Roy sat and took it all in.

"We don't know who she is yet," Paul said, drinking deep. Beginning well before sunrise, he had put in another fourteen-hour day. He was glad to be away from the constant harassment of the media. They were doing special reports now—serial killer on the loose. Dredging up comparisons to the Manson family, who had started out in this same desert before moving on to Hollywood. The FBI—Carter and Hobbes again—was stepping up the pressure to take over the case—but what could they do that wasn't already being done? Everybody was calling at all hours for updates. When will you catch the guy? They all wanted to know. Good question. Nobody in homicide was getting a day off anytime soon. "The damn hands."

"He's making a statement," Jane said. "Talking to us in the only language he knows." Jane picked at traces of clay under her fingernails. She had permanent gray smudges on the insides of her forearms.

"And what language is that?"

Jane said, "The language of parts. A macabre sort of hieroglyphics."

Eileen said, "Please—can't you two leave this at the office?" Her upbeat attitude was no match for this grisly case.

"Don't work well at the office," Paul said, and took a healthy slug. "Too many cops, telephones, crap."

"It's creepy," Eileen said, "to think of that girl being a hostage to that, that—"

"Go ahead," Jane said gently. "They can't catch him until they know what to call him."

"I know what to call him," Paul said. "The bogeyman."

Roy brooded. He wanted to do something and had nothing to do. Paul was drinking way too hard these days. So was he. It wasn't good for either one of them, but it kept him from panicking. Maybe Paul, too.

"Just a few more weeks until finals, right? Then the long hot summer," Eileen said to Roy to change the subject. "You can finally stop putting off that book."

"I'm not putting it off—it's just hard to concentrate right now."

"I'm just saying. You always say I should encourage you more." He could tell she meant well—he shouldn't have jumped on her so hard. Still, she made him sound like a dilettante.

"Summer's a good time," Jane said. "The heat sort of purifies you."

"Sucks the juice right out your goddamned pores, you mean," Paul said, and took another slug.

Down the hill the little gun snapped again. Eileen started. Paul seemed to be concentrating on the sound.

"Two girls dead," Jane said. "Why were they both so white?"

Paul explained tiredly, "No blood in 'em. He bled 'em to death out the carotid artery—decapitation. I told you."

Roy said, "But how—"

Paul quickly moved behind Roy and locked a forearm around his throat. Roy went dizzy.

"Easy!" Eileen said and gently pulled at Paul's arm.

"First knock 'em out, then slice 'em open. Hell of a thing. Could have used a drug, too."

"But why? What would he want with the blood?"

"Good question," Jane said. "Part of the same language."

Paul said, "That case in Cleveland? They asked Eliot Ness the same question. Some said it was cannibals, body parts missing, too. Then there was the mad-doctor theory—medical hocus-pocus, some Frankenstein dissecting fresh corpses. I don't fucking know."

Jane said, "But we know he was a strong guy."

"My guess. But maybe not. What I just did? Eileen could do it. Surprise is the main thing."

Roy said, "All I want to know is where is she."

"Yeah," Paul agreed. "That's the question, all right."

"You're spooking the hell out of me," Eileen said. "Can't we just sit here and enjoy the peace and quiet? Do you have to talk about it so much?" Roy took her hand. All this talk must be bringing back bad memories for her—the California business. Even now Roy had a hard time using the precise word: rape.

"You want spooky?" Paul said. "Here's spooky. The coroner can't fix time of death. For either girl. Says months, maybe. Says number two was killed first."

"But wouldn't they decompose—"

"Please," Eileen said softly.

"Lord, but aren't we a bunch of ghouls!" Jane said, picking up on her mood and changing the subject. "Reminds me of when I was with my archaeologist, pawing over burial mounds in the Yucatán." She'd gotten interested in pottery during a dig in Mexico with him. To her it had all seemed like glorified grave-robbing, but in the pottery she'd recognized a language, a code, that gave it meaning. A language of touch and shape, a world of order that could be read by fingertips. She hadn't seen him in years, but she still had the feel for pottery.

Paul wasn't paying her any mind. "That's the thing. And the kids were playing in that washer last week and it wasn't full of body parts then."

"What's the answer?"

"The answer is the coroner needs to go back to school."

They were quiet for a moment, breathing and drinking. Roy was thinking that all the stories he heard lately were about murder. "The Blue Hotel," he said.

"What?"

"A story we discussed today in seminar."

"Isn't that the one where all these fellows gang up on that poor Swede?" Paul said. "Pretty good story."

"Something like that, yeah."

"I seem to remember that yarn. Wonder where I heard it." Whenever Paul got wound up, his voice went gravelly. "This old Swede comes to town, and they all gang up on him—a cowboy, an Eastern dandy, a country boy named Johnnie, and a gambler. The Swede, he keeps on saying, right from the start, One thing I know, I'm never gonna leave this place alive, and by God the little squarehead was right all along."

"What an awful story," Jane said.

"It's a good story," Roy said, feeling slightly drunk. "Only you didn't get it exactly right."

"How I remember it."

"It's all about the mythical Wild West, Uncle Paul. The old Swede doesn't understand where he is."

"Look around you, boy—this is the Wild West. The old Swede had eyes."

Roy didn't break stride. "He's paranoid. He brings it on himself."

"How, exactly?" Jane asked.

"You're missing the point." Roy was thinking, When a story's right, you just can't explain it.

"Didn't that fat old bastard Hemingway murder a Swede somewhere, too?" Paul asked. He was loosening up, and it was good to see. But he was always doing that—making fun of what Roy took seriously.

"It's a motif in modern literature," Roy said. "Kill the Swede. You see it in practically every story."

"I remember now," Paul said. "I remember what the Swede did."

"Then tell us, for God's sake."

Down the hill the air gun snapped again and a child squealed. "He talked too much."

This time there was no duststorm, and they remained on the porch long after sundown, nibbling tacos and burritos and finishing up the scotch.

Long ago the BB gun had quit. From time to time Esmeralda slipped down the hill to attend to her kids. Zack, too, had a clandestine habit of slipping off into the near shadows. Once, he hunkered at the edge of the veranda and cracked something between his jaws, then swallowed it.

At ten o'clock Paul told Esmeralda, "Go home to your bambinos. I'll clean up." Esmeralda put down a glass pitcher of fresh margaritas. She trimmed a clay kerosene lamp inside the house and set another on the low porch table, unlit.

She smiled in the ambient desert light, and Roy had a sudden curiosity to follow her home. What would be waiting for her below? Cranky kids who must be fed? A black-and-white TV screen flickering with snowy reruns of old sitcoms? Zapata was off on a trip. She must be lonely.

Esmeralda turned from them, tossing her dark head. She has an instinct for catching a man's eye, Roy thought. He watched her descend toward the soft lights of the trailer and heard the coyotes start to yip and bark up in the high places. Zack stiffened his ears and then flattened them again.

Paul walked off into the darkness and pissed onto the hardpan. Roy listened to his footsteps scattering gravel as he returned. The coyotes, the restless dog, the darkness—all of it unnerved Roy. He said, "Way out here, beyond the lights."

Jane said, "It's like a curtain is pulled down. Anything might be going on behind the curtain."

"Sure," Roy said. "He's got until sunup to do his dirty deed. All bets are off."

"It's true." Paul admitted, "Murder is a nighttime thing. Not always, but there are things, things . . ."

"Things that only come out at night," Roy suggested.

"Don't start up again," Eileen said.

"I was going to say that there are things we simply would not do in the broad light of day."

Roy couldn't help thinking about Cindy Callison, the bagging of the other woman's hands. That part would never seem right. Where was Cindy Callison tonight? What was she seeing?

Jane said, "The old shamans used to believe that spirit leaked out of body all the time. After the sun had gone to sleep. Whatever force was holding spirit inside loosened its hold and spirit floated free." She fluttered one long hand. "Then spirit, which has no color, took on the color of the night. Became corrupted, lived a life all its own, no boundaries, no limits."

Eileen said, "That's the biggest tub of bullshit I've heard all night," and laughed nervously. "Thought you were a scientist."

"Go ahead, make fun." It was clear Jane didn't mind her joshing. "That's what nightmares are, though. Your soul flies out of your body and does awful things."

Roy said, "You tell your patients that?"

"It visits the nether regions."

"And what it sees there," Paul said, "scares the hell out of it." Paul laughed in a tired way, letting the air go out of his belly.

Roy wasn't laughing along. He was thinking of the stories again, of Hawthorne's wandering spirits, about poor Young Goodman Brown, the naive Puritan going out in the black woods to rendezvous with the devil.

Was that what Cindy Callison did?

In Hawthorne's story, Goodman Brown finds a witch coven in the woods—and with them is his own wife, Faith. She, too, is making a bargain with the devil. But in the end Goodman Brown prays for deliverance and wakes from the nightmare—but was it only a nightmare?

Cindy Callison was missing. The others had been hacked to pieces. As long as he lived, Roy would see that head rolling off the stretcher. The coyotes yipped back and forth.

Paul said, "Never underestimate what people know. You'd be surprised." His head swayed a little as he said it.

"What rule is that?" Roy said. He was losing track.

Jane said, "Go on, Paul, I'm listening." The kerosene flame strobed weakly against the window at their back.

"Think of what you have to know to get away with murder."

Roy said, "He hasn't got away with anything yet."

"He's gotten away with it so far. So far." Paul belched. "He knew where to find her alone. All of the girls. He knew how to dump the bodies without being seen. He knew to get rid of the fingerprints. And railroad timetables, maybe he knew them, too."

"I don't get that," Roy said. "Why he left her like that."

"That's enough," Eileen said. She was trembling. She lit the other lamp and Roy watched it burnish her face under the shadows.

Jane rose and walked past everyone into the house, throwing a quick shadow against the adobe wall. She returned with her cigarettes. Roy wished he'd remembered to bring along a cigar. He stared off drunkenly down the hill toward Esmeralda's dark trailer. In the lamplight Paul's face was livid, cratered with shadow. His cheeks hung in fleshy jowls. His eyes were squinting slits. Roy snuffed the flames, and they all stared out at a desert now boisterous with racket. As if the light had been muting the noise, had frozen all that surreptitious movement into and out of burrows, through the tangled palo verde thickets, under flat ancient boulders.

The coyotes resumed their complaint and the faint breeze carried it out of the foothills down the dry washes and into their ears. In Uncle Paul's desert yard, Roy could swear he heard now the scrabbling of little clawed feet, now the rasp of snakeskin over rock, now the erratic flutter of bats' wings.

And from every crevice, every safe hole, strewn like jewels among the stickers and burrs and spines, shining eyes.

Head clearing. Does that sometimes. Buzzing stops, pictures quit flashing by so fast. Hours go by like that, days. I swim along on top of things, light and invisible to all of them. Normal as shit.

I hear so hard. Walk into the light from the darkness. Watch her in the cage.

Hear so hard, hear her breathing, even when I'm not down there with her but out in the high wide desert, where the sky is blue and cold. I hear so hard I can feel her blood beating in the little tubes under her skin. Feel her skin vibrating with the pulse of life. Feel her skin on my hands.

For a long time it cleared up and I learned things. Thought I could learn my way out of here, but you need solid state for that and a system that don't crash, see?

I'm all tubes, top to bottom and inside out.

Glowing in the dark.

Don't remember all the things I learned. Something called calculus and another thing called chemistry, which I liked because of all those powders and bottles and tubes. And there were faces. Clean faces. Her face is always dirty, though I beg her to be clean.

I know I terrify her. I want to terrify her. I see it all day long, and I want to do it. Do you know what? What it feels like? Like chocolate melting in your mouth.

I would like to be terrified, too.

But when the buzzing starts again and the pictures come I just do things. I just do things. I just do. Hurts at first and then I buzz along with it.

When it clears, don't know what to do with her. Get excited.

Helps to listen to the blast of the gun against the air—blows out the pipes. Makes her scream. She sounds like metal screaming. I'm out but going in.

When I'm in, I hear voices all over the air. Sometimes my voice is in there, talking just like I was out. Talking up a storm, as they say. A storm of talk, over.

Can you read me?

She was bound to a tree in Library Park downtown. A maintenance man found her. By the time Paul and Roy arrived, the TV people were already shooting. The uniforms were keeping back a crowd of gawkers—most of them minor bureaucrats from the nearby state office buildings. The police station was just around the corner.

They left the T-bird at the curb and walked out among the transients who made the park their home. Gray people with sallow skin and runny noses. Junkies. Crackheads. Blue-flamers. Plain old winos. They wouldn't remember a thing, and if they remembered they'd never tell.

"There," Paul said, pointing. "The poor girl tied to it, standing up."

Roy nodded, breathing deliberately. Frank Stein was shooting her from every angle, like she was a fashion model. Billings was scribbling notes with a bandaged hand. "Heavy date last night," he explained to Paul. "She bit me."

"Maybe you shouldn't prowl so much."

Jane Featherbead stood off to one side, the crowd at her back, just staring, as if entranced. Roy noticed everything. "Where's her head?"

"Unknown," Paul said. "This is all we got. Hey—take it easy. She was a blonde. Body hair. The Callison girl is black Irish."

Roy nodded, grateful and guilty all at once. Thank God this one and not Cindy Callison was dead?

"Like some damned Indian thing," Roy said.

"Real Indians don't do this shit. Her hands are missing, the torso slashed. He was out of control."

Roy heard scraping up in the canopy of flat pithy leaves. Billings saw him look up. "Rats," he explained, grinning.

The cops were all over the place. A team of FBI special agents took Paul off to one side to argue. Paul was saying, "As long as it's a murder investigation, you take your lead from me." And the special agent in charge, Howard Carter, was saying, "We'll see about that." Carter had close-cropped red hair and freckled hands. Hobbes, the other agent, looked like an Ivy League car salesman.

Paul left them and came back over to the body. A young TV reporter dressed like a prom queen grabbed him by the elbow and shoved a microphone toward his face, but he shrugged her off and the uniforms hustled her away. Her crew set up next to a dry fountain ringed with little marble cherubs, their heads cracked off by vandals.

Paul said, "Let me guess—nobody saw anything."

Billings closed his notebook. "*Nada.* She's been here all night, at least. No I.D. Ligature marks on the neck—what's left of it—indicate strangulation." His hands clutched the notebook tightly, as if he were afraid somebody might try to take it away. "But we don't know for sure."

Hoff, the coroner, peeled off his latex gloves. "Blood in the body this time. If that's any help. Can I get some coffee here?" A uniform handed him a Styrofoam cup. "I can tell more after an autopsy."

"Right," Gino agreed. "No discoloration. Not white, like the others." He spoke without inflection, like he was lecturing. Roy still felt dazed.

Hoff said, "A fresh kill."

"Yeah," Gino agreed, "a fresh kill."

Paul stared off into the distance. "Now, how do you like that."

Billings tapped his pen on his notebook. "Something else—she's all chewed up."

"Rats," Gino said, pointing up into the date palm. "Big suckers."

"Find out where he got the rope. What is it, clothesline?"

"Dollar ninety-nine at any supermarket in town," Gino said with certainty. "We'll never trace it." Roy thought, Everybody sounds so sure of himself, yet we don't know anything.

"Try anyway."

"Righto."

"You want to examine the body here?" Hoff asked. His steady voice irritated Roy—he wanted shock, anger, outrage.

"I'll see her on the slab."

Paul, Roy, and Jane Featherbead adjourned to a little Mexican joint in the Guadalupe district. Paul was hungry. And when Paul got hungry, he dropped whatever he was doing and went straight for food. They sat over tacos at a linoleum table and Roy stared at the oil-on-black-velvet portrait of Jack and Bobby Kennedy on the far wall.

"You look like shit," Paul said. "You need a drink?"

"I'm okay," Roy said. "I think I've just had enough of this. You don't need me anymore."

"Stick around. Humor me." Paul tapped out a Pall Mall and lit up, then went into a coughing fit.

"Take it easy on those coffin nails."

Paul gulped a glass of water. "You just keep your eyes on the road." He puffed on his cigarette. "What I need's a reason. A motive."

Jane said, "You still believe you can find her."

Paul was musing. "This is a frontier town. There's always a transparent motive—sex, drugs, money."

We're in the desert, Roy was thinking. In a city in the desert—does that have anything to do with it? Paul was right. This was the Wild West—stripped of its hearty promise, left with only its outlaw brag. The American Dream left out in the sun too long. "How about a cult? Like the Manson family, you know."

"You've been watching too much TV. This is not that." Paul lit another cigarette off the first. "Did I tell you the first two bodies were washed before they were dumped?"

"This guy doesn't want to get caught."

Jane said, "Not necessarily. There are a lot of contradictions here."

"That's no help," Paul said. "Is it?"

Jane didn't touch the food on her plate. "That's all human behavior is—contradictions."

"So where does that get us? I'm tired of philosophy."

Jane pulled out a notebook. "I've been working up a profile. Every time I think I've got him, a new dimension is added. Something that throws me off."

"Go on."

"First, his I.Q. is probably through the roof. Genius-grade, in raw brainpower."

Paul nodded through the haze of cigarette smoke. "Sure, I figured. Smart guy. Too smart for his own good."

"Also, socially awkward. Shy. Quiet. Speaks only when spoken to. Listens hard."

"Schizophrenic," Paul said. "Don't forget that."

Jane cradled her head on her fist and leaned it to one side so that her long hair fell loose onto the linoleum tabletop. "Yes, but something more, too. Not your classical case, exchanging personalities. Though he can probably do that."

Roy couldn't help asking, "How do you know all this stuff?"

Jane smiled. "Just an educated guess. But there's a body of literature. I spent a few hours calling up case studies."

Paul said, "Tell me about our schizophrenic."

Jane sat up straight. "Well, when he's not out hacking up pretty girls, he may lead a normal life."

Roy said, "How's that?" He couldn't believe what he was hearing. The guy just went home, popped a beer, and watched the ballgame?

"There have been cases where the subject can switch it on and off." She snapped her fingers.

Paul said quietly, "So he could be walking around right under our noses, acting innocent as a nun."

Jane slowly nodded. "His neighbors probably think he's a swell guy. Quiet, unassuming, no trouble. His co-workers, too."

Roy said, "Co-workers? He can hold a job? When does he find the time?"

Jane said, "Listen to me, both of you. You think you're looking for a monster, a bogeyman, some creature out of a horror matinee. But what you're going to find is an ordinary guy with a day job."

"Lee Harvey Oswald meets Dracula," Roy said. "You're serious."

"He may go for days without any sleep, maybe as long as a week at a stretch. He runs on—I don't know—some weird kind of adrenaline. He has incredible energy. No outward signs of fatigue or stress, unless you're trained to look for it."

"And if you're trained?" Paul asked.

"Preternatural alertness. Very slight slurring of speech. Mood swings. Sense of humor may take a bizarre turn. He may talk to himself—kind of a jazzy patter. Nonsense to anybody but him. Or he may talk to somebody else."

"His victim?"

"Or somebody totally imaginary. There's just no way to tell."

Paul said, "Textbook psychotic behavior. Sounds like a crack-head."

"Not too far off, at least outwardly. Physical movements can get a little herky-jerky, like he's trying to move too fast. In the last hours before the crash, coordination may suffer."

"Outwardly," Paul mused.

Jane said, "Right. Who the hell knows what actually goes on in his head. Maybe nothing. Maybe everything."

"And he can run for a whole week before the crash?"

She shrugged. "Could be longer. Nobody's ever tested the limits. Nobody knows for sure what the chemistry is. Hard to study it while it's going on. But then he snaps out of it." She snapped her fingers again. "It's like it never happened. A dream. Maybe less than a dream."

Roy thought, Young Goodman Brown. He wakes up, and he'll never know.

Jane flipped through her notebook. "Maybe here's something you can use. Just a hunch."

Paul shoveled in his taco and said between bites, "I can use a hunch."

Jane leaned over the table. "My hunch is, he's a homebody. Has one special place where he does all his victims."

Does, Roy thought—what an innocent verb to describe that horror. A cop word. He stared at the portrait of the Kennedys, their waxy, cartooned faces, the Day-Glo Stars and Stripes rippling in the background. "Then that's where Cindy Callison is? That's what you're saying?"

Paul shook his head and pushed away his plate. "Shrivels my balls just to think about it."

Roy sipped his water and heard the animated Spanish voices rising all around them, hard syllables tapping the air. Paul was still talking, too, but Roy could only watch his thick lips move and his big face flex and fill, like he was underwater. His words made no sense.

Paul shook his shoulder gently. "You're looking green—let's vamoose."

Outside, the sky was white with sun. The heat made it hard for Roy to breathe. Jane got into her four-wheel-drive and left. Paul and Roy stood facing each other across the landau roof of the T-bird. A low-rider pickup rumbled by, blaring salsa with a bass throb. Roy said, "If Cindy Callison isn't dead, then what he's going to do to her now is worse."

"That's pure truth. Get in the car."

Inside the T-bird Paul turned on the air conditioner. First came the hot blast of stale air off the manifold, then the cool draft that raised gooseflesh along Roy's bare arms.

"A pattern," Paul said. "That's what I need. Figured you'd be good at recognizing patterns—isn't that what you literary critics do?"

Roy thought about his book—how every audience clamors for a happy ending. But an ending has to connect up with what went before. And all words written on a page or spoken out loud were just a pattern. "If we do it right," Roy answered. Everything he saw out the window was ugly, cars, buildings, people—rundown, worn out, used up. That was the only pattern he saw. But the murder was a kind of story, so there must be a pattern. The story began when a body was discovered. Maybe it ended that way, too. Something was being played out, and it had meaning. The pattern would tell them what it meant.

Paul steered the car back over the dry riverbed toward Tempe. The road ran right through the river. After every flood they had to repave it. "Number one was killed last. Number two had her eyes scooped out and an undertaker's prosthesis sewn into her mouth. Number three is missing her head. Two and three are missing hands. Number one had her hands practically burned off. No prints anywhere, none we can use."

"Cindy Callison is the key," Roy said quietly, still looking out the window. There was a transient family camping among the palo verdes in the middle of the river, a stone's throw from traffic. Didn't they realize? "She's the only one who can identify him."

"Don't get your hopes up. First she's got to live through this." Paul lit another cigarette and puffed on it. "Never seen so many potential leads that come up zero." Paul counted on his fingers, waving the lit cigarette and managing the wheel. "We got zip on her car. Zip from her apartment. Zip on her old boyfriend. Zip on her new boyfriend. Zip on where he grabbed her. Zip, zip, zip. It ain't right."

"Jane says this killer's practically a genius. And he's lucky."

"Every serial murderer seems like Superman until you catch him."

"What about the ones you don't catch?"

"Let's keep a good thought, shall we. But it makes you wonder. Those three dead girls—it's like they never existed. Erased clean. Missing persons can't even come up with their names. Who were they? Where did they come from?"

"You're asking me?"

"And another thing. I've been thinking about those railroad tracks. Where we found the first girl. They run awfully close to the university. I mean, remember where we found her car—right outside the gym."

Roy sat up, alert. "So what are you saying?"

Paul stubbed out his Pall Mall. "There's every chance it's a face you've seen in your own office doorway."

If Paul was deliberately spooking him, it was working. "Take me home, Uncle Paul. I've got to see my wife."

"Count your blessings," Paul said. "I don't blame you."

For the few minutes it took to get down Mill Avenue to Roy and Eileen's apartment complex, Roy sorted out the variables: bagged hands, undertaker's smile, clothesline around a date palm. Killer rats and winos and a missing head. And Cindy Callison waiting her turn in some special murderer's place. There had to be a pattern.

Grand, Central, Library.

Day Fifteen

"All my life," Paul was saying in between shots, "I've tried to prepare myself." Roy reloaded the .38 special. Paul was popping off miniature liquor bottles, offhand, from twenty yards. Each report snapped his wrist, brought his shooting hand up in a half-arc that never varied. Then the weight of the long barrel would drop his hand back to firing position.

"Don't you ever miss?"

Paul reloaded. "All my life I've been living toward that moment when everything I've ever done." Blam. "All I've ever learned." Blam. "Will be focused for one dangerous critical instant." Blam. "And do some good." Blam. He fell silent and fired off two more shots.

Paul turned and ejected the hot shells, his left thumb working the tab of the ejector rod. "This old Colt was designed over a hundred years ago by a guy who understood the working muscles of a man's hand." Paul reloaded, spun the pistol around his trigger finger twice, cocked, and fired at nothing. "Won't wear out your hand or your eye."

He holstered the gun and they trudged along the arroyo back to the house. The sky over the mountains was coming up opal, and there were at last shadows across the shimmering desert. Hard to believe that just over the ridge a few miles was all the racket of the city, the incessant clamor of official people wanting answers.

"Listen to what I'm telling you," Paul was saying as they hiked along the rugged bottom. Leg-breaking country, he called this.

"I do not cheat at cards. I have never hit a woman. I always pay what I owe. I keep my tools sharp and clean. I tend my house. I never drink before noon. I have never in my life taken a bribe."

Carefully, Roy picked his way over the boulders and around the prickly pear. "You're a man's man, Uncle Paul."

"Shit, that's what I'm telling you—it's not enough anymore." He was breathing hard from the labor of walking. "Maybe it never was."

They hiked up behind Esmeralda's trailer. She stood in the yard hanging clothes on a sagging line. The kids played around her feet without making a sound. When she arched on tiptoe to lift a sheet onto the line, Roy watched the long curve of her back under the white cotton sundress. When she saw them, she dropped the clothespins into a bag and went behind the trailer.

"What is she to you, Uncle Paul?"

Paul wagged a finger at him and Roy felt suddenly ten years old. "I know the difference between right and wrong, son. Don't think I don't." Roy thought, can't he ever say anything straight out?

On the porch Eileen and Jane Featherbead were playing backgammon and drinking margaritas. Jane Featherbead was spending a lot of time at Paul's lately. Maybe she just wanted to be close to the drama. Roy was getting tired of the drama.

"Sit down, boys, adjust your attitudes," Jane said. She clunked ice into two glasses and poured from a new bottle of scotch.

Paul backed heavily into the seat between the women. They put up the game board. Roy pulled a chair to Eileen's elbow. It made him a little on edge to be this close to her in public. He was sure it made the trouble between them transparent to everybody.

"You ought to invite Gino out here some time," Roy said. "Might loosen him up."

"Gino's a good boy. I tell him what to do and he does it. Doesn't talk back, just makes it happen. But this is my home, not the squad room." He was the only cop he knew who didn't socialize with other cops. He had built a life out here separate from the lurid reality of the job. But not any more—this case was living here. Now he kept the cellular phone handy outdoors. It rang for the umpteenth time today and he listened to more flack from the mayor's office and refused, one more time, to promise a quick solution to the crimes.

"Tell me a story," Jane said. "Get our minds off murder."

"It was a good story today in the seminar," Roy said absently. Some days the stories preoccupied him, as if hidden in them was some crucial clue that could save Cindy Callison. Crazy, he knew. "Listen: An old man with wings falls into the backyard of a poor peasant. They don't know if he's an angel or what." He drank. "They shut him up in a chicken coop. People come for miles around to gawk at him. They poke him, pinch him, pull off his feathers. Watch him sleep and eat and groom and flinch from pain. He's their geek, see?"

"All the world loves a geek," Jane said.

"Exactly. Well, you guessed it, they get tired of him, and then one day he grows new wings and just flies away, over the sea. The woman of the house, she watches him go. The farther away he flies, the better she can see him. When he's out of sight altogether, way over the horizon, she sees him most clearly. And that makes her smile. The end."

"Sort of poignant," Eileen said. "I like it better than the blue hotel one."

"Nobody dies?" Paul said, hanging up the cellular phone. "How can it be a story if nobody dies?"

Jane said, "What do you do when an angel falls into your own backyard?"

Up the hill came Esmeralda carrying something in her arms. Zack followed close at her heels, yipping and whining.

"What have you got there, Ezzy?" Paul said.

She came into the shade of the ramada and laid a bundled blanket on the stone floor. She looked scared to death. Paul kept the dog off. "I found this at the dump a little while ago." She bent reverently and unwrapped the blanket with quick fingers. She drew away the last flap and there against the bright colors lay the white shapes of bones. "I waited till you came back."

"Good Lord," Jane said. "Were they wrapped that way when you found them?"

"*Sí.*" She stood, shivering. Roy wanted her to do something—to move, or make the sign of the cross. Something. Roy held Eileen's hand tightly and watched Esmeralda stand at the edge of the porch, between him and the light, and recover herself. The light breeze stirred her white skirts.

Paul stood and bent over the bones. Then, carefully, he knelt and touched a large, misshapen, flat fragment. Roy recognized parts of a skull and a broken jaw. Also there were several long bones—legs? arms?

"They did not look like an animal," Esmeralda said and folded her arms under her breasts. Roy turned his eyes back to the bones.

"I've seen this before," Paul said. "Now where have I seen this before?"

Roy shook his head. "Shouldn't we do something?"

"Finish your drink. There's no light for a search. Those bones have been dead for a long time—clean as stones in a crick. Morning will be soon enough."

Jane said, "This can't have anything to do with anything, can it?"

Paul said, "Everything has to do with everything, sweetheart." Then he sighed and added, "Don't get too worked up. Desert's full of old bones."

After Esmeralda walked back down the hill to mind her kids, Eileen knelt by the blanket and reached for a bone.

"Don't touch them," Paul said with sudden authority.

"Just curious."

"There's always the chance of contagion."

Eileen yanked back her hand. "Why didn't you tell me?"

"Just did."

"Roy. Wrap them up carefully and put them where the dog ain't. The shed will do, I think. I've got some calls to make." He went inside to use the house phone in private.

Roy carried the bundle of bones out to Paul's toolshed, where he locked it in. Zack followed and watched every move. He sniffed around the closed door awhile, whining, even growling a bit. Roy dragged the dog back by the collar.

When he returned to the veranda, Jane had brought the kerosene lamp out and now lit it and replaced the sooted chimney. "We're not going to sit here and talk about those creepy bones all night long. I brought out the story lamp."

Roy said, "You mean you're just going to sit here like nothing's happened?"

"What else you going to do?" Paul said. "Come first light, we'll get to work. I've got a call in to the coroner—he's on the road somewhere. All we can do now is wait."

Day Fifteen, Night

The sky was going dusky, the air thickening. The green of the palo verdes in the arroyo was flattening to gray, and the White Tanks were two-dimensional sawtooth cutouts of rusty iron. It was shaping up to be the kind of night you needed a story to get through, Roy thought: they weren't so civilized, just cavemen gathered at the edge of light.

They talked about the bones for a few minutes and got nowhere. Paul had made arrangements to get a lab crew out at first light. He saw no pressing need to be working in the dark. Esmeralda was down the hill with her kids.

"Okay," Paul said, helping himself to more scotch. He poured the liquor and then floated two ice cubes in it. "So here's a story. Once upon a time there was a Mexican whore. A good one, too. Young. Sweet and sassy and savvy. Let's say she lived in Nogales."

Roy was surprised—Paul wasn't one to tell stories. But he'd been telling him lots of stuff lately, like he'd been storing it up. Like it was time to come clean.

Paul rubbed his palms. "She's got a little English, but mostly she talks in Mexi, caters to the tourist trade down from Tucson. Has herself a little crib off Revolution Street—not much, but clean. She's quiet, not one to make a fuss. Family's poor as a hole in your pocket, country people. Campesinos. She salts away every buck and dreams about going to Hollywood."

"Hollywood?"

"Tinsel dreams. It's not a bad life. Some of the fellows leave American money. Dollars. Real money. Overpay her on purpose. All this goes into a cigar box stashed under the mattress."

"I was wondering," Jane said.

"Going too fast for you, sweetheart?"

"Not at all."

"Anyhow," Paul said, "pretty soon she has a whole cigar box full of money. Almost three thousand dollars.

"One day a young American comes along. Married, but so was everybody. He likes her, he comes back. Two, three, a dozen times. Saturday nights, ain't hard to get away. Life on the home front's pretty grim.

"And she likes him. What's not to like? He's a good-looking boy, he's never rough with her. She starts reserving her Saturday nights special for him, waits even when he doesn't show. He teaches her English words. Pays her too much. He ain't rich, but like lots of folks he's got more than he needs. Someday I'm going to be a movie star, she tells him. Right. On the Coast she'll be just another busted bimbo hustling the creeps, waiting for the break that never comes. He knows this. But why spoil it? He bides his time.

"So one Saturday night our Yanqui shows up on schedule, and there's this Mexican tough working her over, see? Beating her up but good."

"I knew we'd get around to the wham and the bam sooner or later," Eileen said.

Paul pulled out two maduro Churchills and offered one to Roy. "Now where was I. This muchacho is whaling the bejesus out of her. Then our Yanqui shows up. Chops him a couple of good ones and sends him off spitting bad teeth. What he doesn't realize, this bandito already glommed her cigar box and made off with the goods." Paul narrowed his eyes and let that sink in, as if it were some kind of lesson.

"He stays with her there for several days, he can always make excuses back home." He smoked, looking serious. "He washes her face, cuts bandages, sends a boy out to buy penicillin. Sits there with her and holds her hand. Bakes tortillas for her. Brews tea and soup, takes care of her, see?

"At night he sleeps beside her. Doesn't touch her. Lies there in the dark and listens to her breathing and feels proud of himself.

"Wasn't long before the bandito comes back. They always do, you know. It's night. Our Yanqui's lying with the girl and the door's kicked open. Guy standing in the doorway has a shotgun, looks like. Our Yanqui grabs his pistol—"

"Hold the phone—you never said he had a pistol," Roy objected.

"Why should I? In those times, and a man like that going to a whore? Do I have to spell everything out?"

"Go on."

"He fires—pop-pop, pop-pop. Just like that. Guy in the doorway is gone. The girl's awake now. No screaming, though—not her style. They go to the door together and he's rolling round out there in the dark, howling to wake the holy dead. All the shots hit the guy's legs. The shotgun? It's a baseball bat."

"So he overreacted?" Roy said.

"I don't see it," Paul said. "You can kill a man with a baseball bat, easy."

"What happened to her?" Eileen asked.

"What d'you think? She couldn't stay there anymore. But she didn't have any money. Our Yanqui was facing hard times in a Mexican hoosegow, and he lit out." Paul turned away into the dusk. "You figure it out."

Nobody said anything for a minute. Roy looked down the hill toward Esmeralda's trailer and saw that the lights, predictably, had already gone on.

"That's all? That's the end?"

"It's a good story," Eileen said. "But what happened to the Mexican guy?"

"Who cares," Roy said, still looking down the hill, watching for the shape of her in the window.

"I care," Eileen said. "Who was he? What did he want? Why did he come back, if he already had the money?"

Paul said, "I need another drink. Roy?"

"Me, too," Roy said.

"Right. That's all you need," Eileen said. "Clear up your thinking."

"I'm thinking just fine." Roy poured the scotch and thought about all the things Paul had left out of the story at the end. Did the Yanqui help her get away? What about the wife up north? What did the girl do for money? Did she ever make it to Hollywood? But something in the cellar of his mind told him that, as usual, he was asking all the wrong questions.

"I was thinking of the bones again," Jane said. "The blanket. It seems almost new."

"Yes," Paul said. "Wasn't out there long. But the bones are old."

"Bones, bones, bones," Eileen said mostly to herself, and drank.

The coyotes started up on cue. There was a dark-gold smear behind the mountains now, all that remained of the sun. Roy could swear at times that being out here was like living on a movie set. The stillness was uncanny. Roy saw a shadow move out from behind Esmeralda's trailer and into the arroyo. He still looked for her silhouette in the window. Paul's story wasn't much to go on tonight. Esmeralda had found the bones. What secrets was she keeping?

Something big moved in the darkness beyond the porch. Zack heard it first, stiffened his ears and growled a low, rattling growl. They all listened. The stamp of hoof on hardpan was unmistakable. The thing moved off slowly down the arroyo and Zack got up once and saluted each of the mesquite posts supporting the ramada, then lay down again, restless, at Paul's feet.

"Javelina," Paul said. "Desert pigs. Mean little dickens, always rooting."

Roy looked down the hill at Esmeralda's trailer, quiet and glowing with soft internal light. What, precisely, was her story?

And who had gone away from here and left behind these murdered bones?

At first light the cops met them at the dump, a natural sink among desert-bald hillocks.

"Show me," Paul said, and Esmeralda fired off something in Spanish. Paul nodded. Zack was already way ahead of them, pawing at the base of an overturned bathtub. "For crissakes, Roy—get ahold of the dog."

The dump was a local one used only by a few neighbors—not for regular trash but for those items hard to dispose of: old refrigerators, sofas, tires, household junk. Paul walked carefully among the heaps to an overturned bathtub with broken legs.

"Here?" he asked. Hugging herself, Esmeralda nodded.

Meanwhile uniforms cordoned off the area with yellow streamers and Stein was shooting every inch of the place.

Paul signaled for Gino and Billings. "Roll away the stone," he ordered. They lifted the old tub and rolled it on its side, and Roy caught a whiff of vile-smelling air. On the oval of desert it had shaded lay a heap of bright bones.

"What I was afraid of," Paul said. "It's an old crime. Years, probably."

Stein said, "Hold it," and snapped their picture beside the tub, like it was a photo op.

Paul waved Stein out of the way. "Call the coroner over here."

"It is not right to leave the dead unburied," Esmeralda said.

"Amen to that," Paul replied. "Now go on home. We've got work to do."

After a preliminary examination, Hoff said, "The hands and feet are missing. Hacked off—how about that? Jaws smashed by blunt force. A few loose teeth. No evidence of clothing—rot, animals, whatever." He wore latex gloves and gave a pair to Paul so he could handle the bones.

"How many?"

"Three skulls. Caucasian. Slightly built. Either young or female or both." He handed one to Paul, who turned it in his upraised palm.

"How long?"

Hoff shrugged. "That clean? A year. Longer. We'll know better after we get them to the lab."

Paul nodded, as if remembering something. He put down the skull. Roy watched the men work quietly among the debris as the sun rose over the brown hills and the sky bloomed with light. Jane looked on impassively.

"Gino," Paul said sharply. "Get a map. Take as many uniforms as you need. Wade, help him. Canvass every house within a five-mile radius. I want to know if anybody acts nervous or has unusual habits. Or was ever arrested. Or ever spent time in a rubber room."

"Righto."

"Or butchers their own stock, anybody with a smokehouse or deep-freeze. Do it today."

"Righto."

"Call me."

"Why don't you ever write this stuff down?"

"Already did."

"I'll be at the house with the coroner."

Roy followed Paul up the north hillock overlooking the dump. They stood there in the sunlight and Paul appeared to be listening to the light breeze moan across the desert floor. He slowly swiveled in a compass. "Not a goddamn thing out there," he said after a moment, his words lost in too much blue sky.

"Desert, sand, and rock."

"Sand, rock, and bones." The whole grisly business had followed him home after all. "Come on."

Roy had a sudden vision of bones, thousands of them, strewn

across the desert, bleaching to dust. It had something to do with the immensity of the land around them, the hard unyielding surface of things, the lack of boundaries in any direction. Something was loose and had an infinite range.

Jane joined them at the T-bird. Paul drove them back along the rutted track, sucking on a Pall Mall. "Five years ago, more or less, some flower girls disappeared. You know, those kids who stand on street corners with roses and daffodils and run out to cars at red lights."

"That's a long time ago." Roy saw them every day, wearing skimpy shorts and halter tops and working alone with a folding chair and a plastic pail of flowers.

"Four of them in a nine-month stretch. If I were a betting man—no bodies were ever recovered. No witnesses ever came forward. Lot of them are loose kids—runaways, living on the street."

"Come on, Paul. That's a long shot. What are the chances?"

"Four. Four flower girls, four sets of bones. If that's a goddamned coincidence, then horses shit peanuts."

Paul parked below the house and they climbed up to the shed and unlocked the door. On the floor lay the blanket, open and torn to shreds, the bones scattered all about. Roy had the impression some were missing.

"Christ, that's all we need," Paul said, and bent to pick up a long bone. He turned it, and even Roy, looking over his shoulder, could discern the bite marks.

"Something got in here," Jane said.

"I don't see how."

But Roy saw: at the back of the shed was a burrow coming up under the wall. Pebbles and sand were splashed all over the blanket. "The dog?"

"Too small for the dog." Paul led him around back of the shed to the other end of the burrow. "Notice anything, nephew?"

Roy didn't see anything peculiar. A burrow was a burrow. "No."

"Look again. Where's all the dirt from the digging?"

There was no fresh sand outside the shed. "How can that be?"

"Whatever it was, it was already inside. The burrow was how it got out."

Roy recalled his visit to the shed the night before, how Zack had remained sniffing at the door after he had left the bones inside, had had to be dragged away. "Coyote?"

"They'll tell us at the lab. Dammit! That shed has always been safe as a lockbox."

"You couldn't have known," Roy said.

"What gets me is all the stuff. All the evidence that comes up zero." He sighed. "Sometimes too much is not enough."

"Somebody always knows something. You said."

Paul lit up a Pall Mall and hunkered in the dust. "At this point in time we're just collecting bodies. We need a new theory. A whole new way of looking at the world."

Jane didn't comment, only nodded.

Roy squatted down beside Paul, feeling the creak in his knees.

"Twenty-four hours after a homicide, the chances of catching the killer go down by fifty percent. After five years? Shit."

"But this is mass murder."

Paul squinted into the smoke and the sun.

Jane walked closer and said, "He will do three things. One, tamper with the body—which includes moving it."

"The first bundle of bones. The new blanket."

"Second, revisit the scene of the crime. Third, live near where the body was dumped."

Roy said, "Maybe he wants the attention. Maybe that's why he put the bones out in the open."

"Then why go to such trouble to hide the bodies in the first place? To cover up the identities of the victims?"

"Maybe he changed his mind. Maybe he gets off on the media hype."

Paul said, "We'll never know if he raped them. All we've got is bones."

Jane said, "He's probably impotent. If he uses his victims for sex, it's probably self-abuse. He tortures them and masturbates."

Roy said, "How can you even talk about this stuff?" Somehow saying it out loud made it more real and frightening.

"One thing's for sure," Paul said. "He's not going to see this on TV. Nobody knows what we found out there, and nobody's going to. Not yet."

"Can you do that?"

Paul flicked away his cigarette. "We can do whatever we want. We're the cops."

Eileen met them on the porch, her hair up, the brown curve of her neck still glistening from the shower. Roy put his arm around her and could not help running his hands over her ribs, her spine, the back of her skull. He kissed her hair. "Hey, what's all this?" At first she had pulled away.

"Nothing," he said. Paul went by them into the house.

"What did you find out there?"

"Later," he said. He took her hand and pulled her into him, embracing her too hard. Something was very wrong in the world, and he needed to feel her warm, living body. They kissed. He held her, listening to the dry wind rattling the palo verde.

She stepped away but kept hold of his hand. "It's got to stop sometime. It has to. Paul will figure it out."

Roy nodded and followed her into the house. He wished he could be so sure.

Time is the air I breathe, over.

Carried her out in the rosy mist and laid her down. Wrapped her up and laid her down—must wrap the package, copy?

Before you begin sewing, clear the mouth and throat passages of any blockage. Insert the prosthesis with thumb and forefinger of right hand while steadying the subject's jaw with the left hand. You will hear it click into place over the teeth when positioned properly.

The stitches must be loose enough not to tear and tight enough to hold firmly for forty-eight hours—longer, in extraordinary cases when the subject must travel.

In that eventuality, dry ice is recommended (see Chapter 9).

A basting stitch will work nicely, but be sure to lead the needle into the gum inside the lip; otherwise, the thread will show. Waxed nylon #4 is recommended, along with a #2 Benson's needle.

You can do careful work when you're thrilled.

Believe it.

You can focus and concentrate. The air becomes a humming cone and you spiral down to the pinpoint at the bottom of the cone where everything weighs a hundred times more, and sound is a needle prick deep in the hump at the top of your neck. You should've seen her smile.

Felt how she bled warm all over me.

I stole her voice. Now it's mine. Kind of voice that tickles your chest. Swells your eardrums with a deep low hum.

Radio voice.

Wouldn't talk to me, over. Scooped her eyes out with a dessert spoon.

Angle of repose is reached by calculating inertial moment as a function of friction and gravity. Do you copy?

Say again, angle of repose.

White dog crosses my dreams and wakes her up. White dog on my trail, over. Digging bones. Digging up my girls.

No more. Doggie fixed.

Man follow doggie, over.

I dream barking and whistles. Have followed her in and out of the places of this city. She has a light around her that makes her untouchable. I get so close and no closer. Once I brushed her sleeve and felt the warm glow of her flesh. Remarkable.

He's with her often, and he tells her stories. Stories are like a dog whistle blown way up high. You have to have the right ears. I heard him, and believed.

Here is a long place that winds and winds. Her skin is on my hands.

I am her—copy?

Got a date with the dreamboat behind door number three.

Listen: Can make her scream like a cat, over. Squeal like a rat. Sounds like the fucking monkeyhouse in here, copy?

Day Twenty-two

The following Thursday, Paul's voice sounded shaky on the phone. "Come up here when you can," he said.

Roy was in his office grading his first batch of essay exams, most of them unfocused, full of dimly perceived ideas and misremembered facts. Hadn't they been listening at all? Or had he simply not told the stories well enough? He knew his own focus was suffering lately.

"You got a break in the case?"

"Just come up when you can. Tomorrow too soon?"

Roy stopped up at the departmental office long enough to retrieve his mail, then went across the street for a sandwich and read the paper, knowing Eileen would not be home yet. This week her client was a big credit-card company headquartered downtown. The company had fragmented into little feuding fiefdoms and profits were nosediving. Her job was to redraw lines of communication within the office—setting up everything from circulation routes for memos to an employee grievance procedure. She taught the bigwigs how to get along with the mailboy, the secretary, the receptionist—the ones she called the "invisible people." Crucial, but hardly noticed and rarely appreciated. Her business was efficiency.

She's always been talented, Roy reflected, at getting other people to talk things out to a solution. Yet she wouldn't even go with him to their counselor anymore.

As he ate, Roy bided his time watching the students, tan and young and good-looking, and thinking about Cindy Callison.

After lunch, he walked down College Street to where it dead-ended into the stadium parking lot, where her car had been recovered. Beyond that were the tracks, a spur of the line that ran along Grand Avenue. He walked the right-of-way toward Mill Avenue, half a mile. The gravel of the roadbed held the heat—Roy could feel the burn through his desert boots. The steel rail was polished from recent use. He stopped and looked and listened. He did not know what he was after here. He walked on.

"I can do the work," she had said the last day he saw her. At his office an hour before the seminar. Then the rest, and he had said nothing to help her. What could he have said?

Where had she spent the last hours of her freedom?

He tried to imagine it. She walked out of class and down College Street. That would have been Wednesday. He had watched her across the table as he spoke, listened to her answers about the stories, wished he could talk plainly with her. Watched her brown glowing hands, their answers. Her eyes bright and full.

What did a man say to a woman to lure her to a place where he might murder her?

Jane had said the flower-girl murderer would dump the bodies near his own home. Was he really the one who had taken Cindy Callison? How could he be near all those places at once? Was he on the move? Was it even the same man? It all seemed so preposterous—the impossible happened, and kept on happening.

He walked the six blocks to their apartment in a contemporary adobe cluster. Eileen was already there. "Canceled my last appointment," she explained. "God, I just can't concentrate on anything anymore. I look at faces, you know. I look at their eyes and hands. I listen to their tone of voice. I think, Is that the one? How about him?"

"Two beers," he said. "One for you, one for me. Then we go for a ride."

"Good. I feel like moving." She handed him a can so cold his sweaty fingers stuck to it. He popped the top and took a long draft.

"Missed you," he said and leaned against the fridge. "No kidding."

Eileen stared out the window over the sink. "I've been dreaming about those bones," she said. "You know? Skeletons up and walking around. Creepy stuff."

"I won't let the bogeyman get you," Roy said and hugged her from behind.

She turned and drew back. "I want a gun. I've decided."

That's what she needed, all right, a gun. She'd asked for one before, but he'd talked her out of it. But just now he'd give her anything she asked. "All right." He crumpled his can and flung it away. "Grab the checkbook."

Roy drove Eileen to the pawnshop downtown where Paul had taken him. The pawnbroker was a one-armed man named Junior who wore a turquoise bola tie. Roy mentioned Paul's name, and what he wanted. The one-armed man handed the five-shot nickel-plated revolver to Eileen.

"What's this?" she said. "Is it big enough?" She held it and pointed it, closing one eye. "Don't I want an automatic? Don't they have more bullets?"

"This is simpler. You can't shoot yourself, and if you have to shoot somebody else all you do is point and pull the trigger. No safety, no cocking, no clip to fall out." The same speech Uncle Paul had given him, years ago now.

"A hundred and a quarter," the pawnbroker said. "For Paul, make it a hundred even plus tax. Okay?"

"Write the man a check," Roy said.

"Don't I have to take a test or something?" Eileen asked.

"Sweetheart, this is the Wild West. Just don't shoot nobody unless they got it coming."

"Something's wrong," Roy said as they pulled up to Paul's house. The drive was full of cars—the T-bird, Jane's Bronco, Zapata's Pontiac with mag wheels, and a red Jeep. They parked and hurried across the porch. He was expecting news about the case, but all the commotion was on account of the dog.

"Goddamned javelinas," Paul said, opening the door. He had

been drinking. On a small mattress in the middle of the floor lay Zack. The vet was bending over him, palpating the dog's shaved pink stomach and hinquarters while Jane gently held him still. Zack's ears were taped and one eye was patched. Both hind legs were in splints.

"Goddamned pigs," Paul said, and paced.

The vet said, "He's hanging in there. Hate to move him. The stitches I put in this morning are holding, but he's all busted up inside."

"What happened, Uncle Paul?" Roy took his uncle's arm. Eileen had already stationed herself next to Jane, to be of help.

"He was out all night. I run across him this morning, just laying there in the wash. You could see the blood and the tracks of his broken legs."

"Jesus. I'm sorry."

"He was trying to get back. I carried him here, me and Ezzy. Goddamned javelinas got to him. Whole goddamned herd. Pulled him just about limb from limb."

Jane and Eileen were petting the dog's head, carefully. He wagged his tail and feebly licked their hands.

"Look at him," Roy said. "Jesus."

Paul pulled something black and rubbery out of his pocket, and laughed tiredly. "Look at this," he said, holding it in his open palm. Roy could see now it was crusted with blood. "Old Zack bit off one of their noses. Bled him to death. I found the carcass."

"Why did they leave him be?"

Paul shrugged. "Something scared them off, I guess."

It was a long night. With a hundred twenty-nine stitches closing his wounds, Zack slept fitfully, yipping and growling in a subliminal voice, front paws scraping the floor, clickety, clickety, as he chased around in his nightmares. They all sat inside and kept an eye on him, and at some point it got too late to go home and it was understood they would all keep Paul's vigil with him. From time to time the dog woke and tried to rise, then thumped his tail almost in apology, it seemed to Roy. His eye was red and lacked luster. His breathing was heavy and rough.

"You'd think that old hound would've learned something in ten years on the desert," Paul said. "Worthless old coot."

"He'll be all right," Jane said. "Wait and see."

And indeed by morning Zack was sleeping more or less peacefully. "Drugged to the eyeballs," Paul said. He slept in a chair next to the dog. Eileen and Jane had the couches, and Roy lay on the rug.

Paul roused him before it was light. "I think he's going to make it." Zack was awake and licking himself. "Does my heart good." They took turns scratching the dog under the chin.

They went quietly to the kitchen and had coffee. Then Paul led him to the back bedroom where his gun locker was and selected a Winchester .30-30 for Roy and an old Garand .30-06 for himself.

"Take plenty of shells, nephew."

Paul strapped on his matching Colts, then locked home a clip in his rifle. Roy fed seven shells into the Winchester's tubular magazine, the way Paul had showed him when he was still a teenager. He hadn't fired a rifle in years, but it all came back to him easily. Outside the house, Paul cocked his weapon and flicked on the safety, and Roy jacked a round into the chamber, then let the hammer down gently.

Already a light shone in the window of Esmeralda's trailer, silvered in the crepuscular glow. Zapata's gray Pontiac was still there.

They tracked down the arroyo in the gray light. There lay the carcass of the pig Zack had killed. Already the coyotes had stripped it to hide and skull and a spiny cape.

"I know where the herd keeps," Paul said. "A mile or so. There's a little sinkhole they like and it's all high-cut banks. If we can catch them in there." Paul sniffed the dawning breeze that was blowing into their faces. They moved on. Roy tried hard not to scrabble loose rock with his footsteps. He tried to plant each step on soft sand or clean rock. Ahead moved Paul, silent and heavy.

When they got to the place, they waited and listened. They lay flat on the bank, downwind, on either side of the arroyo where it fed into the sink. Roy did not move. He held the trigger as he cocked the hammer silently, released the trigger, and laid the rifle flat on the ground beside him.

Time floated above them across the sky, washing it with blue and gold and pink. Not a cloud anywhere. Roy heard the birds, cactus wrens and grackles, then silence. Pretty soon there was another sound, a trick of the ear at first and then more definite—something moving down the arroyo. He lifted his face high enough that he could see.

Five black shapes rustled out of the brush and into the sink. To Roy, from above, they looked like five enormous bugs. They snorted and chuffed around the muddy water, jostling for position. Ever so slowly, Roy raised his rifle. Out of the corner of his eye he could see Paul rising as a gray shadow across the arroyo, a morning ghost. Roy sighted through the iron ring.

They fired out their magazines together.

With the first shots, the javelinas moiled about in confusion, grunting and clacking their fangs. Some tried to climb the steep banks and slid back, squealing. One rushed toward the arroyo opening, and Paul cut him down with a head shot. Roy put three rounds into a little one before it ceased flopping around in the mud.

The last wild desert pig, foaming and snorting, charged right up the bank toward Roy. Its sharp little hooves gouged out the loose sand and clay, slipping, spraying scree, but on it came. Roy could see the shine of its eyes, the black wet snout, the bristling cape. He could hear the bared, foam-flecked tusks clacking. He was out of ammo.

From the other side, Paul fired once more and blew it back down into the sink, then slid down among the slaughtered herd. He drew one of his long Colts and, barrel to ear, put a round into each of the dead pigs. He shot the last dead pig twice.

"There," he said. "Goddamnit." Paul was breathing hard.

Roy stood a minute to let the adrenaline go down, feeling sort of ashamed. He tasted the sour hot juice of his stomach. He didn't know what to say. All he could think of was how Paul had trained him to shoot only what he planned to eat, never to waste. Take life to make life. So he said, hesitantly, "Do you want the meat? I didn't bring a knife."

Paul walked away from him to the blank rise of the sink. He stood there among the carcasses and Roy watched his back. He couldn't see the man's face. He watched the T of sweat on the back of Paul's blue shirt. Paul seemed to be mumbling to himself, then he coughed and spat out a mouthful of phlegm.

"Do you want—"

"Fuck it." Paul turned and tucked the rifle under his arm. "Would make me sick to eat it."

Day Twenty-three, Morning

Zapata's Pontiac was gone when they got back. Without a word, Paul clomped across the porch and into the house. Roy sat now in a hard chair on the porch, watching the day get hot. "Off your ass and into the Bronco," Jane said, bursting out the door and moving past him in a blur. "It may be nap time on the Ponderosa, but I've got pots to deliver."

"How's the dog?"

"He'll sleep all day. I just gave him another dose."

Roy had no classes today, so he climbed into the Bronco. Gravel and sand sprayed under the fenders and wheel wells as Jane pulled out in a hurry. When she was behind the wheel of a truck, there was something loose and easy about her. Wearing jeans and a chambray shirt, dusty brown hair pulled back in a neat ponytail, she looked almost pretty.

They loaded the pots from Jane's studio at the edge of the Gila Reservation and made four stops, dropping off the last crate at a walled-in mansion at the foot of Camelback Mountain. "My clients get a kick out of seeing their finished work," she said.

"Why don't they take them home on their regular visits?"

"I don't let them near the kiln, for one thing. A lot of amateur work just explodes—air bubbles in the clay. They find it devastating. My clients are people who are just barely hanging on. It can set them back months."

"I thought the pot-making was just therapy. You know, sort of a hobby to relax them."

"For the therapy to be real, the pots have to be real."

"So you show up with the successes."

"Right. They learn to take what comes. Not to count on things too much. But whatever they do get, it's the real thing."

"What if everything they make blows up in the kiln?"

Jane just gave him a look.

They were headed back to Paul's. Roy was feeling the fatigue wash over him and, with the sun glazing the windshield, he had to fight off drowsiness. Jane wore aviator glasses. "You like making pots?" he asked.

"I like living in the desert away from all this crap. I like working when I feel like it and not having to be with anybody I don't want to."

"Fair enough. But why pots?"

"As I said the other night, I was involved with an archaeologist. He was into dead things. Bones and dust."

Roy shook his head. "Not my style." He liked his stories alive, in words.

"Not mine, either, as it turned out. Got tired of potsherds, fragments, broken pieces. The curve of the whole pleases me more."

"Is that what pottery is?"

"That's what psychology is."

"The curve of the whole," he repeated, liking the phrase. He would have to remember it for class.

She nodded. "Most psychological problems are problems of integrity. Literally. Things are in pieces instead of connected into some coherent whole. When you turn a pot, it's all one thing. As the French say, the craft enters the body. Integrity becomes a practical habit."

Talks just like Eileen does about offices, Roy thought. Connecting all the pieces into one working whole. The way Paul talked about this case. "So this killer we're after lacks integrity?"

"In a word, yes. His consciousness is fragmented. Look, most of us can compartmentalize our lives to a certain extent. You're at the office, you behave certain way. At home, you relax. And so on. But you never stop being who you are. That arc of connection is personality."

"Are you saying this murderer doesn't have a personality?"

"I don't know what I'm saying. I'm in the dark, just like you and Paul. But if I had to guess, I'd guess his personality is a black hole that sucks in other personalities and mimics them in perverse ways."

"Mimics? Like an actor?"

"Like a method actor. The emotion is false, but real to him at the time. Then, click, he's somebody else."

"Just like that?"

"Just like that."

The drive seemed to take a long time. Roy drowsed, waking whenever the Bronco stopped at a red light. It was a pleasant, just-below-the-surface dozing, untroubled by dreams. His eyes swam in the filtered light.

"You know what all this is about, don't you?" Jane said all at once, rousing him.

"Sure. It's about catching a maniac." He didn't say the rest: before he kills Cindy Callison.

"Ask him about Linda," Jane said as they headed at last out of traffic and into the open desert west of town. "That's who this is about. Linda and Paul."

Roy straightened in his seat and yawned. Paul's wife, his aunt. "I know she was killed, but nobody ever talked about it. Paul especially. I think I was in, what, first grade. One of those years we were in Colorado."

The White Tanks were visible in the distance. Roy watched their golden peaks swell as the Bronco closed the miles.

"It's an awful story."

"My parents told me about it in a general way." But not the details, he thought. Whenever he'd asked for details, they'd changed the subject. Everybody had gone to a lot of trouble to forget. As he'd gotten older, even he had put it out of his mind—just an old family tragedy, vague at the edges.

"She was kidnapped. They found her out by Chandler—buried alive."

"I remember the kidnapping part." Buried alive, he thought. One of the details they'd never mentioned.

"Case of mistaken identity, that was the theory. They were after the rich Popes, not poor old Paul. Buried her in a box, gave her a canteen and a flashlight. There was an air shaft, but somehow it got plugged up. She suffocated."

"Jesus." He knew they had killed her, but he'd always just assumed they'd shot her, that it was sudden. He fixed the picture in his mind's eye. "How long was she in there?"

"Took them two weeks to find her."

"Did she—was she—how long did she survive down there?" In an odd way, it mattered to him: how long had she suffered, hoping, at last losing hope? How long did she know she was going to die?

Jane kept staring straight ahead behind her sunglasses. "You always want the gory details, don't you. Four days, maybe five. Who knows. The water was gone and the batteries were dead. They never did get the guys who did it."

Roy imagined that—boxed in, thirsty, choking on dust, lungs filling up with darkness.

"It was a bad time for everybody."

"You talk like you know."

"I knew Paul before Linda. I introduced them." She got quiet, as if overwhelmed by memory.

Roy sat up, wide awake now, and watched her profile. "Were you in love with him?"

She smiled wanly. "Everybody falls in love with Paul sooner or later."

They turned into Paul's lane and passed Esmeralda's trailer. There on the porch sat Paul.

"Howdy," Paul called hoarsely. Drink in hand, he looked old and slack and loose-boned. Jane kissed him on the forehead and patted his shoulders. Roy knew Paul should be working. "How's the dog?"

"Just hunky-dory. Still looks like hell, though."

Eileen appeared at the door. Her dark hair was gathered in a ponytail that bared her brown graceful neck. She flung her arms around Roy and kissed him passionately and long. She looked at Jane and nodded hello, her arms still wrapped around her husband. But Eileen had marketing to do, and when she left Roy sat down next to Paul.

"Look at that," Jane said, watching Eileen go. "My Lord, that woman's got curves."

Paul nodded. "Kind of raises your confidence in Roy here, don't it."

Paul looked defeated. His face had a gray, sagging cast to it. His eyes squinted. His hands were white and unsteady on the glass. He wasn't even drinking from it, just holding it. For the first time Roy started to think of Uncle Paul growing old. He'd always thought of him as ageless, powerful, the biggest and smartest man in any room.

Jane went into the house.

"What we did," Paul said after she left. "Been studying on it." He put down his glass. His eyes settled into a brooding stare.

"What are you making it such a big deal for? Forget it. You've killed desert pigs before."

Paul stared out into the desert. His eyes betrayed agitation, but his hands were clasped tight in his lap and his body stiffened in an effort at composure. "I don't say we did wrong. I have never regretted anything I ever did in this life and I don't intend to start now." He said it too loudly.

"You're making too much out of it."

Paul exhaled a long breath and all the starch went out of him. "It flushed me out, though. I do say that. I feel all used up and hollow. I'm sitting here just trying to fill up again."

"Uncle Paul, they were just pigs . . ."

"It's not just the pigs." How to make Roy understand how the killing had frightened him? "It's all of it," Paul said.

Roy sat there a moment before replying. "I understand."

Paul said, "You sure find out what you're made of. I've been on the job in this wicked world so long, I don't go to the john without packing iron. I live that way, no apologies. I have killed one of ev-erything that lives in this desert, including men. But until this morn-ing, I never killed in anger."

What difference could it possibly make, Roy wondered. Dead pigs, dead men, they didn't care what was going on in your mind. They just died. He was getting impatient with Paul's maudlin preoc-cupation with a bunch of pigs. "The pigs hurt the dog, and we took care of them. It's done. And you've got more important things to worry about."

Paul shook his head, not hearing him. "Can't put it into words."

Roy listened to the air sing with the heat. Though it was mid-morning, it was already hot and bright. Evening was eight hours away, and night itself seemed impossible in such a landscape under a sky as blue and hard as bottle glass. Roy thought of Linda, Paul's young wife, buried alive in dust. He hated seeing Paul this way—it shook him up. If he couldn't rely on Paul, then who?

Paul said, "Thing is, she may be still alive. The Callison girl. Feels like she is."

"Then she's running out of time. We ought to be out looking—"

"I got twenty-three detectives and two hundred officers out look-ing. I got Gino on the other end of a phone."

"But nobody's looking in the right place."

Paul nodded and then tapped an index finger against his temple. "I am."

Day Twenty-three, Evening

At noon, when the civil-defense sirens in Phoenix blew, Zack had lifted his muzzle and weakly sung along. His feeble howling entered Roy's dreaming as a clear, wavering note, carried away on the wind. Roy slept in his hard chair on the porch. Between the shooting and helping Jane make her deliveries, it had already been a long day.

He woke for good late in the afternoon when the veterinarian arrived to check on Zack. Without opening his eyes, he heard the boots clacking across the stone, the low voices murmuring confidentially. He could tell by the sound that everything was all right. It was pleasant to listen to the voices. He had watched the vet work with the dog yesterday. When he laid his hands on, even in his pain Zack had not balked. Paul always said the dog knows a sure hand.

Roy did not have to open his eyes to see it: the one-eyed dog, pink belly and flanks crosshatched with black stitches painted with a film of orange antiseptic, settled and quiet under the probing hands, hind legs bound stiff in splints. Roy could smell the antiseptic, like overripe pears.

They came out onto the porch. Paul must have slept too: he looked sober and washed, and he was wearing his silver Stetson. It seemed like ten years had come off him.

Roy stood and yawned. The light was beginning to go.

"You're good to come out," Paul said to the vet. He walked him out to the drive.

"You do what you can. I'm sorry it couldn't have been more." Then the vet got into his red Jeep and drove away.

When he was gone Paul said, "Let's walk."

Roy stretched his legs and stepped off the porch. The two men ambled down the hill and then west, toward the foothills, where the light was draining slowly into color. Roy had expected Eileen to be back by now.

"You missed some phone calls while you were asleep, but that's okay," Paul said. The desert lay before them, unbroken, all the way to the mountains. Underfoot the earth was hard and littered with sharp stones.

Paul continued, "The flower-girl bones, the other two, were all hacked apart by the same weapon. A big, heavy knife. Machete, hunter's Bowie."

"You're sure they were the missing flower girls?"

"No positive I.D. Gino's team is going through dental records all over town, but that's a long shot. There are almost four hundred dentists. We may never know for sure."

"Then what good is that?"

"Means he's been at this for a long time. Do you know how many people disappear in a town like Phoenix and are never missed?"

"You keep calling it a town—there are half a million people in this valley."

"That's why I live out here, so I can forget them."

"How could he get away with it all this time?"

"This fellow is amazing. No pattern to any of it. No way to predict him."

"It's obscene." Roy tried to picture it, but his imagination balked. A man choking a young woman unconscious, then cutting her head off while she was still alive. Then methodically hacking her limb from limb. His mind's eye blanked.

"Victims one and three were frozen. That's why fixing time of death was so tricky. It's not something the coroner sees much of in this place. And you'll love this: we found prints. Two sets. Two."

"An accomplice? But I thought—"

"Hoff says no. Too small. Plus, get this: They match the prints of two of the dead flower girls. They had to get fingerprinted for a vendor's license."

"But that's impossible!"

"Don't tell me. Most of it seems impossible. But it's what we have."

Roy didn't say anything. He felt as if they were descending deeper and deeper into some cellar of the human soul. He had no light down there. He felt like a character in that Edgar Allan Poe story, being led into those deep catacombs planted on either side with the skeletons of generations. The one in which Montresor chains Fortunato to the dungeon wall and then bricks up the opening.

They spotted the dust of a car coming up the dirt drive. "There's Eileen," Roy said, hearing the relief in his own voice. "We'd better get back." Jane's Bronco was right behind Eileen's car.

"Take your time. Give them the run of the kitchen a while yet."

Roy managed the rough terrain easily in the running shoes he was wearing for a change. Paul had on western boots—sensible in this country, a coarse wilderness of prickly pear, sidewinder, and scorpion.

"I've said it enough times, but one of these days I'm getting a pair of roans," Paul said. "We could ride out all the way to the foothills, you and me."

Roy's answer was the familiar refrain. "Haven't had a good horse under me in years."

"Nephew, don't let me pry into your business. What goes on under your roof is between you and your own wife."

"It's complicated, Uncle Paul."

"Something happened, then."

Roy nodded. How do you tell somebody that your wife was raped, and that you made it worse?

"You don't want to say."

"Right." He didn't, but he did, too. If he could ever think of a way to tell it so it would come out right.

"That's okay, boss. I don't go in much for this Fraudian shit anyways." He deliberately pronounced it wrong. He trusted Jane because she had common sense to go along with her book sense. And Jane was a friend from the old days. But in general he thought psychology was overrated. "Some things a man best keep to himself."

"Right."

"But then again, sometimes talk simplifies things."

They walked on, enjoying the last light.

"Let me ask you a question," Paul said. He stopped and rubbed his temples. Quail broke into low flight from the scrub thicket to their left. "What can excite such hatred in a man?"

Roy pondered a minute and watched the quail alight fifty yards off. They dropped in a volley toward the cover of a wash, then went invisible, all at once, like a magic trick. "I don't think this is about hatred. When you hate you lose control. I think our killer only seems out of control. I think he has plenty of control."

Paul nodded, watching a cottontail bound out of the arroyo, a flash of white and brown. More magic. "That's a good answer. That's what I would have said. But think about this morning."

Roy remembered how they had held in their anger and then deliberately gone to a specific place for the purpose of killing. How they had fired carefully and left nothing in the little sink alive.

"You don't think it's the same?"

"It gives me pause. I mean, we were sort of out of control."

"Remember how bad you felt afterward. And they were only pigs."

"That's what saves a man," Paul agreed. "Our killer doesn't feel that, though, does he. All he feels is hate."

"Not hate. Something else. Something we don't even have a name for."

Paul nodded and listened to the desert. Roy heard the birds now, busy and chattering in the thick air—grackles, cactus wrens, woodpeckers, quail, dove.

The quality of desert light at this hour never ceased to astonish Roy. The air held the dust in a deep screen fine as vapor. When you walked through it, you felt the space your body opened up and then felt that space close behind you, an invisible wake. You could stroke the air and feel a silky friction.

"If only the whole world were like this," Paul said.

"You loved her very much, didn't you. Linda."

"That was a lifetime ago. The less said, the better."

Roy shook his head. "I would have broken."

"There's a reason I never told you. Didn't want pity."

"You have Jane. You have—"

"Jane is not my love. I don't expect you to understand that, and I don't expect you to bring it up again."

"I'm not old enough? You can't tell me that anymore."

"Maybe, maybe you're right." He watched the desert and listened and didn't look at Roy. He took a step away and stood there. "A good woman completes a man, that's all."

"I know that." He thought about Eileen—what would he ever do if he lost her? How could he go on without her?

"No, you don't. You may believe it, but you don't know it. Someday, though. God willing."

The birds swam in the thick air, hovering and dipping, wings blading graceful arcs. Maybe it was about time he told Roy. The murders had made them close again in a way they had not been for years.

"You always want to know things. All right. When Linda was killed, I dedicated myself to her revenge. I know what a cliché that is. Knew it then, but I didn't care. I'd catch every killer on earth if I had to. One of them would be hers. Maybe I'd never know, but if only I got them all. If only." His fist closed fast, then loosened again.

Roy waited for him to continue.

Paul rubbed his eyes. Cottontails and big gray jacks were popping up all over the place now, feeding before the coyotes came out. "Watch out for snakes," Paul said. "Right time of day."

Roy looked at his flimsy running shoes. He never thought about snakes. He walked carefully, which made him clumsy. "Revenge," Roy said offhandedly, to prod him.

"You can't hold on to it, though," Paul said. "Revenge is a fine thread, starts unraveling. Pretty soon one day you wake up and it's flat gone."

"Why do you keep on doing it, then?"

"If I knew that. There's still the mystery. Haven't gotten too far with that. Sometimes I think I'm closer. Something will scratch behind my eyes and I know I'm almost there. If I could only know. If I could. This case, who knows."

"What? What would it change? What would you do?"

Paul sighed long, as if he'd been waiting years for the question. "I'd stay out here and watch the birds at sundown. I'd lay my tired carcass on this stubborn place and let the varmints pick my bones clean. And be at peace."

"A hard land to rest in peace in."

"One of these days I'll be gone, and this place'll be yours. Have you thought of that?"

"What in the world are you talking like that for?" Paul looked a bit tired, but nowhere near played out. He smoked too much and had that hacking cough, but it didn't seem to slow him down any. He'd always been cranky and careless about what was good for him. "You just need a good night's sleep, away from telephones."

"The past is a funny thing—it fills you up, but it also eats you up."

"I shouldn't have pressed you about her."

"Like you said, you're old enough now. Pay attention to things."

They walked back knee-deep in shadow.

"Whatever you want," Roy said.

Paul laughed and clapped him on the shoulder. "We both talk too much. But shoot, what else is any better."

On the porch they walked into the yellow lantern glow spilling out of the kitchen. They could smell the meat cooking.

"Come on in here and wash your hands," Eileen called. "Then park your butts and choose your cuts."

They sat down to a supper of prime rib au jus, steamed garden broccoli, and baked potatoes. Eileen's midriff was bare and brown between jeans faded to powder-blue and a pink man's shirt whose tails were tied under her loose breasts. Her dark-brown hair was combed out long. She said, "You're both turning to skin and bones, and I won't have it."

Her hair shone and her eyes sparkled, and any man seeing her there, Roy was certain, would fall in love with her at a glance.

They bowed their heads for the silent blessing. Paul stared at the meat platter a moment, then chose a small slab and passed the dish on. Jane speared a big cut and piled it onto Paul's plate. "You heard the woman," she said.

Roy claimed a slice thick as his finger. Eileen poured rich plummy Beaujolais into four stemmed glasses and left the bottle on the table. Roy ate and tasted the sweet blood.

Base Station #5

Sometimes, when I'm out, I turn the radio off, and there's no sound at all.

White noise.

I am the heart of a rock. Hear no one, no one can hear me. Watch the doors breathe in the heat, leaking light at their edges. Watch the air settle in a fine dust over the books, the furniture, my tools, my fingers.

Can do this for almost half a minute.

She was a voice in my ear before she was anything else. I wanted one of her. I saw around her a light, pink and dazzling. Electric, over. Neon Freon.

Walked beside her, made my legs keep up. Touched her hand and could almost feel it. Patted her on the back, stood close enough to smell her hair.

Sucked her into me with eyes nose ears. But couldn't keep her, not the way I keep her now.

I sit here alone, and wonder what it's like to be lonely. That what I am?

Closed your eyes. Don't look at me, babe. Just lay there still and don't even breathe. This hurts me more than it hurts you. Don't watch.

Love this heat, over? Love the blasted wasteland outside, all bright and hard. Cooking up my brown ass, over. Sizzling my brain yolk, over. Over easy, over?

Just turn myself off at night and go to bed. She'll still be here in the morning. Radio is mine now. My voice. Me.

Wanted to find out what was inside her, little flower girl. Go in there and take it. Have to open her to the light, see? Then it all spills out, but it was nothing, man. Nothing! Where'd she go? Where'd her voice go? Where'd her sunny light go? Her engine of joy? Thought it would be inside her, but no. Shucks.

Nothing, over. Power failure, copy? Pure blackout.

Say again, no engine of joy.

She always listened for the trains. I watch her sleep and make dreams for her. Only a dream myself.

Saturday night Roy and Eileen stayed in Paul's guest bedroom, as they often had in the past—Paul insisted. Roy could sense
more than ever that Paul was gathering his friends and family around
him, keeping them close.

Sunday was the last gathering of energy for the start of the work-
week. Paul was up early for a long, lone stroll in the desert. Eileen
slept in with Roy. When they rose, Paul was sitting over Zack, talking
to him as if he were an old drinking pal. "When you were just a
wet-assed whelp," he was saying, stroking the dog's head, "you could
run pretty good in those days."

At breakfast, while Esmeralda served them chorizo and eggs with
coffee, Paul said, "Call me every day. I want to hear from you."

"Sure."

"I'm not thinking straight on this. Keep me straight on this."

"I'm not a private eye, Uncle Paul."

"I don't expect you to do any legwork. Sit in your air-conditioned
office and fire up your thinking muscle. Savvy?"

"Sure," he said, but he knew he wasn't much help. At least he
could offer company, and moral support. Maybe that was all Paul
really wanted.

Esmeralda hovered in the background, refilling coffee cups and
putting down hot toast.

After breakfast the three of them went shooting while Esmeralda
cleared up the dishes. Paul admired Eileen's little nickel-plated gun.
"It will do," he said. Paul unloaded it and handed it to Eileen. "Point

it and pull the trigger." She threw her arm as if she were pitching a baseball and snapped the hammer.

"Goddamned Annie Oakley," Paul said, chuckling. He covered her right hand with his own and steadied her arm. "Now wrap the first three fingers of your left hand over your right." He took away his hand and she did so. "Now close your left eye and breathe. Listen to how you breathe. Aim at the fence-post. Squeeze the trigger very, very slowly."

The hammer snapped. She lowered the gun.

"Now load. Push the little tripper by your thumb." She did, and the cylinder swung out. She fitted in the bullets. Paul put bottles along the top rail of the fence. "Get closer. Closer. That's it."

"At this range I can't miss."

"Right. Can't miss. One, two, three—"

She raised the revolver and fired off five quick shots and hit nothing.

"Try it again."

She reloaded, and this time when she brought the barrel up she sighted. It took a second longer, but the bottle burst with her shot. She sighted again, fired, and hit a second bottle. The third bottle she missed, but she got it on the fourth try. The last shot cut the neck off a Coke bottle.

"I'm still missing," she said.

Paul laughed. He was looking at his watch. "Twelve seconds, for all that. Don't fret—a man is bigger than a Coke bottle."

For Roy there was an undeniable excitement in her form, the quick percussions at the end of her hands, the wild look on her face, as if she had it all under control, but just barely. But it made him anxious, too.

"That's enough for one day," Paul said.

In the car on the way down the drive, out of the blue, Eileen said, "Did you ever sleep with her, Roy? Cindy Callison?"

"You have to ask? You of all people should know better."

"All I know is that you've been acting pretty damned strange ever since all this got started. What am I supposed to think?"

"It's not like that at all."

"Then what is it like? Tell me, Roy. You never talk to me about what's going on."

"I never talk to you? I can't even get you to go back to the marriage counselor."

"That wasn't helping." She fussed with her hair, pinning it up off her neck, keeping her hands busy. "We need to do it ourselves."

Roy held the steering wheel in both hands. "Tell me what will help," he said softly.

Eileen stared out the window as the dust swirled around the car. "I don't know," she said. "God, it's hot."

"I'm so tired of all this," Roy said. He reached over and caressed her bare neck. Maybe if they could get away by themselves, somewhere isolated from all this, somewhere romantic—maybe that would help. "Let's get away for a couple of days," he said.

"But Paul needs you . . ."

"Just to take a breather," Roy said, more enthusiastically now. "Just to clear our heads and cool off."

She turned from the window and nodded slowly. "Maybe you're right." They were on the highway now and the car hummed on the smooth road.

"Of course I'm right," he repeated. "Let's go cool off somewhere. Then, when we get back, we'll be fresh. Paul doesn't need me—I'm no good at this. He'll catch this creep pretty soon."

Eileen said, "It could go on for years. Have you considered that?"

He hadn't. He had assumed a mystery came with a built-in clock that started when the body was found. At some point either they would beat the clock or an alarm would go off and they would lose. Lose what? What was the prize? Cindy Callison. The penalty? Cindy Callison dead. What if the clock was set for twenty years? A lifetime? Those flower girls had already been dead for years. Nobody had solved that mystery.

"That's why Paul came to you, you know. He's afraid."

"What do you mean? Afraid of what?"

"Afraid of being afraid, I guess. How should I know. It's harder, when you're not used to it."

"He doesn't scare that easy."

"Being brave takes practice. At his age it's a lot to take on."

"He's not that old."

"Age isn't a matter of years. It's a matter of when certain things happen to you. How much space you have left inside."

He could agree with that. When his own parents had died in that plane crash, the world became different overnight. It shrank for a while and then opened up again, but when it opened it was all changed. Everything was fragile. Nothing was certain.

"He's afraid he won't see it through. He needs you."

"I read books," Roy said, both hands on the wheel again. He needed to hold on to something solid. "I read books and then I talk about them." Eileen looked over at him. "Sometimes I even think about them a little first. That's all I do."

Eileen scooted over the console between them and sucked on his neck, then kissed his ear and ran a hand through his hair. "Then pretend we're all in a book, and that anything can happen," she said. "Even a happy ending."

Where'd you grow up? she'd ask me. As if I did. Los Angeles. Sunset Boulevard. William Holden.

Memory's a slippery hole.

Mother, says I, was an actress. My old man was a jockey. She dug that, the jockey part. Crushed by a jumper at Fairhill, and she grabs my arm and says how sorry etcetera. Me, I'm soaring.

I could picture my old man, you know. Green and gold silks flashing in the sun, all those jumpers pouring over the hedge. Bright like water over a fall.

Could hear the gunshot crack of the leading leg, hear my old man grunting as the big horse slammed on him and rolled. Could hear the high whinny of the busted horse chopping the air with his hooves.

She bawls, over? Priceless.

I was there, says I. Saw it all. The men in taupe jackets rushing out across the great sloping downs, working over the fallen horse and my old man. They take him away and I'm riding with him in the ambulance. He sure didn't finish in the money this time.

They push this gigantic needle into the horse's neck and he stays down. Hook chains around his back hooves and winch him up the ramp into the trailer.

Twelve hundred pounds of thoroughbred gone for dogmeat, copy?

So she's bawling into my jacket. You tell it good enough, feels just like it happened to you. For real.

Let's go somewhere and sit, she says. You can disappear into a crowd.

Mother, says I, she couldn't take it. Swallowed half a bottle of barbs and split the scene. Choked myself all up. Sad fucking stuff.

Oh hon, she says, I understand how you feel. She's turning white. I really do. She hugs me like it was true. And right then, at that moment, it is the truest thing in the fucking world. Copy?

Thrilling how my old man died. Now I knew. Talked my way into knowing it. And Mom, that bitch. Now I knew that, too.

Had a bungalow out in West Hollywood, I say. Place called Laverne Terrace.

Never heard of it? *The Big Sleep*, I say, old Bogart movie—she still doesn't get it. I'm making this stuff up as I go.

Bank took the house, I say, and I'm actually missing it. Christ.

But now I have this new place. End of the rainbow. Last Chance waterhole. She squeezes my hand, won't let go.

Didn't sleep last night. First time. Or not. My memory, man, fucking player piano score. Rolls right up.

One fried motherfucker, copy?

Patrolling the hills, lone goddamn ranger. Kimo-fucking-sabe.

Had me a roast to carve. Barbecue al fresco.

Came this close, copy? Then she bang-banged me, man. Shit.

The other one sleeps, but not where I left her. They put her on the TV. Fucking train never mashed her. Left her face. Now she keeps coming back, watching me.

Will the real cowgirl please stand up? She doesn't say much, over. Just sits in her cage and grins for daddy.

Sometimes, when I go down there, deeper and deeper down, I can hear all their voices. Whispering in the walls. The fucking walls have ears, over. Good place for them—not out in the world. Not her face.

My old man made his last jump, over.

Green and gold flashing in the sun. Flying horsesweat and leather. Beautiful crush of bone and flesh on the muddy track.

Mud all over them pretty silks.

Jump higher, faster, stay up, grab air.

When I told it to her, it happened. Keeps on happening now, just like everything else. If you make it up good enough, it's true.

My old man falls from darkness into light, over. And so do I.

Day Twenty-nine

They were already well out of the city, speeding toward water.

Roy drove up Route 60 through the Superstitions and the Mescal range, past Miami, Claypool, the turnoff for Globe.

Miami was practically a ghost town, a survivor of boomtown strip-mining days. The ore in these hills had yielded copper, silver, even gold back before the big wars. Now the rocky, shadeless land lay scabbed, reduced to slagheaps and runoff seeps that shimmered blue and red and green under the fat sun.

Farther on, Claypool. Leftover men hung out in the sparse shade of street-corner awnings. Ragged kids played with sticks and stones in gray alleys. Empty stores rotted in the sun. The Ford dealership had just two hard-used cars on its pitted lot.

The land here was ruined, dug up and sifted through and relieved of its treasure. The people here were all used up. The unrepaired road twisted along ridiculous grades and blind curves, ducked into cool narrow tunnels, and flew back into daylight over steel bridges that erupted out of nowhere between impossible canyon walls, rocky dry creeks scoring the canyon floor hundreds of feet below.

Something had been fought over here. The conflict had been mapped right into the countryside, the people, and it could not be gotten out again.

After they had left the wasteland behind, out on Route 88, they climbed the Sierra Anchas between Rockinstraw Peak on the right and Castle Dome on the left, then descended. As they rounded a turn, they saw it shimmering below—Theodore Roosevelt Lake, sky-blue and cool-looking on the floor of the brown valley. Roy felt gravity pulling them down to it. They were three hours from the hot hustle of Phoenix.

Within the hour they were outside the buoys and raising sail on their rented sloop, reaching up the lake toward the dam and eventually Horse Pasture Bay, fifteen miles of good motion. The whole lake had once been ranch land, pastures. Barbed-wire fences still stood, forty feet underwater. The old sinks among scrub hillocks had been flooded into coves, private and safe from big wind.

Roy settled in, back against the coaming and watched the scenery drift by. The boat was heeled just so, and the water sang lightly in his ears. He drank his beer. He glanced aloft to check the sails' trim, shielding his eyes from the slick white glare. The sails curved into the opal sky like glazed ceramic wedges, blades between wind and water. Eileen was steering a true course.

He listened to the water. Eileen was humming "Frankie and Johnny." This was one of her sterling moments. He watched her clean profile, brown hair riffling in the breeze under a loose red bandanna. The words came into his head with the tune: Frankie and Johnny were lovers, Lordy how they could love. She opened her peasant blouse and took the sun on her breasts.

They passed Rock Island to starboard and entered the strait near the dam on a beam reach. In the strait, the wind freshened. It came up hard through the sluice of the Salt River, climbing a thousand vertical feet against the river's current. Then it broke over the dam between sheer rock walls and spilled into the lake. They took a gust that strained the jib and laid the lee rail underwater. Roy eased the sheets. The boat picked up speed and they screamed through the strait in twenty minutes. Whitecaps flecked the water ahead. Roy grinned. It was good to be on the water—cleared the crap out of your head.

The wind blasted in waves over the old masonry dam that Teddy Roosevelt had built. At either end of it rose a Gothic turret.

If you stood on the narrow top of the dam, 280 feet above bedrock, he knew, you could look down a hundred miles of river valley falling away like one of those National Geographic shots of the Himalayas—prehistoric, beyond human imagination, the scale all wrong.

On those rare occasions when he drove over the dam on the precarious road built for democrat wagons and Model A Fords, he held the wheel tightly and kept himself from looking over the edge, as if to look would be to fall into that infinite landscape—he would lose himself and never hit bottom.

"I always forget," Eileen said, eyes closed.

"What's that?"

She opened her eyes and hugged his arm. "How handsome you are. What a good sailor. I always see you with books and papers. It's good to be outdoors."

"Feels good to be on the water," he said. "Everything's better outdoors." It was a relief to have his hands on something actual—not ideas or words. Maybe that's how Jane Featherbead's therapy worked.

"Know what I think," Eileen said, letting go of his arm. "I think you're going to be surprised at the way this thing turns out."

"I'm surprised about every twenty minutes, these days."

"Bad things happen. Grow up, sweetheart."

"Yeah. But not up here."

They were nearly past the dam, out of the strait, and the wind steadied. "You know who built that dam? Apaches, Geronimo's children. No kidding. And drifters, hoboes from the rail yards down in Phoenix, Tucson. Rounded them up, loaded them into freight wagons."

"So you don't want to talk about murder today. I can take a hint."

"Talk about murder—bake a man to death in the sun, crush him under timber, pour a thousand tons of stone on his head. Some of them are buried right in the dam."

Above, the sky was untroubled. But to the west dirty cumuli hung on the rims of the Mazatzal Mountains, not moving—an illusion, Roy figured, of distance and direction. He uncapped his third bottle of beer of the afternoon. "Slow down, kiddo," Eileen said playfully. "I don't want you passing out on me while we're having a romantic evening."

Roy grinned and felt the excitement he always felt when he was pretty sure she would make love to him later.

With hours of fair skies yet, they sailed fast across the Great Salt Bay. The cove Roy wanted was at the other end, just at the entrance to Horse Pasture Bay. They motored over the bar and dropped anchor in ten feet of water, protected on all sides.

It was very quiet, but for birds twittering. A few dappled cows stood in the lee of the east hillock, staring down at the boat.

Later, down in the shade of the double settee berth, he asked softly, "Why do you leave me all those times? What can I do?"

Her hair was spilled all over the cushions and she was smiling. "Never mind." Her eyes remained open. "I love you. You know that." He felt absolutely captured by her. The boat rocked ever so gently. Outside, he heard the breeze in the rigging. An ancient sound, fossilizing wind.

"What can I do? That's all I want to know."

Eileen pulled his head down and wet his ear with her tongue. "Shh. Pretend we're not married." They lay like that, embracing, for half an hour.

Later they dove into the cooling water and splashed around, naked, before climbing up the swim ladder and toweling off. The sky had turned dark. The rain was coming. They could watch it advancing across the hills, bending the palo verde and juniper before it, pushing a cold wind right into their faces.

Cold actually had a color, Roy realized. It had never occurred to him before. Cold was a midnight shade of purple with a roiling black heart.

Eileen shivered and he gathered her into a large towel. The breeze was a wind now, raising gooseflesh along their arms and legs. Eileen went below but Roy stayed up on deck awhile. Staring into the gathering gloom on shore, Roy thought he glimpsed a shadow moving among the scrub juniper. Probably a steer, he figured. Cattle still grazed the open range on this side of the lake. But somehow it didn't look big enough—moved upright, mannish. He watched the place for a long time but could not be sure he actually saw movement. He wished he'd brought binoculars. But they'd been in such a hurry. To get over to this side of the lake a man would need a boat, unless he wanted to drive for an hour along a rugged four-wheel-drive track, like the diehard bass fishermen did. They'd seen no other boats.

A trick of the eye, he told himself. Paranoia. Up here, of all places, they were safe. But he kept watching anyway.

Then the light went, and it was no use watching anymore.

He wouldn't tell Eileen—that would spoil everything. Tonight he wanted things cozy and untroubled, no phantom bogeymen prowling the hillocks. Still, before retiring, he scouted the place once more, squinting through the dusk, blind.

Christ, Roy thought, if he was out there—

But no, he couldn't be. It was crazy to think so. He just couldn't be. Get a grip, he told himself. Don't let your imagination get the better of you. He wouldn't follow you eighty-five miles. Why would he be following you at all?

Down below they made a nest out of the settee berth with blankets and clean towels and all the cushions they could find on board. The boat was all buttoned up—sails stowed, halyards and tiller tied off, forehatch battened down, ground tackle secure. The boards were ready to seal off the companionway, if necessary. They drank a bottle of champagne that had been chilling all afternoon. They listened to the wind and felt the boat rock.

They ate cold tacos and snuggled together. Roy forgot about the shadow up in the scrub. Outside, thunder boomed from mountaintop to mountaintop, but in here all was safe, all was secure. Chain lightning flashed across the portholes. Eileen was letting him touch her, gently, slowly, both of them pretending not to notice.

Suddenly they heard a sharp wailing sound, a keening cry from the hills, and Eileen grabbed him. "What the hell?"

"Nothing, an animal. Lie still."

"Tell me there's nothing out there."

She shivered in his arms. "There's nothing out there. Relax, honey." Roy flashed on the shadow he had seen earlier, out of the corner of his eye, and then, looking hard at it, lost track of. He wished he could be dead sure that nothing, no one, had followed them up here. That was the point, to get away from it. But a thing like that, it got under your skin. "Just coyotes and cows. Shh."

"I hate storms. Hold me."

"There's nothing to be afraid of."

"Hold me anyway."

"It won't last too long."

There was nowhere to go. They were surrounded by water, with two miles of stormy lake between them and a deserted mountain road.

Already darkness had fallen, the darkness of a land without cities. Lightning flashed intermittently, like headlights, across the portholes and the open gap of the companionway. They did not need any more light—they could reach out their hands and feel the contours of the little cabin. And each other. Love was something Roy could put his hands on tonight. In the safe dark, to the dreamy movement of the sailboat, Roy caressed her and started again to make love to her. As he moved carefully on top of her, something bumped against the hull, and she started. It bumped again, and she pushed him off her.

"For Christ's sake—"

"Where's the flashlight?" she demanded. "Where's my gun?"

"You brought your gun?" He tried to hold on to her. "Take it easy, it's all right."

"There's something out there."

"Look, you don't want to go out there in that storm."

"Well, I'm not going to listen to that all night long."

"It's only a log or something, got loose in the storm." He let go, and she pulled away, rummaging in the storage bin for the flashlight.

"The hell with the flashlight," she said, and slipped out through the companionway. Before Roy could stop her, she was standing in the cockpit. As lightning arced across the sky behind her, she held out her pistol at arm's length.

"Hey!" Roy yelled. "Take it easy." He grabbed for her arm but she shook him off.

"I see something—there!"

He looked toward shore, but in the lightning flashes he saw only shadows and scrub. "There's nobody out there. For God's sake." He took firm hold of her arm and the gun went off. The flash blinded him. The concussion made him temporarily deaf. He hugged her tight. "Come on below, honey. Out of the rain."

He steered her below and tucked her in against the inside curve of the hull. She insisted he put the companionway boards in place, and he obliged. "Try to relax." Had she hit anything out there in that wild storm? He hoped to God she hadn't. How would they ever explain it? Adrenaline was rushing through him, making him giddy. "Relax," was all he kept saying, as he waited for the ringing to go out of his ears.

"Why did you have to grab my arm like that?"

Roy couldn't tell if she were blaming him for making the gun go off, or for spoiling her aim. He couldn't think straight. He sure couldn't sleep. They lay awake together, not touching, and listened to the regular bumping against the hull as the storm blew itself out. Roy finished the bottle of champagne all by himself.

Once he dozed and awoke to the uncanny sense that someone else was on the boat with them. He held his breath and listened. Over his head, on deck, he heard a light tread—or was it? It could be the wind, the creak of rigging. He listened hard, but he heard it no more. Then the boat rolled once, gently, as if a wake had just passed under it broadside, or as if someone had just stepped overboard. Roy listened for a splash but heard nothing. The log, or whatever it was, kept bumping against the hull.

He dared not wake Eileen, who had finally fallen asleep in his arms. The gun had fallen from her hand, and he stowed it away within reach. What had come over her? Out of the blue, she had gone hysterical.

Now he himself was beginning to feel cornered, at the mercy of whoever was out there in the storm. If anybody was out there. But no one could be. He was letting his imagination play tricks.

Very late, he fell asleep but did not realize it. At dawn, when Roy awoke, Eileen was gone.

He felt a cold panic and scrambled topside into the gray and windy morning and found her, leaning against the lifeline, quietly sobbing. "You okay?" he said, but she didn't answer and she didn't turn around. She just lifted a limp arm and pointed to the water.

There, spread across a half-submerged log, were Cindy Callison's clothes.

Can't keep still. Lie here staring straight up at the light and want to be in motion, going someplace, going there fast. Lie here in a tangle. Movie rolls by like a train. All aboard!

Long drive through all that gouged-out country, but they showed me the way, over.

Valley of ashes, over?

Wild Fucking West—copy?

Stood on the dam and watched across the windy water. The wind burned my face. Looked over the edge and could see for a hundred miles. Wanted to leap onto the air and let it carry me down there, far down there. Away. Could see the air hanging brown and dirty, like smoke, and I could ride on it, I swear I could . . . just spread my wings and soar in gentle swooping turns, spiraling down and down.

But could not let loose of the hot rusty iron railing. Water below was a hard silver track, an ooze of quicksilver off the mighty trembling dam.

Felt the stones shudder, like they knew.

Felt the hollow heart of the dam, beating slowly against all that water.

Felt it breathing and beating.

If I didn't look over, I could follow the road off the dam onto the hill and watch the sailboat. Took a long time passing the dam.

Blue-silver water, white boat, tiny as a fingernail. Wind buzzed in my head. Almost took a flyer.

Storm covered me with noise. Should have seen that cradle rocking, over—plankety-plankety-plank. Could smell her coconut sun-tan oil.

Should've seen that shit float, man.

Watched her come out in the storm. The wind was me. The dark wind. The eye of the storm. The thing at the nursery-room window, babes.

When my eyes hurt, I left. The sun pulled me home and here I lie, over. Still in the movie, over. Staring over the edge—copy?

Forty-mile stare.

Can you imagine sailing on that brown air? To leap over the long fall of the dam and dive into a shimmering vein of quicksilver?

Lying here, I've done it over and over. The railing's at my back. I spread my arms, lean forward, arch my spine, and kick off from the stone wall. The air holds me in its cold breath and I see stars and light. See the flash of quicksilver at the bottom and soar right over it, tumbling in air.

Splashdown murky and dark and feels like whipped cream—no pain, no burn.

Almost had her, copy. Till she bang-banged me. Pulled me a Swamp Fox.

Run away to fight another day, over? Stay up. Grab air.

The log was snagged somehow against the hull. Roy knew they were her clothes—the distinctive colors. A geometrical print blouse of bright blues, reds, and yellows. Lemon slacks. The image of her that last day clicked on in his mind with certainty. She'd worn that outfit to his seminar.

The log was too heavy for the boat hook, so he slipped over the side. He looped his arm over the log and was towing it toward the swim ladder when something soft and solid brushed his leg—a bass?

The thing popped to the surface all at once and it was no bass. Roy screamed and splashed, trying to get away from it. It was a human leg.

Eileen shouted down to him: "What? What?"

Roy fluttered his lips, but he was scared beyond words. He reached out his hand so Eileen could pull him out of the water. "The radio," he said.

Paul's helicopter landed on the south hillock and he made his way down to the edge of the water, eyes on the ground. Close behind Paul came Gino, then Hoff in suntans. A boatload of sheriff's deputies was already on the scene and had bagged the evidence. A deputy handed Paul a plastic bag full of clothes. "Did you photograph it in the water first?" Paul asked. He was wondering what was taking his own photographer so long to get here.

The deputy looked puzzled.

"Goddamn amateur hour," Paul said. "Where the hell is Stein?"

"We didn't fool with 'em none," the deputy said.

"I was hoping to see a pattern in how they were laid out on the log," Paul explained gruffly, losing patience. "Where the hell are my people? Where the hell's Billings?"

Gino said, "Couldn't get hold of him. And Stein took a personal day."

Roy said, "Pattern? Jesus, Paul—what about the goddamn leg?"

Paul draped an arm around Roy and said, "Get a grip. Talk to your wife."

Hoff examined the clothes and the leg with a magnifying glass. Then he pocketed the glass, drew the severed leg out of the bag, and handled it gingerly. "Well, what do you know about that."

"I didn't want to know she was really dead," Roy said quietly to Paul. He was shaking all over and couldn't stop. Eileen stared at him in a sort of daze. There had been something out there worth shooting.

"It ain't hers," Hoff said. "Not the girl you mean. This leg and foot belong to victim number two. Bet on it."

"Then why—"

"Something is being said here," Paul said. "So little decomposition—how come?"

Hoff held out the leg. "See how white it is? The green pallor? It was frozen. He used chemicals again, too. Clever, very clever. You got to admire this character—in a perverse sort of way."

Roy kept wiping his hands on his trousers, unaware he was even doing it.

"And notice this," Hoff said. "No blood on the clothes. None that I can see without a microscope, that is."

"Is that a good sign?" Roy was still confused.

"Never know. He could undress her first, then whack her. But all the other clothes have been bloody."

Eileen stood out of the way in a terrycloth robe, hand to her mouth, sobbing quietly. She said, "He was here, then. Wasn't he?"

"We don't know when," Paul said. "Just take it easy."

One of the deputies called out, "Lieutenant—get a load of this."

Roy followed Paul to a boggy sink between hillocks. "Hoff—get over here. Now."

In the mud lay the carcass of a heifer, headless and neatly disemboweled.

Hoff hunkered down against his cane and dipped his hand into the muck. "Blood," he pronounced. "A christly lot of blood."

"So he butchered it right here."

"About four, six hours ago," Hoff agreed.

"Organize your men, deputy. Grid search. Gino—"

"Yo."

"Get on the radio and fly more people up here. I want a tire track, a footprint. Anything."

"Righto."

Eileen stole up behind Roy, no longer sobbing. "Don't you get it?"

"Get what?" He reached for her gently.

She pulled back. "You're not after *him* anymore. He's after *us*."

"Calm down. Get a grip."

"He was on the boat. All that mud on deck."

"We don't know for sure."

"If he can follow us all the way out here—"

"Eileen, please. Take it easy."

"You don't know a goddamned thing, either one of you." To Paul, she said, "Are you going to catch him now? Can you promise me?"

Paul held up his hands, palms out.

"What good is that," she said, and walked away.

Paul grabbed Roy's wrist as he started to follow her. "You're in this now in a way you weren't before."

Roy nodded. His legs were all rubbery and his mouth was dry. "We came up here to get away from it," Roy said. "We never thought for a minute."

"I'll look out for you as best I can," Paul said. "But keep an eye on each other. That's the most important thing now."

The sheriff's boat would tow the sloop back to the marina. The police chopper flew Roy and Eileen back to their car. They rose over the little cove in a whir of wind and noise. So Eileen had scared him off. Roy knew what she was thinking: while they slept, he was out there. All night. Watching. Using his knife. Doing it for them, to show them something. Like they were part of it now. Accomplices.

Day Thirty-three

Roy continued to meet his classes in preparation for final exams. Eileen began phoning him at the office every two or three hours. He didn't want to tell her to stop. Things were different now. She was in danger. They both were. Now the case was out to solve *them.*

"Nothing urgent," she'd say. He knew she just wanted to hear his voice. And he needed to hear hers. If he was in class, the secretary would give him the message. When he returned her call, she'd say only, "Just wanted to make sure you're okay."

"I'm fine," he'd answer, grateful beyond reason that she'd remained safe in the few hours since he'd left her. "Is there anything you need?" He wouldn't hang up right away, even if it meant being late for class. They'd linger on the line, listening to each other breathe. He missed her. He wanted to make her feel safe, but he couldn't. He didn't feel safe.

She left notes for him in the morning before she left for appointments and signed them "love." Their marriage had not been this good in many months. But it was still curiously mannered, like a formal dance.

They locked their doors and windows. They paid attention to the rearview mirror. Every time the phone rang, they jumped. Every stranger was a suspect—the mailman, the paper boy, the Mormons coming door-to-door on Sundays. They let no one in the apartment except Paul.

Each evening they watched the news together at six and ten—something they had never done. They held hands over the bad news,

clucked in relief over the unchanging weather map that always fore-
cast hot and sunny weather. They rented videos of old movies with
happy endings.

After a night of staring, rapt, at the television screen, Roy would
lie in bed next to his wife, aching to make love to her but afraid to
press her too hard. He kept a baseball bat next to the bed. Eileen slept
with her pistol under her pillow, which scared them both. But she
didn't know where else to put it so it would be handy in the dark,
when she would be too terrified to think.

Roy drove himself crazy with listening. He heard real sounds—
people coming and going along the outdoor corridor of their apartment cluster, cars rumbling by on the street. He also heard imaginary
noises: the bump of that log against the hull, the soft footfalls of a
murderer on the deck overhead. When he closed his eyes, he could see
again that quick, man-sized shadow dodging among the juniper.

In the slant of moonlight across their bed, he would stare at their
locked bedroom door, wondering who was out there tonight. Their
lovemaking never got beyond nervous foreplay. They were always
alert, always listening for someone at the door.

What would become of them? Roy wondered in the swimmy twilight before dead sleep.

Sometimes they'd wake trembling in the night and cleave hard
together, hearts pounding, as if they'd both been rescued from the
same nightmare. They knew it was melodrama, but it somehow ele-
vated them, drew cleaner lines around their lives. Reduced their lives
to this minute. Right here, right now.

They were frightened all the time. Their fear exhausted them. It
was a kind of tuning, a tensioning of heartstrings. When they were
together, they watched each other. Roy thought Eileen's long, brown
hair was miraculous, the way it shimmered. She moved through the
air like a swimmer. He couldn't get over it.

He listened to her voice—he had never noticed how husky it got
when she was tired. If he noticed goosebumps rising on her brown
arms, he would turn up the thermostat.

Apart, they imagined each other with clarity. Roy began to put himself in her place mentally—he wrote whole scenes in his head in which he was Eileen, entering an office, interviewing a manager, conducting a seminar on data-transfer software. He knew nothing about modems and fax machines, but he imagined whole speeches in her voice using words like "autodial," "downloading," and "mail-merge." Words he'd heard her use but never paid much attention to.

He found himself doodling flowcharts and writing memos to himself. It was the first time he had ever really paid attention to his wife's work. He missed her. He was inventing her life during all the minutes and hours she was away from him.

For the first time, too, he forced himself to imagine what she had gone through on the side of a highway in California. The thing they never talked about. The thing the counselor was for. The thing that was a spike driven into their marriage. He still didn't have the words, but he felt closer. He felt they were moving together in some kind of tenuous rhythm. He felt their lives pulling toward a happy ending, but only if they made exactly the right choices.

He was terrified of her death. He was more terrified of his own. For the first time, he experienced the remarkable concentration that comes with terror for one's life. In class, Roy noticed everything and remembered nothing. Every face in the room, the color of eyes, the texture of hair, the ripeness of young skin. He had no idea what their names were.

Once a student showed up for his afternoon seminar fresh from the stables, and the reek of ammonia and horse sweat nearly made him faint. His eyes watered, then cleared. The odors of dung, hay, and saddle soap distracted him so much he could hardly get through the stories.

Other days he taught the stories with such intensity and absorption that the class was spellbound. The hour was up and there they sat, not reaching for books or shuffling backpacks. He would keep talking until something snapped him out of it. It was like coming up from underwater, his ears suddenly clearing.

He'd slip his books and notes into his book bag and disappear out the door. His students didn't dare approach him after class. He'd glide down the hall and feel the sweat cooling his bare arms and neck.

The students seemed to sense they were witnessing something extraordinary. Attendance was perfect.

And Cindy Callison's empty seat haunted every seminar.

Base Station #8

They'd wait for me on corners.

Me in that big white gas hog, copy? Ditched that mother in the river long time gone.

They'd come to the smoked window smiling and brown and ready for the pitch. Carried a wad thick as my fist in those days. Soon as they got a load of that I could take 'em anywhere. Chicks dig moola, over.

They were cute and giggly or they were sassy and punk, I didn't care. Wore Crayola mascara and ruby lipstick and smacked gum in my face so close I could smell their sweet peppermint breath—yum, yum. Could lick 'em right down to the stick.

Their chompers were white and clean. Their tongues little red clams. I'd crank up the air and suck in a tape and head for Marlboro Country.

You got a copy on that?

When I looked over the dam, there was nothing on the other side. Just plain nothing, man—zero, zip, and zoot. Panoramic eighty-six, man, over. Out of sight, really gone, just plain removed, over? Scarier'n shit, bro.

She wore red hotpants. Keep them under my pillow.

Her sister wore lime-green satin gym shorts—man I could go for that in a big way. What a pair. Put a swing on that porch, over.

Once we hit the hungry stick, we didn't stop for man nor beast. Passed up the hooters and the honkers, the zooters and the zonkers, the tooters and the tonkers. Squealin' wheels and scrubbin' the rubber, man oh man.

Out in the high wide and handsome we'd punch up about a nickel's worth of moonlight and hunker down in front of a mesquite fire, watching the saguaros lift their fuzzy arms against the sky. Camporee-city, babe, lead in my pencil and the love-snake all coiled and ready to strike. Blood in my pumper and Hank Williams on the box. Tap me a Lonestar, honey-do, and saddle up—leapin' lizards and happy trails!

Expected them both to last longer, but they crapped out on me. Rode hard and put away wet, pard—just don't make 'em like they used to, over? Just don't make 'em.

Creepy. Look over the damn dam and there's nothin', man. Absolute zero. A fucking hole in your eye, dig? Like looking in the mirror at a barbershop—zap, zap, zap, zap, bouncing back and forth between the walls. Pretty soon you're all used up. Flat gone. Like the little green light in the center of your TV tube when you turn the set off—zi-i-ip, and out. Just like that.

Boat crawled over the silver water—man, could have snatched her off right there and then, don't tell me I couldn't. Could have reached down and plucked out her horny beating heart.

Ol' bossie didn't give me no fuss, though. Sirloin on the hoof, woof.

Toss the flowers on the backseat, honey—that's a roger. We're on for the long haul—roger and out.

Day Thirty-six

With the semester over, Roy had time on his hands. He walked the streets, soaking up the heat. All week the temperature never dipped below a hundred-five. The low gray clouds of the gathering monsoon pressed the heat into a dense, palpable ether and magnified the sun to ridiculous proportions. Pondering the red notebook Cindy Callison had left behind, Roy sweated through his suntans. He sweated a new band into his panama hat. His face burned crimson and then tan, and his wrists and hands and forearms stayed red. He felt the heat radiate from them at night when he tried to sleep, feverish.

Sometimes, walking, he hallucinated: there was Cindy Callison up ahead on the sidewalk, a shopping bag on her arm, stepping onto a bus. There she stood in a crowd of sorority girls coming out of the ice cream parlor.

As he walked, he felt dizzy. He had trouble focusing his eyes. The world hemmed and hawed, the sidewalk tripped him up. He worried about Eileen. He drank Mexican beer after breakfast and felt light-headed. He had another Bohemia for lunch and felt lighter still.

He sensed himself rising, as if he would dissipate into spirit. Who was he? Away from Eileen, he wasn't sure. Was that love—defining each other? He stayed away from his office. He'd never made much of an effort to get to know his colleagues, and now he hardly saw them at all. If he needed something from his office, he'd slip in at night when no one was around. Without students he wasn't a teacher. He hadn't touched his book in weeks, so he wasn't a scholar. He wasn't even a real detective, just somebody who'd gotten sucked into a ghoulish world of mass murder.

When Paul retired, he would still be Paul, but less so. Eileen was always herself. Roy knew he was different in class, different in meetings, different with Paul. Different with Cindy Callison. What things, taken away, made him more himself? Or less? What things, taken away, changed nothing?

He wondered if even Jane knew the answer to that.

To keep himself grounded in the here and now, he bought Eileen a present every day, something small and intimate: perfumed soap beads, a bright-yellow scarf for her hair, coconut-oil lotion for her hands. Every evening when he gave her his present, she took his face into her two hands and kissed him.

Paul invited them for an overnight. "I like it better when you two are where I can keep an eye on you," he said on the phone.

On the way they stopped briefly at a cocktail party Roy's department chairman was having. Roy hated such affairs, but Eileen insisted: getting out might do them both good. Eileen wore a sleeveless dress of earth tones and blues. Roy admired the curve of her neck, the clean outline of her figure, the sharp definition of her dark-brown hair ribboned against her neck. He himself felt vague and undefined, a smudge of dull khaki.

The chairman's house was high up on the side of Camelback Mountain, overlooking the city. The party was out back in the desert garden among potted succulents and three standing saguaros with uplifted arms. They moved through a crowd of men in shiny suits and women in too-bright dresses. The men laughed so heartily that Roy could barely stand to be among them.

"Haven't seen much of you lately," they said to him by turns, and he murmured some excuse about working on the book. He shook hands that seemed too soft and listened to chatter about course loads, tenure, and sabbaticals. Compared to what his life had become, it all seemed trivial. Nobody mentioned Cindy Callison in his presence. He could hear them discussing the grisly murders freely until he entered the circle of conversation. Then he could hear them deliberately changing the subject. He felt apart from them, a kind of ghost.

They drank champagne from plastic flutes and watched the shimmering grid of lights below. "Phoenix," Roy said to no one in particular. "The city that looks best from the sky, at night." Down there, in the dark alleys and barrooms and bedrooms, murderers were stirring. He watched the bright lines of traffic, how the city twinkled through the dusty atmosphere. A beautiful illusion of light staining the desert floor, gone by morning.

The other guests had moved into the house, where food was being served. Roy and Eileen stayed in the desert garden, watching the luminous cityscape below that filled the whole valley.

"Don't hit that champagne too hard," Eileen said.

He had already drunk more than he realized. The grid of streets lighted by sodium-vapor lamps reminded him of airport runways. He was thinking about his parents—videotaped news footage of rescue workers swarming over the wreckage of the DC-9 six miles west of Dallas–Fort Worth. "Identity," he said. "That's the key. Don't you get it? That's all there is." Collecting body parts: a shoe with a foot in it, a couple of loose fingers, a skull, a leg. His parents had been dashed to bits and buried together in a single plastic bag. "They died strangers to everybody," he said more softly. "Even to themselves."

"You mean those girls?" Eileen asked.

"Yes," Roy said. "Those girls."

"This isn't the place," she said. "Let's get out of here."

Roy gathered her in from behind and softly kissed her ear, her neck, her hair. She let her weight fall against him. Her bosom filled and emptied, filled and emptied, and she made no attempt to move. Then they slipped out through the garden gate.

Heart of the rock. Can you imagine how a single voice echoes in this place?

Walls don't hold it, rock doesn't hold words. Everything bounces back in your ears, nothing absorbed, just comes back at you louder and louder.

Other voices come back. Hang in thin air like colored streamers—red, gold, blue. Floating, tangling. Stone sucks in the light.

Of all of them, she's the only one who stays with me. Yet I gave her to the train—remarkable!

The other one was a beauty, too, crisscrossed in bars of shadow. If only she had washed, over. She would just sit there by the hour, by the day and week, and whimper, over.

In the end, didn't even whimper. Didn't eat the open cans of food I set before her—copy?

Her water dish was fouled. Her eyes were red and deep and ferocious.

She fought me with the strength of roots.

Cut all day and boiled her away, over. But am beginning to believe there's no battery. Say again, no battery. Exploratory incision on chest revealed nothing.

Nobody home where the heart is.

When she was down to clean sticks, I bundled her in a blanket and hauled her out into the sun.

She was light in my arms.

Nothing new there, over.

Laced her up behind the saddle and went for a ride. High noon. Bleached-white cattle skull kept watch out of big blank eyes, over. Gone to join her sisters under the white grinning tombstone of my love.

Day Thirty-six, Night

It was late. They sat on the veranda at Paul's house—Roy, Eileen, Paul, Jane, and Esmeralda. Paul was wearing his gun. He'd always worn a gun, but now Roy noticed. The long veranda was washed by the monsoon breeze. The house was completely dark and the stars were sharp in the sky.

Eileen was sitting close to Roy, as if he could keep her safe. Esmeralda sat across the semicircle of rattan chairs from Roy. Zack lay in the perfect middle of them all.

"Is there anything else you remember about what happened on the lake?" Jane asked.

Eileen said softly, "I could feel him. His presence. Like a bad smell."

"He must have followed them up there," Paul said. "You're surprised he left his home range?"

Jane shook her head. "Not really. Look how much ground Ted Bundy covered. I just wondered why he would go to all the trouble—"

"You mean it would be easier to get me at home," Eileen said.

"I didn't know quite how to put it." Jane touched her arm.

"I'm okay," Eileen said. "If he shows his face, I'll shoot him. Worked once."

Paul agreed. "Gun probably saved you both."

"If you recognize him," Roy said. He'd had too much champagne, and now he was drinking scotch.

"Meaning?" Paul asked.

"This is going to be good," Jane said. "How much did you drink before you got here?"

Eileen pursed her lips, but she did not move away. Esmeralda folded her hands.

"Meaning, those girls were not just killed—they were erased. Their identities ceased to exist. Maybe that's what this is all about—identity."

"So what are you saying?" Jane asked. "That he manipulates his own identity, too?"

"Maybe. To be what his victims want him to be. What they will trust."

"It has the ring of truth," Jane said. "Fits the profile."

"We're all different people, depending on who we're with. On whom," Roy corrected himself and belched. "We all do it." He thought he was making sense. Getting to the bottom of something important. "We all wear costumes. We all play roles to get what we want. Maybe he just does it better." Roy realized dimly he was using his hands, but he had no control over them. "In a way, this is the perfect crime."

"No such thing," Paul said.

"A perfect crime is an absolute crime. Never mind if it's solved—the damage, the absolute damage, is done. Sharing the knowledge of it only makes it more perfect." He was thinking as much about California as about the murders.

"Perfect is perfect," Jane said. "It can't be more so."

Roy laughed sharply and drank. "We're talking absolutes, that's the key. Nobody talks about absolutes anymore."

Paul agreed. "Nobody believes in good and evil these days."

"Come on, good and evil," Jane said.

"Guilty and innocent," Roy said.

"Some people are pure guilty," Paul said. "And must be punished. That's what civilization is. That's all it is. Look out there." He yanked a thumb toward Phoenix, invisible behind the house. "That's not civilization." He stamped his foot. "Here—here is civilization."

The scotch burned Roy's raw tongue. He would have another and listen to the nighttime racket of the desert. They stared into the black hills, knowing he was out there, close. Eileen had hold of Roy's arm.

They all sit on the porch, staring across the desert at me. White dog knows I'm out here. Pig killer. Can't go in too close.

Wish I could lie at their feet in place of the dog.

Their faces are yellow in the light, their hands move like white birds, back and forth. Their hands are talking about me.

She was suffering, so I hit her gently, fump, with the bag of gold dust. Had no idea she would suffer. Had no idea it would matter. It was the first thing ever I could not watch.

Her eyes were open when I drew the blade across her throat.

The other creatures slink around me, gliding along at the edge of moonlight. Invisible, like creatures under the sea. The starlight burns their dark scaly hides. They hunker beneath rock and sage, avoiding it, waiting for the milky monsoon clouds to wrap us again in night. Their business is nighttime business, over.

In this serene hard place, we are killing one another.

Silver trailer flashes like a bullet under the low moon. Voices carry on the silky wind. Murmur of company.

Desert voices clamor. Wind carries the damp breath of the Mexican sea. Night is full of lurking eyes, red pinpricks in the shadow of the land. My breath is a coarse draft and comes out black.

They sit in fear and safety. The dog at last goes in to bed.

Think I'll just watch for a while.

Day Thirty-seven, Morning

Roy and Paul were on the highway early. Paul gunned the big Thunderbird toward the city, the sky in front of them aglow with the dawn. He smoked two cigarettes before he said anything. Then he said, "Your head clear?"

"What do you think." Roy's eyes were dry and his head hummed. He had not slept enough. He sipped on a plastic mug of coffee, heavily sugared.

Paul was cranky. "We didn't find anything at the lake. Not a goddamned thing."

"Getting tired of hearing that."

"You're getting tired! This Cindy Callison, nobody saw her at the gym. The waitress at the yogurt place never saw her. Like she's the Invisible Girl. Now you see her, now you don't."

"None of the victims had any family. Don't you find that odd?"

"Lot of rootless folks in this city. That's one of the main things wrong with it. They're heading for the coast, the old clunker breaks down, and here they are. Or else they make it to L.A. and get slam-dunked, turn around, wind up here."

"What about the bundle of bones Ezzy found? Or the ones under the bathtub at the dump—"

"Here's a flash: the bones Ezzy found don't match up with the ones under the bathtub, timewise."

"Timewise? So it wasn't the flower-girl murders?"

"I didn't say that. But the one victim was older than the three under the tub. Death was more recent. And get this—the flesh boiled off the bones."

"Jesus—boiled?" So that's why they were so clean.

"Stewed meat. Fucking soup."

"Take it easy, Uncle Paul."

"That's our connection to the here and now—old bones, new bones, same knife. Ain't that just ducky. And where was flower girl number four between the time she was abducted and the time she was killed? For all that time?"

"How long we talking?"

"Hoff says months, at least. Maybe years. He's running more tests."

"Like he kept her someplace?"

Paul nodded. "Like he kept her someplace."

Roy thought about that. Was he keeping Cindy Callison? It gave him an odd surge of hope, though God only knew how she would be suffering.

There was some chatter on the police radio, nothing Paul had to answer. "You tell me, Roy. You got the brains in the family. What are we doing wrong?"

Why did he always talk that way, Roy wondered? *Summa cum laude* and two years of law school and he was still playing the bunkhouse billy. "Somebody always knows something, that's what you tell me. What about the boyfriend?"

"We had a tail on our buddy Loomis. Then, yesterday, he disappears."

"You're kidding."

"Goes into a biker joint. Couple of guys start throwing punches over a pool game, our guys get mixed up in it. He vamooses out the back."

"Maybe he is your guy. Med student and all."

"Before he vamoosed, he was making the rounds. Every stud bar on Van Buren. Likes guys in leather, chains, fur-lined handcuffs. Real pervert."

"Being gay isn't a crime anymore."

"Jane says these macho guys often go queer." Roy wondered if she had used that word. "Bodybuilders, big muscle-heads. According to her, there's a thin line between the locker room and the bathhouse."

"Did he cut anybody up?"

"Not that we know. We're waiting to see what turns up."

The road stretched on, level and straight, past Perryville Prison and a crop duster's airstrip. On either side were bare fields stripped of their cotton, and farther along pecan groves and beanfields, irrigated relentlessly.

"You said you'd tell me the story about my father, how he shot that guy in Mexico."

Paul lit another cigarette and his laughter ended in a fit of coughing. Then he said, "I already told you that story."

All at once Roy understood. "You're kidding—Esmeralda's story? I thought you were making that up."

"Nephew, this world is crazy enough. I never make anything up."

"I just never figured."

"Your father and Ezzy. She's older than she looks. How about that."

"I have to think about this a minute."

"Don't blame him for what he did, son. It was a long time ago. He was young. Hell, in the end he helped her."

His own dead father, visiting a whore in Mexico.

"Time he got back across the border, he was thinking straight again. He knew what he'd left her in for. And he knew where she'd go."

"Hollywood."

"Right."

"You went down and got her." So Paul had rescued her—that's how she eventually came to live in his trailer.

"Does it matter who went? He was sick about her, never seen him like that. Couldn't leave her there. He'd have mourned her all his life. A man has obligations. Doesn't matter if he wants them."

"So you bailed him out."

Paul shrugged. "It was only money and a little time."

"After doing that to my mother? Going to a whore?"

Paul stopped the car right there on the highway, left it running, and leaned over the smooth white seat. "Listen up. Get it straight. Your father was a good man. Period. My only brother. He and your mother were having some problems, the way people do. He did what he did and he tried to make it right. He asked me to help and I did. A man owes that to another man. And as for your mother, she never knew."

"You can't be sure."

"Yes, I can. He was never to see Ezzy or call her again, never to speak her name to me or anyone else. That was the deal. And to remain faithful unto death, savvy?"

"Or else what."

"Don't ask stupid questions. He treated your mother like a queen for the rest of her life. That's what he did. And made her a happy woman. Got it?"

"Got it."

"Good." Paul levered the shift into drive and sped off down the straight highway, the sun in his eyes now.

Roy finished his coffee, gone lukewarm. Paul smoked another cigarette.

"What about Ezzy's kids? Did my father—"

"Don't be an ass. They're strays. Orphans. She takes them in."

Roy brooded for a time, trying to wake up. "The one he shot—did he die?"

"You can't just listen, you always got to ask questions? Yeah, of course he did, we all do—what difference does it make? Three years later got his belly sliced open in Juarez."

They were hitting the outskirts of the city now and were in thin traffic. On either side were long low blocks of adobe houses, then storefronts with Spanish signs.

Paul said, "Life's a sloppy business, amigo. Live with it."

"Just so he loved her. My mother, I mean."

"The world doesn't stop because you love your wife. Other people still tangle you up in their life. You don't have to sleep with a woman to owe her something."

Roy wondered what Paul meant by that—Cindy Callison? How much did he know? "I don't owe anybody anything."

"Then what is it you're not telling me?"

"Hey, I'm suddenly the bad guy?"

Paul blew out smoke. "You're right. Shit. It's the job," he said, shaking his head. "Sometimes you forget how to talk soft." They were into steady commuter traffic now. The buildings were getting taller.

A little time went by. "If we can be personal, then why don't you tell me about it?" Roy was looking out the window as he said it, never doubting that Paul would know exactly what he meant.

Paul sighed and lit another cigarette off the one in his hand. He nodded before he spoke out loud, as if he were talking it over with himself first. "Okay, okay. You got me talking this morning. I don't want to tell you, but I've wanted you to know. For a long time now. You ought to know."

"Don't tell me if it's too hard."

Paul jammed his fresh cigarette into the ashtray and immediately lit another off the dashboard lighter. "Christ, if it were easy it wouldn't be worth telling—don't you know anything? Just don't interrupt me."

"Sorry."

Paul got a good deep lungful of smoke, then coughed it out. "They took her on a Friday afternoon, right off the campus. We were supposed to meet for happy hour at a little joint on Apache, like always. I waited an hour, then walked across the street and all over campus looking for her. I knew something was wrong, always had a feeling for that. She'd been seen in the library but never made it to class. Now, Linda never missed class. Never.

"I called the police. She hadn't been back to the car, she hadn't been back to the house, she hadn't called any of her girlfriends. She was just gone." Paul drove for a few minutes. His cigarette burned in the ashtray. Roy didn't say anything, just waited.

"The ransom note came on Saturday. Right away I knew it was a mistake. They meant the rich Popes, the ones who own all that real estate downtown, the bankers. One hundred thousand dollars. We tried to stall.

"The rich Popes refused to get involved. I went down there myself and begged for the money. I'll make it up to you, I said. Old man Pope, big shit banker. Said he sympathized with my predicament, but what could he do? Never mind that it was his name got us into it. His money. I stood there on his soft carpet and begged him.

"I would have done anything—absolutely anything—to get her back. I'd already come to terms with that. I was willing. If killing Mister Pope would have got my Linda back, I'd have done it with my bare hands.

"Maybe I should have done it anyway. He could read me—the man had scared eyes.

"We stalled. They started sounding desperate on the telephone. Shouted, then hung up quick, out of breath all the time. You could hear the panic in their voices.

"Finally the police agreed to set up a fake drop. It was our only chance. But something went wrong, and they never showed. That was Wednesday. She'd been in the ground for five days. How could we know?" Once again he paused. Roy marveled at how flat Paul's voice sounded through all this.

Paul spoke very slowly and quietly. "Thursday went by, Friday, Saturday. Nothing. I was crazy. The whole world was a spike driven right between my ribs. I couldn't talk. Couldn't think. Couldn't see straight. I ached when I breathed, do you understand? I ached.

"I think, by Wednesday, when they didn't show, I knew she was dead. Something had gone wrong. Maybe they'd intended to show up, I don't know. On Sunday morning I got a call from a voice I'd never heard before, a high young voice. Sounded scared, maybe, and tired.

"That's how we knew where to dig. Still it took us a couple of hours to find exactly the right spot. It was a junkyard, you know. All that stuff lying around, cars, junk. They wouldn't let me dig. Four of their detectives did it, fast. Man, they wanted to get her out. It was a shallow hole, but deep enough."

Roy watched him light another cigarette and marveled at the steadiness of his hand. "I knelt by the hole as they dug, and I kept calling her name—to give her hope, you see?"

Roy nodded, looking straight ahead, the sun in his eyes.

"Soon as they got the lid pried off, they pulled her out. But it was plain she was dead. They had a doctor standing by, an ambulance, but it was no use." Paul stopped the car for the red light and put his head on the steering wheel. "Her hands were bloody, and her mouth was open. Her eyes were open, too. They found dust in her lungs, dust in her stomach. Her face was covered with dust. That's how she died."

The light changed to green, but Paul didn't move and Roy said nothing. Behind them he heard horns. When the light changed back to red, Paul accelerated through it, narrowly missing a pickup truck, and continued downtown.

"You wanted to hear it."

Roy realized he'd been holding his breath. He let it out now. "They never found who did it?"

"No. Disappeared. Like they'd left the planet. Every lead turned up blind. Nobody saw anything, nobody knew."

"Maybe someday—"

Paul laughed hoarsely, then coughed. "That's what I thought, I guess. For a long time after. Years, even. You think that way because you don't know what else to do. They're not supposed to get away with it, you think."

"Sometimes—"

"You said you wouldn't interrupt. I thought that way for a long time, but each year it got thinner. From the moment they put her in that box, they got away with it."

"But—"

"There ought to be justice. True. I believe it. But you know what? There hardly ever is." Paul reached over and clapped him on the shoulder. "You're too young to be listening to an old man talk like this," he said. "You're thinking, Then what the hell are we doing here?" They pulled into the police parking garage. "You're thinking, Why bother? Well, we do bother. It's about something else. I don't know just what yet, but something. Trust your uncle."

Where I'm from. Okay. After L.A.? Lot of places, I told her. Pictures and smells.

First a place of fish and cold docks, slippery concrete piers at the edge of a gray sickle of a bay. Like walking on oil. The voices spat and cut the air. Black and gray shaped people, birds everywhere, laughing at me.

You receiving this?

Then a wooded place with dappled cows. Walking was hard in the hills. Snow as big as the house. The sky hung down right over our heads, propped up by the bare bones of black trees. At night, the timber wolves howled for love.

After that a swampy place, over. Full of snakes and gators with mouths like the chrome grills of Chevies. Air was water, water was mud. No sky. I'd hang them up by their legs and let the blood drain out, then fillet the back meat. Preferred it high and full of sweet juice, over.

Other places, but I don't always know them. At night, the pictures just come to me, all at once, lightning.

Shack by the warm flat sea, brown girls in floppy white hats.

Highway going round the bend out of sight, taking all the cars with it.

Apartment across from a beer warehouse—the trucks racketing in and out all night long, men named Joe and Bill and Harry with leather jackets and cigars.

Here is the best place: home. The sky way up there, blue clear. The moon lights my way. The rock is hot, hard, secret, deep.

She sat there and would not speak, day after day, week after week. Her face was black and mean, over. She did not move. She would no longer look me in the eye. My ears buzzed all day long, I felt them crawling on me and swatted them away. The cans of food increased and I did not bother to change her water. She did not comb her hair.

She was not clean, over.

I watched over her as she slept. Into her dreams I whispered a village by the sea, an old gray barn, and a clear brook that sang over the rocks. Then I whispered a bedroom I have seen with my own eyes, a pitcher and bowl and brass bedstead standing clean in sunlight. Bedroom was in a gold frame.

Where I was born, over. Where I entered the fucking story. Out of all that suffering came only moi. Copy?

Think about her almost all the time now. She changed everything.

Nobody recognizes me. Sometimes I walk along by the trains to hear the roar of the planet groaning in its bed, to feel the great wind. Have tried to let it take me, but it will not, over?

Press this key to transmit.

Day Thirty-seven, Afternoon

Hoff had his lab in the basement of the state building down-town: thoroughly air-conditioned, the block walls blank of windows, the ceiling a bank of sunny fluorescent lights. The whole place, Roy thought, was a sort of cave, a den to which Hoff retreated out of the sunlight.

"You're going to love this," he said to Roy as he walked in and felt the chill. Hoff grabbed papers off a metal desk in the corner of the lab and riffled through them. "Here, I'm going to simplify things for you." He put the papers down and led Roy and Paul across the lab to a bank of three stainless-steel lockers. He opened one and pulled out a long drawer with a body on it—the girl found in Cindy Callison's costume.

"We estimated time of death approximately eight hours before you found her, correct?"

"Yeah," Paul said, drawing out a cigarette but knowing better than to light up down here. He stuffed it back into the pack and the pack into his shirt pocket. He fidgeted and didn't seem to know what to do with his hands.

"I was wrong, but it was an honest mistake."

"How long then?"

"Almost a month, I'd say."

"What?"

"I have to be approximate, but plus or minus a week."

"What in the hell are you talking about?"

Hoff slid closed the drawer and clicked shut the stainless-steel door. "I told you it was simple. The body was frozen shortly after death, so the ordinary progress of lividity, rigor mortis, decomposition, and so forth, were halted. They began again when the body thawed, several hours before you found it. Easy to miss, if all you're doing is gutting the poor girl to count organs. You have to have seen this sort of thing before to recognize it."

Roy said, "All sounds pretty hokey to me."

"Look. Did you ever hear about the Explorers Club's woolly mammoth roast? Back in the twenties, some fellows found a mammoth frozen in arctic ice. They cut it out, ice and all, and shipped it home. The meat wasn't even tainted. They roasted and ate the sonofabitch! A carcass over ten thousand years old! D'you get it? They *ate* him. Don't tell me what's hokey."

"The other girls, too?" Paul asked.

"Except the one in Library Park. Same sort of thing, although apparently number two had been thawed for a little while and then refrozen. In her case, time of death was at least two years ago, probably longer. The thawing business, you see, interferes with accuracy."

"What the hell kind of killer are we looking for?" Paul said, to himself, it seemed.

Hoff laughed. "Anybody with a deep-freeze. It's a fairly simple matter. That's what I meant when I said I'd simplify the thing for you. While it all seems a bit farfetched and complicated, actually it spreads the murders out—three flower girls five years ago or so, two to three years ago the girl in the washer."

"And a few months ago the girl on the tracks."

"Right. The Library Park victim was fairly fresh."

"What about the one whose bones—"

"Almost impossible to say. At least a few months. Beyond that, who knows."

"How does this make anything simple?"

Hoff shrugged. "Shows how easily one guy could have done all the dirt himself. Kills them quick and then takes his time with the rest." His voice had that melodramatic leer to it. He sounded like a man who enjoyed his grisly job a little too much.

"What bothers me," Paul said, "is that you make some kind of sense."

"Come over here," Hoff said. From a jar of saline solution he plucked a translucent tube. He handed it to Roy.

"Looks like a condom," Roy observed. "Feels like one."

"A finger," Paul said. "The whole skin."

"Right," Hoff said cheerfully, and Roy dropped it onto the table.

"S.O.P. for getting prints off floaters."

"Jesus Christ!" Roy said, and wiped his hands on his trousers.

Hoff laughed and retrieved the tube. "See the nail?" He put some gel on his pinky, stuffed it into the tube and fleshed it out. An exact fit.

"The girls' prints," Paul said. "Now I get it."

"Fucking science fiction. Double fucking chiller theater."

"Now tell us about the girl's toenails," Paul suggested.

"You mean the burro shit? That's a funny thing. At first we didn't pay much attention to her feet. The hands were a good bet, but came up zero, eh? But the bottoms of the feet were dirty, and I got good samples under the toenails."

"Indicating?" Paul prodded.

"Indicating she had spent some time on a dirt floor, probably, full of limestone and fossilized shit. Oat and alfalfa fodder, desert forage. I thought horse at first. But a buddy of mine at the university says burro. A cave or a hole or something. And I saved the best for last— gold dust. Just a trace, but there it is. Unmistakable. So let's call that hole a gold mine."

"Do you know what still gets me?" Roy said. "That they weren't missed. I mean, a year? Two years? And nobody notices?" Was that the best measure of a life, how much of a hole you left in others' lives at the end?

Paul said, "Like I told you, lot of rootless people. Don't belong to anybody. Live out there on the margins. This city eats them up." Despite the air conditioning he was feeling closed in. He took a deliberate breath and felt his chest tighten. Just nerves, he told himself.

"I'll tell you something else to simplify things."

"You and me don't mean the same thing by simplify," Paul said. He wanted to get out of this place, up into the fresh air. Get a grip, he thought.

"This fellow you're after has a headquarters. When you find it, you're going to find a knife, rope, embalming instruments—all the tools. And God knows what all else. Unspeakable things, probably."

"Headquarters." Roy got the feeling Paul was a little overwhelmed by all this. Roy sure was. Jane had come to the same conclusion.

"And you may find something else there—more bodies."

"How can you predict these things?" Hoff was really showing off today.

"He's keeping the bodies a long time before dumping them, that's how. It's all in the book."

"You people are amazing," Roy said, pacing. "Truly amazing. Doesn't this sicken you?"

"Sit down," Hoff said. "Lighten up."

Paul said, "I've never seen anything like this before. I've never even heard of anything like this before."

"Hey, you okay?" Roy said.

"Fine. Just fine. Too much coffee."

"Everything's happened before," Hoff said, "a hundred years ago, or a thousand, back in the Bible. Maybe even the Bible is just the history of things that kept happening over and over."

Twice-told tales, Roy thought, all of them. Paul seemed shaky today.

Paul called his office. "Round 'em up," he said. "And get hold of Frankenstein, too." He put down the phone abruptly. "Let's get out of here. I want some daylight."

"If you need me," Hoff said, grinning.

"My office, half an hour."

They climbed the concrete stairs up to the main floor and Paul paused to light a cigarette before they pushed open the glass doors and stood in bright sunlight on the high steps of the main entrance.

The heat was oppressive. Paul opened his collar and took deep breaths of air and dragged on his cigarette till he coughed.

"What do you make of that guy?" Roy asked.

"Hoff? Salt of the earth. Loves his work."

"Loves his work. Exactly. Don't you find that a little weird?"

"Everybody's a little weird."

"You know what I'm getting at."

"Come out and say it then. You think Hoff cut up our girls—" Paul started coughing and didn't finish.

Roy clapped him on the back. "It would explain a lot of things. Like the killer's expertise in pathology. Like why we haven't caught him yet."

"You're dreaming. I've known Hoff for years."

"What's his house like?"

"What?" Paul dragged on the cigarette "I don't fucking know. Never been there." Outdoors, he felt calmer. His chest loosened up.

"Where does he go to church?"

"How should I know."

"See—you don't know him. He could be anybody."

"Could be, but he's not. Don't give me this. I don't need it."

But Roy pressed. "He could control it all, right from that little horror shop down there." He pointed back into the building. "Don't you see it? And he's even been on campus. Could have seen the Callison girl there a dozen times."

Paul was suddenly listening. He waved the cigarette. "What? What was he doing on campus?"

Roy felt a small satisfaction. "You heard him talk about his buddy at the university. Hoff teaches an adjunct course every spring. Physical Anthropology. You know—bones, organs, muscles, blood."

Paul said, "Shit, don't tell me stuff like that."

"You have to hear it. Jane said, whoever it is will love tampering with the bodies. Don't get sloppy in your old age."

"Maybe it's about time I hung up the spurs," Paul said, not moving. "Had about enough of this shit." The claustrophobia downstairs—or whatever it was—had thrown him. Usually he was unflappable.

"Come on, you're just tired. It's getting to you."

"No, it's more. It's something new, that I don't recognize. That wasn't there before."

"You can't quit. You're too good at what you do." Another three years, Roy thought—then what?

"What if I am? Is that any reason to go on doing something?"

"You got a better one?"

"I know what I'm looking for now. I think I even know where. I just wish I knew who."

"It's the same one you've been looking for all along, isn't it."

Paul nodded and smoked. "Yeah, all along. The ones who got Linda. All the other murderers. Years and years. But something's different. Something's changed, or I've changed."

"You left something out of the story this morning, didn't you?"

Paul stared out toward the traffic. "You always leave something out of a story—that's what makes it a story." Roy wasn't sure what he meant by that. "I've been telling you stories all day," Paul said. "Now you tell me one."

Paul was right. What they had just seen had jarred something loose inside. "Okay," Roy said. "I should have told you this. Wanted to, but . . ." It took him a minute to get started. He took a deep breath. "About a year ago, Eileen got pregnant. We couldn't be sure I was the father. She had an abortion."

"Aw, Roy."

"She wasn't unfaithful—that's not what I mean."

"Go on."

"It was rape on the side of a highway. He beat her up."

"My God, Roy. I had no idea—"

Roy held up his hands so Paul would let him tell it while he had the nerve. "Just before we moved back here and I took the job at the university. We were arguing about money. I said she was spending too much. She said I was cheap. Like that, shouting back and forth."

How had they come to be so bitter with each other in those days? Was it something that, sooner or later, every couple went through and just had to hold on tight and come out on the other side of? "We were in the car. I was driving, fast. Out to some shopping mall, way out in the middle of nowhere. You know the kind with outlet stores."

"Every couple quarrels."

Evening. Roy could picture it, but not clearly. The road, the mall, the weather, all were blurred at the edges. Not real memory but only the reconstruction of visual truth. Eileen's eyes hard in a way that scared him. His own voice mean and loud, saying things he could not believe he was hearing—words neither one of them had used before or since. They were quarreling about money. But what they were really fighting about was love, hard as a nut.

They fought meanly and recklessly, with words, and said things that could never be taken back. He told Paul the details, slowly and accurately, because he knew Paul had no use for sloppy testimony.

"Stop the goddamned car!" Eileen yelled finally, on a two-lane road in the middle of nowhere. He punched the brakes. "I'll walk from here. I can't stand to be in the same car with you!" She bolted off into the desert. Roy didn't try to stop her, never even called out her name.

A gas station stood on a corner half a mile up the road. He accelerated so violently the rear tires splashed gravel all over the place. He floored it and felt the little engine strain and knock and didn't give a damn if it exploded.

He drove for only half an hour.

"I went back to the gas station to look for her." Even now, his mouth went dry as he told it. Even now, it seemed like someone else's story, like something that could not possibly have happened in real life, in his own life. "Figured she'd have made it about that far and called a cab. I found her, though, where I'd left her, sitting right in the dirt, bawling like a kid. Something was wrong, bigger than our quarrel."

She looked shapeless, a blot of dull color off the roadway, pink on brown. He pulled the car over and jumped out, eager to ask her to forgive, full of remorse.

She looked up. Her blouse was torn, her skirt was all dusty, her face was bruised, like somebody had punched her over and over. She held her panties in her left hand. She said, "Take me to the hospital."

"He must have come along only a few minutes after I left her there," Roy said very quietly. "A big blond guy wearing a tractor cap and driving a red pickup. They never did catch him."

This was the first time he had told anybody, except the police. "I wanted to tell you, Uncle Paul," he said. "But I was too ashamed."

Paul seemed stricken, his legs suddenly cut out from under him.

"She went to the clinic."

"Your idea?"

"Who can say. I admit, I pressed her. I couldn't help it."

"At least you're honest."

"That doesn't help fix it, though, does it?"

Paul sighed and stubbed out his cigarette and turned his back to Roy. "No, I don't suppose it does. But it's a start."

"And there's another thing. That day Cindy Callison came to my office? The day she disappeared? She told me something. I don't think it matters, not to the case."

"But it matters to you."

Roy looked away. "Yeah, it matters to me. She told me she was in love with me. She wanted—she wanted to do something about it."

Paul nodded. "So you're the genius. You've been a long time telling me. What did she mean?"

"You know damn well."

"Not that part—the love part."

"She was in love. I don't know what she meant. What do people usually mean?"

"What did you tell her?"

"I didn't tell her anything."

"But you didn't sleep with her."

The day she disappeared, before seminar, she'd come to his office. "I've had some trouble lately, but I can do the work," she said. She sat across the desk from him. All at once, she took his hand and held it in both of her own.

"What is it?" he asked, so startled that he didn't remove his hand.

"Don't you know?" she said. "All this time? The way you look at me?"

"Cindy, Cindy," was all he could manage to say.

"I'm in love with you. I want to do something about it."

He started to say, "That's impossible—I love my wife," but he didn't say anything. He honestly didn't know why not. Then or now.

She kissed his hand. She ran her fingertips across his flushed cheek. He was aroused, her hand on his cheek was full of charge. She picked up his hand off the desk and brought it to her lips, kissed it and sucked on the fingertips, till he pulled it away. "You don't know what's good for you," she said. She was trembling. "I'll be back," she said, and left quickly.

Roy shook his head and rubbed his palms together. "You don't get it." He wished he could tell Paul the rest of it—the note he had passed to Cindy in class, the meeting he had kept too late.

Paul nodded again. "I get it, all right. You wanted to. You would have."

"Yeah, I wanted to. I might have."

"All right. Don't go melodramatic. You've got things to fix at home."

"But Cindy Callison, I feel, I don't know—like she counted on me for something."

"For what?"

"I don't know—to know she was alive. To miss her. Don't you see? I had a chance to save her."

"How many people have any of us saved lately? Be realistic. You're doing all you can."

They stood a few minutes, not talking, breathing in the heat. "Okay," Paul said at last, "here it is, the rest of my story." Roy waited while Paul lit another cigarette.

"After they found Linda, I went home. I didn't drink, not a drop. I loaded that old Army Colt and sat in my kitchen. I cocked the gun and it stayed cocked for four days. I sat there with it. Didn't eat, didn't sleep, although there were hours I will never remember.

"I didn't sleep, but I dreamed—you see? Night dreams, but wide awake. The smell of dead earth and dust, the black frame of the coffin box. I smelled . . . flowers . . . and felt my fingers ache. There was no blood in my hands. They went cold, numb, paralyzed.

"The sky was black, no light at all. I could feel it pressing down on me, filling my ears. I choked, tried to push it off me, but it was pressing down too heavy. My hands were bloody, my fingernails broken. I looked as hard as I could, stared till my eyes were ready to explode, but there was nothing, just darkness.

"I dreamed out of her eyes. I never want to do that again."

They both stood in the sun, not talking, not looking at each other.

"I kept the gun in my hand the whole time. Every so often, I'd put the barrel to my temple." He put an index finger to his head. "I prayed for the courage to pull the trigger. Just a slight pressure, a twitch, really, that's all it would take. A twitch. You understand?"

Roy turned and stared at him. He wanted to say yes, but in his heart he believed no one but Paul could ever possibly fathom that moment. Such a moment did not come to men like Roy.

"But I could not." Paul sounded disgusted with himself. "For four days I could not. I believed I was a coward for that. May still believe it. That would have been justice. But here I am, all these years later." He coughed. "A man should die at home."

Roy felt moved and embarrassed all at once. He wanted to say something meaningful, he wanted to touch him, but could not. Any words, any gesture of Roy's would only cheapen the story. They stood together, not touching, each waiting for the other to move first.

Roy started down the steps, trusting his uncle to follow. They had work to do.

Roy installed himself in a straight-backed metal chair at a long conference table in the squad room while Paul sipped coffee. They'd come over from Hoff's lab and it was after quitting time. The rest of the detective bureau was empty. Wade Billings came in looking bleary-eyed and disheveled, as if he were coming off a bad drunk. He gulped two cups of black coffee and poured a third before he said a word. Then all he said was, "Women," and swore. Nobody asked him what he meant. "Getting fed up with overtime."

"You don't like it," Paul said softly, "there's an opening in traffic."

Billings tossed his Styrofoam cup into the wastebasket. "I didn't mean anything. Had a long day, all right?"

Gino drifted in a few minutes later. By comparison to Billings he looked fresh. But by the circles under his eyes Roy could see he, too, was feeling the strain of a long investigation that was going exactly nowhere. Carter and Hobbes, the FBI agents, showed up together in suits. Carter was suffering from bad sunburn on his face. "Fair skin," he said glumly.

Jane Featherbead drifted in and sat down next to Roy.

"What's she doing here?" Carter asked. "For that matter, why is this professor always hanging around? This place is turning into a seminar."

Paul said, "Meet special agents Carter and Hobbes, FBI."

Billings said, "Doesn't the FBI have any plain old regular agents? What makes you guys so special anyway?"

Hobbes said, "A bit irregular—letting civilians get involved in such a sensitive case."

Paul said, "I'll take whatever help I can get. Long as I'm running this thing."

"Well, let's talk about that," Carter said. "We're ready to take over any time. Seems to me you've had your at-bat." His partner Hobbes, hands clasped, nodded. Hobbes was wearing a tweed jacket, which seemed ridiculous to Roy.

Gino said, "Let's have it, Paul—what have you got?"

Just then the door opened and Stein came in carrying a large manila envelope. Hoff was right behind him. "You're going to love what I did with these," Stein announced, spreading eight-by-ten glossies on the steel table. Pictures of body parts, dead women, mutilation.

"We've seen all this," Gino said. "What's the point?"

"I told him to come in," Paul said.

"I spent all last night in the darkroom, reprinting. Going for contrast, you know—sharpening up the edges, opening up the background frames. Underexposing, overexposing. Also, I've got a proof sheet of all the various wounds, so we can compare and contrast—"

"Does it tell us anything new?" Carter interrupted.

"Well, I guess . . . I guess not," Stein said. "But you have to admit, they're beautiful photographs."

"Beautiful? Beautiful?" Hobbes said. "H. Christ. Where'd you get this guy? What the hell kind of investigation are you people running here?"

Billings laughed. "Way to go, Frankenstein." Stein scowled at him.

"Put away the art, Frank," Paul said. "That's not what you're doing here."

Frank Stein sat down, looking hurt. He kept hold of his envelope.

Paul took control of the meeting. "Tell them what you told me, Hoff."

"The first victim had interesting stuff under her toenails. Took a while to sort it all out. Burro shit, for one. So she was barefoot, but where?"

Jane Featherbead spoke for the first time. "Nobody's used working burros for a hundred years or more. Mostly they had them in the old Spanish mines."

"Half the state is copper mines, or used to be," Hobbes said.

Hoff said, "Not copper—gold. There was gold dust under her toenails. Just a trace amount, hardly even showed up."

"How is that?" Carter asked.

Hoff shrugged. "You mainly find what you're looking for. Nobody was looking for gold. We ran across it by accident."

Jane said, "There are a few abandoned shafts down on the Gila Reservation. Some more gold diggings east of here in the Superstitions. And we don't know how many dry shafts were sunk to look for the Lost Dutchman's gold."

"Gold mines?" Carter said. "You're talking gold mines? The Lost Dutchman's fucking gold? Jesus, you people."

"Why not a jewelry shop?" Gino asked. "They grind gold all the time."

Hoff answered, "It's not refined. Not pure."

Jane said, "Remember what I told you: classically, your post-mortem mutilator lives within walking distance of where he dumped the body."

"That won't work here, though," said Roy.

"Correct. There are too many bodies, too many sites." Paul ticked them off: the railroad tracks, the vacant lot on Central, Library Park, the dump out in the desert. He even counted Roosevelt Lake, the heifer carcass. "But suppose we take just one instance and forget the others." Paul stood up and paced the room.

"Which one?" Billings asked. "How you going to pick?"

"Let's be democratic about it, go with the majority. Look: four bodies were discovered at the dump out by the White Tanks."

"Remains." Hoff slurped his coffee cup dry and held it, as if warming his hands.

"Remains. Bones. But four, that's half."

Roy said, "And that's where a mine shaft would be. Not in town."

"Right," Gino said heatedly. "But we're only guessing it's a mine. And from that we're supposing it's where this hombre hangs out. And that he's the same bad guy who did the flower girls. Don't you see how far we're stretching?" It was the first time Roy had ever seen him angry, even a little bit.

Paul said, "We ever had a case where we didn't stretch?"

Agent Carter wagged a finger. "Not like this. This whole thing sounds more like a campfire ghost story than a murder investigation. You've worked it all out in your head, though, haven't you."

"What I've worked out doesn't get us too far. But we had better damn well stretch if we're going to get anywhere." Paul sat down again and stared at the reports on the table, flipping pages and shaking his head, occasionally sighing. Roy watched and thought about all the coincidences piling up so far, all the outrageous evidence, things he himself would not have believed had he not witnessed them.

Forget the other victims, he told himself—there was still the ghost of a chance of finding Cindy Callison alive.

"Maybe you're right," Gino said, not sounding too convinced. "Still doesn't seem like much to go on."

Nobody said anything for a minute. Then Stein said, "So what do you want from me?"

"Get me a good topo map of the West Phoenix area from the freeway all the way out to the mountains. Get an aerial photo if you can, too—you know, the kind surveyors use."

"Where will you be?" Stein said.

"You're a detective—find me."

"Whatever you kids do," Carter said, pushing back away from the table, "keep me posted. No surprises."

"Don't worry," Paul assured him, "you'll be there when we make the arrest."

Carter crumpled his Styrofoam cup and winged it across the room into the wastebasket. "Who you going to arrest, the Lost Dutchman? No, I just don't want you fucking up any evidence. We'll need it when we take over the case."

Base Station #12

Lights don't reach way down here. My special place. Need kerosene fire.

Don't carry the lanterns back—can find my way in the dark, copy?

Down here is my place. When the buzzing gets too loud and can't climb out of the noise. When head swells and belly balloons and fingers bloom like jellyfish. Rest easy, pard.

Coop and recoop, over.

Don't take no guns down there. Not a place of blasting and noise. But of quiet, the heart of the rock. Air presses me back into normal shape.

Then the needles all over my skin go back up.

Greeting all my friends along the way. In the dark. Rising to the light.

Saw them with their guns. Pretty good against pigs—squealed and disappeared. Bloom of blood and fire. Bright death.

I watch them nights, the man of stories, the woman of light.

She's mine. She's fucked, over?

Day Thirty-eight, Morning

Before it was light the detectives and Roy met back in the squad room.

"Where's the FBI?" Billings asked.

Paul said, "They're not invited."

Stein erected an easel and upon it placed a large cardboard-stiffened aerial photograph of the West Phoenix area. On the desk was laid out a series of connecting topographic maps.

"Finally, somebody who can give me what I need," Paul said, sucking on a Pall Mall in between slurps of coffee.

"Enjoy it while it lasts," Stein said. He was drawn and edgy today, as if he hadn't slept much lately. There was resentment in his voice, as if he felt underappreciated. "Had to boost the photo from the state building, right out of the lobby. Infrared, high-altitude resolution, courtesy of the Air Force."

"How old is it?"

"Mid-seventies. A lot has been built since then."

"No shit," Billings said. "Like half the city."

"Better than nothing," Roy said.

"What we're looking for was there a long time ago."

They stood in front of the photo, and Paul kept checking the map against it until he had found what he wanted. "Here," he said, thumping an index finger onto the cardboard. "This road here."

Roy looked closely, trying to get his bearings on the photo. He did better with the map. "Runs along the foothills?"

"Right. See how it skeins off into lines?" Roy squinted at the map, whose detail was just a grid of gray, black, and white lines. Green spaces showed up in red, and buildings appeared as blue rectangles. He finally saw the lines trailing into the rough terrain like creases in the palm of a hand. "Mining roads, rough as cobs. Look, here's my place. Must have just built it."

Sure enough, Roy could identify it. Paul trailed his finger along the photo to a spot just south and west of his house. "The dump where we found all those bones."

Gino stood with his arms crossed, as if bored. "Where's our man?" he said. He didn't raise his voice. He offered no inflection at all. His wan face was drained of expression. "There's nothing out there."

Roy counted the blue spots along the road Paul had identified: only three. "But there might be more by now," Paul said. "I haven't been up that way in some time. Anyway we're not scouting for a house. What we want is a mine. Maybe near a house?"

Gino said, "I couldn't find any records that old. If there were diggings up there, you'd have to go look for yourself. A long shot."

Paul stood, staring at the photo, nodding.

"You're sure he's up there?" Gino said, looking from Roy to Paul.

"Who's sure? Not me. But we may as well start somewhere, and what have we got that's any better?"

"Why not down on the Gila, those old gold diggings?" Gino said. "Least we know where they are."

Paul lit a cigarette and coughed. "Too many kids and tourists go out there. Four-wheelers, hikers, shooters. No place to hide out. Not to mention the Reservation Police."

"And you're sure it's local," Roy said.

"I told you already what I was sure of."

Gino said, "I'm going to call down there and have their guys walk around the gold mines anyhow, okay?"

Paul shrugged. "Belt and braces."

Gino tapped the map at the point indicating the dump. "Our canvassing turned up zero out there. You know that."

"Let me have your list anyhow, so I know who you talked to."

"None of the ones on that map," Gino said. "Nobody said much of anything."

"Who was with you on the canvass?"

"Billings, me, half a dozen uniforms."

"Then let's take a ride up that way."

"How about if I come along?" Roy said.

"How sweet of you to offer. Where's your Jeep?"

"Out front. Why?"

"Cause we'll never get the T-bird over that road."

As they were leaving, Gino said, "Paul, can I see you a minute?"

"What, now?"

"Yeah—now."

They went into Paul's office and came out a few minutes later without explanation. Paul said, "Roy, give Gino the keys to your Jeep. You ride with me. We'll leave the T-bird at my place."

Roy flipped Gino his keys and followed Paul out to the garage.

The sun was coming up. Paul took a shortcut through the factory district and pulled the car off onto a dirt road that ran across the Salt. Right in the dry riverbed, under a railroad bridge, he stopped the car.

"Why're we stopping here?" Roy had a sudden bad feeling about this.

"Get out—I want to show you something."

Roy stepped out, losing his breath in the sudden heat. The drinking was ruining his wind. Before he could get his bearings, Paul raised an open hand and knocked him down. Roy sprawled on the gravel and broken glass, stunned.

"What the hell, Paul?" His mouth hurt. His hand came away bloody. "Jesus."

"You lied to me." Paul stood over him.

Roy sat up. "Paul, I swear—"

"Stop that! Stop that right now. Whatever you say now is police business. You have the right—"

"Fuck that, Paul. Why'd you have to hit me? Christ."

Paul kicked gravel. "You went down to the club to see her."

Roy rubbed his mouth and looked away. "Just that once."

"Four times, that we know of."

"That what Gino says?"

Paul nodded. "What else have you lied about?"

"Jesus! You think . . . listen, it was only a couple of times." He was sure of that much—or was he? Drinking so hard for so long, things tended to run together. It was easy to lose track.

"Keep talking." Paul gave Roy a hand up and Roy leaned against the hot fender.

"Didn't want to give you the wrong idea."

"Well, I've got the wrong idea now, don't I?"

"I already told you about the office. The main stuff. What more do you want?"

"The truth. All of it."

Roy glared at him. His stomach was hot and churning and his head felt light. He swallowed his sickness. "All right, here's the truth," he said.

Paul said nothing, stood, hands in his belt, listening. He lit a cigarette.

"It was stupid. I ran into her a couple of times out of class. God, she was good-looking." He realized he was talking about her in the past tense. "She had this way of moving—"

"At the club. What happened?"

Roy shrugged. "I watched her dance. I got drunk. The second time, her car was in the shop, so I gave her a ride home."

"Jesus!" Paul whammed a fist down on the fender. "Did you go up for a nightcap?"

"It wasn't like that. I swear." He remembered sitting next to her, inhaling the mingled perspiration and perfume and cigarette smoke from the bar. After a long shift she was beat but restless. Wanted to go somewhere, wind down. "We had breakfast at the pancake place on Sixteenth. She bought. Insisted."

Paul walked circles in the gravel, kicking and fuming. "First, you never went there. Then you did but didn't talk to her. Now you've got a fucking date for breakfast!"

"You don't get it. It wasn't like that!"

"It's always like that! You said so yourself, you wanted her. You wanted to."

Roy rubbed his sore jaw. It was all churning around inside him. How in the hell had he gotten so far off track? He said quietly, "It's not the same, wanting to and doing."

"Tell the jury."

"Come on—all we did was talk for a while."

"You held hands across the table. The waitress remembered you."

"So what? You never held hands with someone you didn't fuck?" How the hell did he know this stuff? All this time, Gino had been checking him out.

Paul leaned back against the car and seemed to relax, but Roy was wary. "That's not the issue here. The issue is trust."

"I know, I know," Roy said. "Then trust me. I was feeling horny and mixed up, okay? I got distracted. And then she disappeared."

"You got distracted. Shit." Paul nodded, taking it all in, lit another cigarette off the first, and said quietly, looking away, "Now, before you answer my next question, think very carefully. You may be tempted to lie but I'll hear it in your voice."

"What?"

"You were supposed to meet her that day?"

Roy was startled. "How did you—"

"A guess. The eye in my gut. Then it's true?"

That's the ball game, Roy figured. Paul would never trust him again. "Yes, it's true."

Paul exploded. "Jesus Christ, boy! What the hell do you think we're playing at?" He shoved the lit cigarette into Roy's face, and Roy leaned backward over the hood to get away from it. "People are dying, Roy! Some psychopath is hacking off heads and you're jacking me around!" He banged his fist down on the fender, denting it. "Shit!" he yelled, squeezing his bruised hand.

Roy gave Paul a minute to calm down. He had a right to be angry.

Roy almost wished Paul would hit him again, hard, if that would fix it. He'd never seen Paul lose control like this. "We were supposed to meet an hour after class. I was late. She never showed."

"How late?"

"Fifteen minutes, give or take."

"Where?"

"The parking lot."

"Why?"

"To talk."

"Come on, Roy."

"To do something about it. Who knows. I don't know what would have happened, Paul. I just wanted to be with her a little while. Does it change anything?"

Paul stared at him, deciding, then crushed out his smoke and lit yet another from his pack. He blew a couple of smoky breaths and looked off down the dry riverbed. "I believe you, I guess." He smoked. "Shit. Been hard on you, hasn't it?"

"Right," Roy said. "I never meant any harm. Poor damned girl."

"Christ. With all your brains. Did you really think we wouldn't find out? Makes you look guilty as hell."

"You know better."

"Yeah, sure. I know better. Maybe I talk up for you. But the judge and jury, they're not family. They won't give a shit."

Roy was scared. "I didn't do anything."

"Didn't do anything?" Paul got angry all over again. "You've been jamming me up all along, that's what you've been doing. Spinning fairy tales. You lied about knowing the girl out of class, lied about meeting her at the club, covered up when you found the notebook—obstructing justice! The FBI goons all over my ass and you're jamming me up. They're gonna just love this."

"Paul, I—"

Paul grabbed him hard by the collar. "Don't jam me up anymore."

"I swear. I didn't mean to cause any trouble."

"You didn't mean to?" Paul squinted into his eyes, and let go of his collar. "Glad to hear it."

Roy caught his breath. Paul leaned on the car and smoked, recovering his composure. After a minute, Roy said, "I'm sorry if I make you look bad to the FBI."

Paul shook his head. "Who gives a shit about looking bad. Those little pricks. I care about the girls."

"You don't like those agents hanging around. Carter and Hobbes."

"Hobbes, who cares. Carter I don't trust."

"How can you not trust the FBI?"

"Guy gives me the creeps, that orange hair, maybe. The pink eyes, like a rabbit. He's been here five years, head prick in the Phoenix office. Had five different partners. Nobody will work with the guy. They all transfer out. That tells you something."

He walked down the riverbed a few paces and spoke without turning around. "Got to ask you something, Roy."

"Shoot."

"Tell the truth now. Don't jack me around." Paul turned to look Roy in the eye. "Where were you night before last?"

Roy didn't hesitate. "At home with Eileen. Watching a movie."

"Which one?"

Roy thought back. "*The Name of the Rose.* We turned it off halfway through."

"If I ask Eileen, that's what she'll tell me?"

"Of course."

"Reason I ask, Loomis turned up."

"Then maybe he can clear up some things."

"I doubt it," Paul said, turning away again. "Somebody cut his throat."

Roy suddenly wanted a drink. "Shit," he said, tasting bile again. This was going to just keep going on and on, with him in the middle. "Must've known something," Roy said.

"Maybe," Paul said. "He was into some shady stuff. Could be a drug thing. Or the gay mafia. May not have anything to do with anything."

"Where'd they find him?"

Paul crumpled his empty cigarette pack and tossed it onto the riverbed at Roy's feet. "Right about there."

Involuntarily, Roy stepped back.

"Get in the car," Paul said. "And Roy?"

"Yeah?"

"You ever lie to me again. . . ."

Day Thirty-eight, Noon

They met Gino and Billings at Paul's house. Paul unlocked his trunk and removed two pump-action shotguns and four flak vests. He reached in under the hardtop and set the shotguns in the rack on the driver's side of the open Jeep, butts facing forward. Gino and Billings climbed into the backseat and Paul got in beside Roy, rocking the frame. He set his binoculars and his cellular phone in the cuddy between the seats.

Billings's face was framed in the rearview mirror. "Get this show on the road," he said.

"Let's do it right the first time," Paul said.

It took the better part of an hour to find the dirt road Paul wanted—there were so many false tracks, loops and detours made by off-road vehicles. The first house they came to was obviously abandoned—a rotting wood shack, paint scoured off the clapboard walls by the incessant desert wind. Part of the roof had fallen in. Once, perhaps, it had been a miner's cabin. The land from the road in was fenced sloppily in barbed wire and posted with a sign warning away strangers:

TRESPASERS WILL BE PERSEKUTED TO THE
EXTENT OF TWO MONGRAL DOGS AND A 12-GAGE
SHARTGUN THAT HAIN'T LODED WITH SOFER CUSHINS.

Paul directed Roy to park fifty yards from the house behind a thick-limbed brown mesquite. He tossed Roy his pump and one of the heavy vests. "You stay here with the horses."

"Aw, come on."

"We're dead without wheels, nephew. You hear shooting, and anything comes out of the house that ain't us, you bring it down, hear?"

"You betcha."

Roy squatted down at the edge of the mesquite cover, from where he could see Paul, Billings, and Gino approaching the shack from opposite ends. The monsoons were coming, the gray days, and clouds were blowing in across an opal sky. They were covering one another as they moved cautiously through the creosote. They were now at the edge of the firebreak, the customary swath a dozen yards in a radius from the house, cleared of brush.

Paul motioned with his hand, and then drew his .38. He hurried across the firebreak and stopped beside a window. Gino, shotgun in hand, disappeared behind the house, presumably to guard the back door. Billings went around the side, out of sight. Paul flicked his head into the window opening, then ducked. Crouching, he made it to the front door, which was ajar, and suddenly bolted inside the house.

Roy waited for a shot. Nothing happened. A turkey buzzard circled the desert out to the east. In the west, a hawk swooped and shrieked. The sun shone. Nothing happened. The shotgun sweated into his palms. He smelled gun oil. Nothing moved in his field of vision. Under the vest his shirt was already damp.

Suddenly a lone figure stood at the door. Roy tensed, raised the shotgun, had him nailed at the end of the barrel, felt his finger twitch against the warm sliver of trigger—Gino. He breathed but didn't raise the gun, kept it trained on the doorway, like a game.

"Don't shoot your uncle," Paul called from behind Gino in the doorway of the house. Billings appeared. All three ambled back, in no hurry.

"Well?"

"Just an old shack," Gino said. "No mine, nothing like that."

Paul lit a smoke. "Having fun yet?"

"Sure gets the juices running."

"That's what it's good for."

Gino turned to Roy. "You ready to shoot something, are you?"

Roy passed it off as a joke. Still, it had been a strange feeling, seeing a human target down the barrel of a gun, a kind of guilty thrill. He could not really imagine pulling the trigger, watching a human being disappear in a blast of blood and smoke. Perhaps, he reasoned, that's what made him different from the one they were after—not being able to imagine it.

In all the casual good humor of the moment, Roy could sense the tension draining from the detectives. Paul took deep drags on his smoke and coughed. Gino took deep breaths and rubbed his palms together, shotgun tucked loosely under his arm. Billings took a piss against the back tire. Paul had high color, looked alert and younger than he had in months. This business, Roy realized, was something Paul had understood for years. The puzzle, the intellectual side, occupied him, sure, but what he really craved was action.

"Let's take a ride," Paul said.

In the course of the afternoon they investigated several side trails that banked up the steep rock hills, treacherous with scree and potholes and boulders. Twice they got out and walked, following the course of tailings —rubble spilled downhill from diggings at the angle of repose, a telltale of mining activity. But each was only a false start, a scooped-out vertical hole with a visible bottom, a vein that had petered out before it had even begun.

They stopped at two more houses along the way, both, like the first, shacks long abandoned to weather and rot. Hours passed.

The road climbed gradually, getting rougher and narrower.

"There's nobody out here," Gino said as the Jeep lurched over the old mining track. "I think we've got to admit that to ourselves, eh, boss? Maybe this guy's just going to be a fishing story. The one that got away."

"What's the matter—you're not enjoying yourself?"

"I'm enjoying myself just fine, Paul. I'm just saying."

"Fuck this heat," Wade Billings said, and spat.

The road had twisted enough so that Roy was disoriented, but they seemed already far out of the vicinity of Paul's house. Hoff might be wrong. The evidence of the toenails, like all the other evidence, might just be one more piece they didn't need to solve this thing, one more superfluous bit of information to confuse the issue—pulverized limestone, burro shit, gold dust.

Yet if he lived out here, Roy considered, it would be the right place. Desolate, hard, away from people, out on the bare edge of the city, on the high ground usually preferred by predators. The only practical problem would be getting in and out, though there might always be another way in that didn't show on the map.

They cornered a jut of rock, crested a hillock, and there, in a sort of pocket valley, was a house. Without being told, Roy immediately stopped the Jeep and killed the engine. Paul was out and ready with his gun before Roy even got the brakes on, Gino and Billings beside him. Together they climbed the hillock, careful not to offer a silhouette. This time there was no shrubbery, only tumbled rock, bordering the track like a gate.

The house was a relic, built of thick adobe bricks, unwhitewashed, and backed right up against the near-vertical rock of the hill. Next to it leaned a wooden shed, its door padlocked. No vehicle was in sight, but strewn about the natural compound were rusted hunks of machinery, coiled cable, broken timbers. Mining stuff.

Again, Paul handed Roy the shotgun. "Wait here." Again he watched as the three men dashed across open ground to the walls of the house, thinking, Hoff had an eye in his gut, too.

Paul rapped on the door and waited. Roy heard no sound but the breeze rattling some dry greasewood nearby, about the only thing that grew out here. Each greasewood cluster was nearly perfectly spaced from the next, growing out from an original plant in a kind of radial colony. Some were ancient.

Paul tried the door handle, then shook his head at the other two. Roy then watched him holster his .38 and play with the latch with both hands—picking it, Roy knew, illegally. He waited.

After more than a minute, it turned. Once more Paul had his weapon in his hand. Gino and Billings followed him through the door.

Behind the rock, Roy waited. He glanced nervously at his back from time to time in case another vehicle should come along, scouted the nearby hills with the binoculars to allay the unreasonable fear that he himself was being watched. He listened for gunfire, for voices, for the smack of fists.

Nothing happened.

He waited for his name to be called, for the sound of glass breaking or a club striking, staccato pistol fire or the big thud of the shotgun.

Nothing.

He looked up and down the hills, spotted two cottontails and four geckos, again sweated slick the stock of the shotgun, listened for the scrabble of feet on loose rock, boots on hardpan, tires on gravel.

When nothing had been happening for nearly five minutes, he found himself walking stiffly toward the house, shotgun at port arms, a round jacked into the breech. Beside the door, he stood and listened to his heart beat. Where were they?

He took a deep breath, tightened his hold on the shotgun, and entered the house.

Day Thirty-eight, Afternoon

When Roy slipped inside the house he went blind. He stood and accustomed himself to the dimness. Light leaked in through the open door behind him, and little sparkles gleamed here and there on the walls. As his eyes adjusted, Roy realized the sparkles were holes in the tinfoil covering the windows. He saw the outlines of furniture and bookshelves, a mammoth TV, another doorway. He waited and wondered where Paul and the others had gone—the house wasn't that big.

He listened for a second breath, for movement or voices, for the shrill alarm of danger in his bones. Nothing.

When he had all the night vision he was going to get, he tiptoed across to the other door, bumping his shins twice on low obstacles in his path. He opened it into a bedroom—a single mattress on the floor, stacks of books piled high all around it. Hundreds of books—hardback, paperback, coverless—and a retractable reading lamp fixed to the wall. Where, he wondered, did the electricity come from all the way out here?

He heard noises, low and vague, and froze. He followed the noise with his eyes and ears and knew that it was coming from a second closed doorway into the bedroom, which led, apparently, toward the back of the house. Shotgun still at the ready, he opened the heavy wooden door and advanced through it into light.

He almost fired at the light. It was a long kitchen, running, he figured, the length of the back of the house, but accessible only from the bedroom, the way the front door was accessible only through the bedroom—the house wound back on itself like a conch shell. Was there a back door?

Yes. Past the deep-freeze and the refrigerator and the stove, all lined along the rear wall, was a door lintel. That's where the others must have gone. The door, oversized and made of hand-hewn oak planks strapped by wrought iron, stood slightly ajar. A chill draft spilled in from the opening.

Beyond was a dim yellow light. Roy eased the door open, hoping it wouldn't creak, but what he got was a shrill cinematic creak of iron on iron. The draft hit him full in his face.

"Jesus Christ!" cried a voice. Out of the darkness in front of Roy a masked face appeared. Reflexively, Roy pointed his shotgun toward the voice.

"Hey, watch where you're pointing that thing," Uncle Paul said. Gino stood beside him. Paul gingerly pushed away the black muzzle of the pump. Paul wore a white handkerchief tied over his mouth and nose—the masked face Roy had seen. He looked like a stagecoach bandit.

"Man alive," Billings said, getting up from the floor and dusting himself off. "I thought you were going to shoot somebody for sure, come busting in here."

"I thought I told you to wait outside. Now get out of here," Paul said.

"Are you all right? I couldn't find you." Roy was shivering with panic and cold. His stomach had turned over and stayed there. He could've shot Paul.

"I don't know if I'm all right. Christ, all right."

"I'm sorry, I'm sorry. I got spooked."

"Okay, you're sorry. Now get your ass back to the Jeep."

Nobody moved. Roy heard everybody catch their breath.

"Shit, he's already here," Billings said and shrugged. "We can use him."

Paul said, "Let's make it quick. We're in deep shit here and it's gonna get deeper fast. Come on." He relieved Roy of the shotgun and led him by the elbow farther along the stone passage. "We're in a gold mine," Paul said. "Old diggings. Hasn't been worked since the war."

"Which one?"

"Whichever one you like."

"Where's that draft coming from?" Already gooseflesh was raised along his arms.

"An air shaft farther on, I guess—all the old mines had one."

"Hurry up," Gino said, his moves quick and sure.

"You got a handkerchief?" Paul asked.

"What for?"

"If you've got a handkerchief, put it on now."

Roy fished one out of his back pocket and knotted it around his mouth and nose.

When it was secure Paul said, "Let me show you what Gino found."

They walked perhaps twenty yards into the cool of the mine, descending only slightly on either side of a narrow-gauge railway, their way lit by dim bulbs strung along the reinforcing timbers, then came to another oaken door framed roughly into rock walls.

Railroad, Roy was thinking: Here's where the tracks lead.

"Used to be a stope," Paul said, holding Roy's elbow. "The door is new. Ready?" Paul pushed it open and, even breathing under the handkerchief, Roy nearly gagged at the stink of feces and urine and chemicals and something else, something dead.

Paul threw a wall switch and the chamber was lit with the same weak yellow glow as the main shaft.

"Don't throw up," Paul said. "Swallow it. We can't have you screwing up evidence."

Roy's stomach was a hot hard ball. His face flushed and his eyes itched. He saw first the table, then the stuff scattered on shelves ringing the high-ceilinged room: a machete, a hunting knife and scabbard, a couple of old pistols, buckets and jars full of floating stuff, other buckets empty and carelessly piled against the far wall, a butcher's knife, a cavalry sword honed and shiny, books and more books, silverware and half-eaten platefuls of food, beer cans. From nails driven into the framing timbers hung cowboy hats and women's veils, flowered dresses and a pair of faded Levis, a thick coil of white rope. A slingshot.

All the stuff looked fake, as if the four of them were backstage in the property room of a rundown opera house.

In a bowl of clear solution floated two translucent gloves. The hands of the flower girls, Roy thought: their whole skins. That was real enough.

Across the room, in an unlighted niche, was a stack of what appeared to be rotting wood.

In the far corner stood a large, filthy animal cage. In it was a canvas cot, some mussed bedding, a plastic bowl of brown water, and an overflowing slop bucket.

"That's where he kept her," Paul said. "Empty. We're too late."

Gino stood in front of the bars, as if lost in thought.

Billings shifted from foot to foot, spooked. "Tell me I'm not in the middle of a frigging nightmare."

Roy stood and took deep breaths, tried to get saliva on his lips. He cleared his dry throat. The stink was overwhelming—what was it? He had to get out of here. His eyes fastened on the brown muck on the floor of the cage. "What's that smell?" Roy said, surprised he could speak at all.

"Over there." Paul pointed his revolver toward the pile of rotten wood. Roy didn't get it. "Arms and legs," Paul said slowly. "Hands and feet. Human limbs."

Roy held both hands over his mouth and counted to five.

Gino said nothing, didn't move. Roy could see how all this was just too much for him. Billings kept spinning slowly in circles. "Where is he?" he kept saying, "Where the fuck?"

"Let's vamoose," Paul said. "We don't know where he is or when he'll be back."

"But Cindy Callison—"

"Gone," Paul said gently, shaking his head. "Lord knows where he dumped her."

"But what if—"

"No what if. Come on, Gino. Wade."

None of the men spoke as they made their way back to the kitchen, through the bedroom and living room, and, cautious of sight and sound, back into the sunlight. Again Roy was blinded, but their luck had held: no vehicle was in sight. The Jeep was still there, metallic blue against the gray rock, steering wheel hot to the touch.

Roy got behind the wheel. Billings started to climb in the back. Gino stood by the back bumper. "Somebody ought to stay here," he said. "Keep an eye out."

"Just what I was thinking. Wade—think you're up to it?"

Billings dropped the magazine out of his nine-millimeter and then popped it back in. He shucked the slide, loading a round into the chamber. "My pleasure," he said.

"We'll leave the bag-phone, but it probably won't be much use in these hills. Keep out of sight."

"You got it, boss."

"I'll send Gino back with the Jeep."

Roy drove. Once they had put a mile or more between them and the house, Paul said, "Pull over." Roy stopped the Jeep. Paul got out, spread the topo map across the hood, then took out a pencil and marked the spot with an X. Roy observed that, in fact, they were only a couple of miles from Paul's house—hard, overland miles, but they could be walked by a man who wanted to.

"So now we know where he is, and he doesn't know we know."

Gino laughed and said, "The whole search was illegal. How we going to fix that?"

They got back into the Jeep. Paul said, "I'll take care of that. Head for my place." Roy drove fast. At every junction or blind curve he expected another vehicle to appear out of the desert and catch them, chase them back to that evil place.

They got to Paul's by a back way Roy had never used. He paid attention to the dashboard compass so he'd remember how to get back there. Esmeralda was nowhere around, but her sheets and clothes were flapping on the line. Paul went inside immediately and used the telephone. Roy sat on the porch while Gino pissed against a greasewood bush. He heard Paul's voice, steady and low, spelling out details, setting it all up.

So it will come to an end after all, Roy was thinking. All the chase, all the superfluous clues, all the philosophy and metaphysics and artistry of reason—it all comes down to some burro shit under a dead girl's toenails. A leathery old coroner playing around with cadavers for fun and profit. He was almost disappointed. They were going to catch the bastard. They knew where he lived. Even if he got away, they had him. They could identify him now, and once identified he could be tracked, hunted down, cornered, captured. They could do with him as they liked, and be rid of him for good.

And they would probably never find Cindy Callison, unless he gave her up.

Roy still felt sick and his brain boiled. From an outdoor faucet at the side of the house he sloshed water over his head and rinsed the dust out of his mouth. Paul startled him and he turned, ready to fend off anything.

"Sorry, nephew. Didn't mean to spook you."

"Never mind." Roy stood there dripping.

"You're in this thing but good, now."

"I understand."

"Wonder if you do."

Gino came up. "Explained it to him?" He stared hard at Roy. Something was going on.

"The warrant," Paul said. "We were never in that place today."

"What?"

"We weren't there. You were. Alone. You were out there driving around in your Jeep and got lost. You knocked on the door and nobody answered, so you let yourself in." Paul pulled out his pack of Pall Malls, but it was empty. He crumpled the pack and stuffed it into his hip pocket.

"The door was open," Gino said. "Open—you got that?" His tone was almost threatening, like he was playing the bad cop in a routine. Roy couldn't understand why he was coming on so strong today. Maybe the whole thing was just finally getting to him.

"You got curious. You saw what you saw and came here to tell me," Paul added.

"Got it?" Gino said. "We weren't there. When we see that place with a search warrant, boy will we be surprised."

"Got it."

"The warrant is on its way," Paul said. "So are the uniforms and a mining engineer. In the meantime I need a drink. Gino, can you find your way back there?"

Gino nodded. Roy flipped him the keys.

Roy, too, wanted a drink, something strong and jolting, to put his mind back on track. He didn't mind the small subversion of the law, this law, for a higher law. He wasn't a cop, and they were dealing with some kind of monstrosity who prowled beyond the pale of ordinary criminal justice.

The blue Jeep raised a rooster tail of dust along the driveway. Roy stared into the desert. Where was Cindy Callison now?

Can smell their bad air in my place. Can feel their hovering presence in these walls. Have to ride this one out on top.

Knew they'd come, that was the point. She knew. Used to watch her sleeping, fill her head with pretty dreams of flowers and light. I'd crawl inside their lives, wrap their warm skins around me, the only booty I cared about. She's gone but she'll never go.

Made a mistake, but I don't know how, over. All that shit I learned. Have my own hands now.

They'll never take her away from me, I've got her but good. Very sensitive dependence on initial conditions—one little thing happens, and the world goes blooey.

Nobody reads me anymore. No more voice. Shut me down but good. Pulled the fucking plug on this radio jock.

The buzzing has stopped—why? Now, of all times?

Quiet as the heart of a rock. Wish I could stay down, but I'm out and staying out, over. Out and staying out. Moving from darkness into light, and back again.

Good night, Mr. and Mrs. America and all the ships at sea.

Houdini Whodunnit, signing off.

Day Thirty-eight, Evening

The time they waited was dead time. Roy sat at Paul's elbow, sipping a neat scotch, swishing it around on his tongue, feeling his gums burn. Zack lay sprawled across the tiles, his flanks a map of survival, panting in the last of the day's heat. The swamp cooler rattled distantly and Paul drank scotch without speaking. He called Jane Featherbead—he wanted her on hand as soon as they nabbed this creep. But she was tied up with a patient and couldn't get away. Soon, she promised.

Roy rinsed the taste of scotch out of his mouth with water and refilled his tumbler twice from a glass pitcher. Roy listened to the ice jingle when he poured again. The dog growled in his sleep and his toenails went clickety-clickety on the tile.

"They'll be here in a few minutes," Paul eventually said.

"About time this was over," Roy said. He counted the minutes on his watch. His glass was finally empty. In a few moments the place would be busy with cops and professionals, and it seemed to him these minutes of waiting were precious. Before the hoopla started, he must get a grip. He had things to ask Paul, but he didn't know if Paul had any answers.

What made it possible for a man to live like an animal, hoarding body parts in a lair, breathing death day after day in his own home? How could he keep Eileen safe in such a world?

He wanted to know many things for sure, and he was afraid that, if he knew one thing for dead sure, it was that he might never know anything for sure again.

Where was Cindy Callison? He wanted her alive, intact—or else he wanted her dead peacefully and without pain.

He imagined Paul's wife Linda, underground, suffocating in dust, and he imagined Paul, aboveground, having to go on anyway. How on earth could a man stand that?

All the cars came at once: two cruisers, an unmarked Ford containing a pair of detectives, a Search and Rescue Jeep with three more cops and a mining engineer, another four-wheel-drive van with a five-man SWAT team. Frank Stein got out of one of the cruisers, cameras looped around his neck and carrying a heavy bag of accessories. They could see him happily fussing with his equipment.

Paul got up and rinsed his mouth at the kitchen sink. He snatched his car keys off the cup-hook. Roy rubbed his eyes and slid off his stool. Paul said, "Ready?"

Roy nodded, feeling none too sure.

A helicopter landed in the desert behind the house and sat there whopping its rotors, a sound like stropping a giant blade on leather. They went to meet it. Agent Hobbes stepped out onto the skid and ducked out from under the rotor wash looking crisp and pressed. "Where's your dance partner?" Paul asked.

"Special Agent Carter had some business. He'll be along shortly. Paul, brief me."

Paul nodded and filled him in while the helicopter took off to reconnoiter.

They waited until the helicopter cleared them to go in. "No sign of any vehicles approaching the site," the pilot reported over the radio. "Just your blue Jeep parked where it ought to be."

"Show time," Paul said, and the motorcade started off.

As they pulled up to the blue Jeep, Gino flagged them down. He was flushed from being outdoors in the heat. His face was dirty from riding through dust in the open four-wheel-drive.

"Where the hell's Billings?" Paul said. "He wasn't supposed to go in alone."

"He was gone when I got here," Gino said. He held up the cellular phone. "Left this behind. Tried to call you, but all I get is noise."

"Jesus H. Christ!" Paul said. "Who does he think he is, John fucking Wayne?"

"Probably circled up for a better view," Gino said. "But I didn't want to be roaming around."

This time they went in with portable halogen spotlights and plenty of help. The helicopter circled wide over the area to warn if anybody approached while they were conducting their search. The SWAT team ranged the hills above the compound and dug in with scoped rifles and radios. On the hill above the house, they discovered a radio mast tall enough to bring in Hong Kong. From up there they could see a graded dirt road that led easily back to the highway south, in the direction opposite from where Paul and Roy had come.

Paul supervised the detectives. They were methodical. They went slow and they did it right. They looked at the big stuff and the little stuff and everything in between. They would make this case in the lab. First they jimmied the lock on the shed, which turned out to be a stall for a horse, complete with hay and droppings and tack. The horse was missing. Behind that was a lean-to, soundproofed with acoustical foam, that housed a heavy-duty generator.

Gino scouted around with some uniforms, then reported back to Paul.

"No sign of Billings?"

"Not yet. Can't figure it."

Paul shook his head and swore. "Got a bad feeling about this."

"He'll turn up," Gino said. "Let's get it done."

They lit the interior of the house like a film set, and Roy hardly recognized it. One wall of the living room was an entertainment bank—two wide-screen TVs, a stereo with monster quadrophonic speakers, belt-high stacks of CDs and records and audio tapes, hundreds of videotapes lined along floor-to-ceiling shelves.

The ratty gray couch was clear of debris, but the two overstuffed chairs and the rocker and both end tables were piled high with books, papers, tapes. Knives and handguns were strewn carelessly about, some loaded, some not. Open boxes of hollow-point .38s and .22-longs and magnum rounds and even armor-piercing bullets lay scattered about in front of the TV. An over-under shotgun and a .30-06 leaned in the corner. A Browning nine-millimeter automatic held open the *TV Guide* on the arm of the sofa. A Buck skinning knife was stabbed vertically into the coffee table. Next to it a rusty scrimshaw-handled straight razor lay on its side.

Roy said. "All the magazines."

American Rifleman lay next to *The New England Journal of Medicine*. *Reader's Digest* shared coffee-table space with *The American Journal of Applied Physics* and *Soldier of Fortune*.

"Can we get an I.D. off the mailing labels?"

Gino riffled through a stack. "Take your pick: R. Oppenheimer, Richard Burton, Jonas Salk, L. DaVinci, Emma Bovary. I'm guessing aliases, eh, chief?"

"We don't need jokes now."

"Sorry. Same P.O. box, Tempe. How about that."

"Good. Call it in and have somebody sit on it."

Gino went outside to one of the radio cars; the rest of the team, Roy included, went into the bedroom. A complicated ham radio was set up on a table on the other side of the bed. "What in the world?" Roy said, noticing the operator's manual.

"Ham radio. Just like Jane said—giving his rap to the whole world."

"Who in the hell was listening?"

Paul nodded. "Yeah. Must be a thousand books here, too. She was right about the I.Q. Where the hell is she when we need her?"

"She sure had this guy's number." Roy looked at titles: *Principia Mathematica*, the *Aeneid*, the collected Henry James in a leather-bound edition. Sir Walter Scott and Scott Fitzgerald. *The CIA Manual of Torture. Cooking Light. The Collected Poems of Emily Dickinson,*

The FBI Story. Shakespeare and Harold Robbins. *Mein Kampf* in German. Markers protruded from yellowed pages.

Special Agent Carter burst onto the scene. "Why the hell wasn't I called first thing?" His red hair was mussed and his tie was askew.

"We did call. Where the hell were you?"

Carter banged his fist against a wall. "I said not to move without telling me first."

"Take it easy," Paul said. "Don't fuck up the scene."

"You're the one who's fucking up. I hear you've already lost one of your people."

"Look, I don't need you—"

"Lieutenant, we found him," a uniform called from the front door. Billings appeared in the doorway. His shirt was torn and he was covered with dust. His face was cut.

"What the hell happened to you?"

Billings looked sheepish. "Fell into a hole. You know, one of those false-start mines. I was circling around up in the hills to get a better observation point and—"

"From now on, do as I tell you."

Carter shook his head. "Discipline. Jesus, your own people don't even listen to you."

"Go get cleaned up. Roy, come on."

They stepped over stacks of books on the floor next to the bed: dog-eared copies of *Principles and Practices of Embalming, The Fractal Geometry of Nature, Nonlinear Dynamics and Chaos, Metamagical Themas.*

The room stank of sweat and stale laundry, of cigarettes and gun oil. A nickel-plated .44 magnum lay on the mussed Davey Crockett quilt, along with an Archie comic and *Shooting Bears—A Hunter's Companion.*

"I want pictures of everything," Paul said to Stein. "From the ground up. I want them clear and in focus and I want it as many times as it takes to get it right. Number your rolls in sequence and develop them all tonight—savvy?"

Stein was already shooting away. "This stuff is going to be gorgeous," he promised, looking through his viewfinder. "Folio quality. One-man show. Coffee-table book of the month."

"Just get it," Paul said.

"Who the hell is this guy?" Roy said. "That's the question."

Paul was busy looking for a clue. "Most of us stay pretty much between the lines, you know? All our lives. This troglodyte, hell. He got outside the lines and stayed out. Jumped the fucking track altogether."

Stein's flashes went off, his shutter clicked, his motordrive whirred continuously. Paul took Roy and the mining engineer into the kitchen.

Gino caught up with them and approached the deep-freeze, laid a hand on it. Paul grabbed his arm, too late. "Dust it first," Paul said. "I want it established that he was the last one to touch it and therefore knew what was inside." Gino handled that.

The FBI agents went with them into the passage, revolvers drawn. Everyone was wearing surgical masks. Paul stopped them halfway down the passage to set up portable fluorescent lights. "You're not going to like what you see," he told the officers and the engineer. "We're going to be brief. A special team is on its way from the coroner's office with decontamination gear." They proceeded.

When Paul opened the door to the chamber, he looked carefully to see if anything had been disturbed since their last visit. Nothing obvious, but that was no guarantee. There might be another way in. Before they touched anything, Paul waited for Stein to catch up and shoot the scene.

Ready as he had been to enter, Roy had exactly the same reaction as on his first visit—violent nausea. Hot flashes dizzied him. His neck constricted. He tasted a chemical burn in his nose and mouth. He concentrated on breathing in and out slowly, deep breaths, on looking at only one thing at a time.

"Get a load of this," Gino said from the corner full of severed limbs. "This goes back a ways, and I see bundles back there." His voice had a high, nervous pitch to it—Roy knew they were all just barely under control.

Paul nodded and seemed to Roy suddenly very tired. During the entry he'd been masterful, completely in charge, no-nonsense and let's do it right. Now he seemed not to want to pursue this, had none of that alertness and keen sense of closing in for the kill that Roy had counted on. "Anything to I.D. him?"

"Not a thing."

They went out of the chamber and into the main passage. Paul turned abruptly, as if his ear had picked up a sound far off down the passage. He asked the engineer. "What I want to know from you is, how far does this passage go?"

The engineer shot his flashlight down the long tunnel, bouncing the beam off the wall where it curved. "At least as far as the air shaft. That's where we're getting the draft from."

"Let's take a look."

Straddling the rusty narrow-gauge tracks, they explored the passage another fifty feet to the end of the string of lights, then past it, slowly descending. Side passages, most hardly larger than crawl spaces and half-filled with gravel and loose rock, branched off at intervals. "Cave-ins," the engineer said. "All the timbering has been stripped from this section of the mine." They lingered beside an ore car so ancient it had a wooden chassis.

Roy said, "Is it dangerous?"

"More or less. I wouldn't do any drilling or blasting in here, but these are hard-rock mines, not like, say, coal mines. It's taken years to knock some of this stuff down. They probably stripped the timber when the mine was played out. Timber's hard to come by out here."

"Terrific." What the hell were they doing in here if the mountain could fall on their heads any minute?

They came to the air passage, a vertical shaft that broke the ceiling and continued through the floor. Paul drew a bullet and tossed it down into the hole and listened for many seconds before he heard it plop into water. "Shit, that's two hundred feet at least."

The stink was suddenly strong again, and Roy guessed what that meant. No daylight came from the shaft above. "It will be covered on top, like a chimney," the engineer explained. "I'll show you when we get out."

At the bottom of the air shaft, water gurgled.

A hundred fifty feet farther on they found another partially collapsed side tunnel. From the rubble protruded a skeletal hand and wrist bones sleeved in rotted red flannel. Only a little farther on, the main passage was blocked by a cave-in.

"What's on the other side?" Paul asked the engineer.

"Who knows."

"Guess."

The engineer tapped his rock pick against the rubble. "Probably unshored diggings right into the limestone. Under the water table. Narrow, wet. Full of noxious gas. Not even bats down there. That enough guessing for you?"

"Then this is far enough," Paul said. "They're going to have to dig up this whole mountain to get to the bottom of this." Roy heard the despair in his voice. "Who is this guy? Who is this fucking guy?"

Once out of the mine, Paul headed back through the kitchen, bedroom, and living room to the fresh evening air outside the house. He walked to the center of the compound and lifted his face to the fitful breeze, turning his head slowly this way and that as if sniffing for a sign. He lit a cigarette and smoked it down, and Gino let him be.

"Guess what we found in the deep-freeze," Gino said at last. His hands were shaking and his voice a note too high. He blew his nose hard. Then he sort of smiled, as if this was the inside story.

"How many?" Roy said.

"Just two. In pieces. Wrapped up nice."

"Women?"

"Girls. Kids. Youngsters. Tenderloin."

"Shit." Cops were all alike—playing hard-nosed to keep it all safely at a distance. Roy wasn't fooled.

Gino said, "Glad to be inside of this thing now?"

Roy just concentrated on breathing.

Paul walked to the radio car and talked awhile. He stubbed out his cigarette and came over to Gino and Roy. "Fucking nightmare," he said. "The paperwork alone will kill us. How in the world can we ever straighten out a thing like this? How can decent people ever sleep at night again? Tell me that."

"All I want to know," Roy said, "is where is Cindy Callison?" Against all odds, he still wanted a happy ending to this thing.

Agent Carter came out of the house. "You find anybody worth arresting yet?" He sounded smug.

Hoff emerged behind him, stripping off a pair of latex gloves and reaching for a fresh pair. His work was just starting. "Man, I'd love to meet this character. Look into his eyes and see if he looks back."

Billings said, "Yeah—you and Frankenstein. He wants to take his picture for *Life* magazine."

"Careful what you wish for," Paul said, lighting another cigarette.

Hoff was agitated. "You know, as ordinary, more or less moral twentieth century Americans, we can only go so far in our mind's eye—right?"

Nobody argued the point.

"This is an opportunity. A scientific opportunity. To go to that point where imagination staggers. Hell, past it. To look over the edge."

"If we get him," Paul said.

"What I'm saying, we take certain things on cold evidence. That Aztec priests plucked out a hundred beating human hearts in an hour. Or that the Nazi Mengele amputated arms and legs from healthy children, without anesthetic, just to see what would happen. But can you really imagine it? Can you really hold such atrocities in your mind's eye?"

Paul smoked and shook his head.

"I can't," Hoff said. "I know that stuff is true, but I can't imagine it. That's why it's so hard to put a serial killer to death. Takes too long to make the case. Eight or nine years after the fact, who can even imagine his crime?"

Roy got the creepy feeling that Hoff really *could* imagine it. That he enjoyed imagining it. "I saw the bodies," Roy said. "I saw the girl lying on the tracks, all cut up. Don't tell me about imagination."

Hoff kept pressing. "But can you actually imagine the moment of death? The last seconds of her suffering? Drawing the blade across her throat?" He snapped his glove.

"That's enough," Paul said. He stubbed his cigarette out on his boot, then put it into his pocket. "Let me lay it out for you. Seventy-two hours, we watch. SWAT in the hills, the chopper in the air, a rotating team of detectives in a camper down the road. We wait for him to come back, then we piss on the fire and call in the dogs."

Carter said what Roy was thinking: "And if he doesn't come back?"

"Then the team comes in and we take this mountain apart foot by cubic foot and start collecting the bodies."

"You'll never get him that way," Carter said. "Figure it out."

Gino said, "Maybe he's right."

"Don't tell me what I won't get. He'll come back. Or we'll find him some other way."

Hoff said, "One more question. How will you know when you've got him?"

"What?" Paul said. "That's not funny, Hoff."

"I'm serious. Sure, if he comes back. But what if he doesn't? If you ran across him sprawled in front of city hall, how would you recognize him?"

"The clock's running," Carter said.

"Don't start with me." Paul called the rest of the detectives out of the house. "Anything with a possible I.D.?"

Billings showed him a shoe box full of I.D.'s—library cards, credit cards, video-rental cards, hunting licenses, club memberships, all under bogus names. Nothing with a photo.

"Here's one that might help," Gino said, snatching a hunting license out of the box. "M. Montresor."

Roy shook his head.

"What?" Gino asked.

"He's in a horror story by Edgar Allan Poe."

Paul laughed for the first time all day. "Ain't we all. Run it down anyway, along with the others. Take them around locally and see if you can get a description. What the hell this joker looks like."

"Won't get us anywhere," Gino said.

"Nothing more we can do here. Let's go back and wait by the phone."

"I'll stick around here, catch a ride with the Feds. You two go on."

It hadn't come together as neatly and surely as Roy had hoped. There would be more time when nothing was happening until, as before, something would happen all at once and require the right action. Roy took the wheel of the Jeep and drove them back to Paul's. In the shotgun seat, Paul rocked spasmodically with the motion over the rough track, saying nothing, staring off into the failing light.

"My Lord it's been a long chase," Paul said halfway home.

"We're close," Roy said, although he didn't quite believe it.

But Paul didn't seem to be listening. "She's a pretty country, this time of day—all that peace and low color. You'd never guess what's in her heart."

Base Station #14

Going down is easier but coming back up is not.
Down there in the circle of light the world is sealed tight. Coyotes prowl over my head, moonlight on their shaggy shoulders.

Yippee-ki-yi-ki-yay, over.

Flames are little tongues and they talk to me.

Him, he just keeps staring. Buddha.

Come down deeper, over. Down where the gold is. Down at the bottom of things. Down where the stories live.

Keep this frequency open.

Day Thirty-eight, Night

Eileen and Jane arrived at Paul's almost at the same time, sharing driveway dust. Paul and Roy were already installed on the porch, drinking scotch over ice cubes. Paul toyed with his matched Colts—he had fired out half a dozen loads earlier just to calm down a little while he waited for word from the stakeout team. Roy sipped: tonight he didn't want a thrashing, foolish drunk but rather a mild and sedative buzz that would soothe him into sleep. Otherwise he'd suffer a waking dream all night long.

Jane was fresh out of the shower, hair still sheeny, her hands and fingernails cleaned of clay. Eileen, hair ponytailed by a red bow, kissed Paul on the cheek and Roy on the mouth and neck. The women sat down with their drinks.

"Missed you today," Paul said. He had the cellular phone next to his chair, and every half-hour the stakeout team was calling in. He had people working the phony I.D.'s, people tracing the P.O. box, people poring over years of missing-persons reports. All he could do now was wait. That was the biggest problem with being in charge—sometimes you didn't have anything to occupy you while you waited. All the real work was done by less important people.

Somebody had already leaked word to the media that a major stakeout was in progress—it wouldn't be long before somebody found out where and the TV cameras showed up. Reporters had been calling the office all afternoon.

"I couldn't get away," Jane said. "Next time you go in, though, I want to be there. See where this creature lives."

"You were right about everything," Roy said. "It was uncanny."

It had rained briefly but violently an hour ago, flash-flooding the arroyos. The wet greasewood lent the air a vaguely medicinal smell that cleared the sinuses. For the next few weeks the monsoons would sweep across the valley and flooding would be a problem on every patch of depressed ground. The rain had left a low, flat line of leadbellied clouds to the west, now gilded with the last of the light.

The breeze had fallen off to almost nothing. Roy sat and watched and sipped and felt the whole world stopped, waiting, suspended in that moment just before, between aim and fire. He noticed Zapata's old primer-gray Pontiac parked among the other cars near the trailer.

Paul said, "Ezzy's got company tonight. We can pour our own drinks, I guess."

From time to time they heard a strident male voice—Zapata's.

"You can hear him yelling at her plain as day. Do you want to do anything about it?"

"Zapata gets wound up sometimes. I don't poke my nose into her business. Give her some privacy."

"Sure mad about something."

"I've got ears," Paul said.

Just then they heard loud cursing in Spanish.

"Maybe we ought to check it out," Roy pressed.

"I'll decide what gets checked out on my property," Paul said. "This is still my house."

For a few minutes, Ezzy's trailer was quiet.

Jane said, "So you have your killer at bay."

"Not exactly." Paul lit a cigarette. "What we have at bay is only his goddamn house."

"I see."

Roy said, "It's only a matter of time now. He'll come in."

"Unless we spooked him. One thing I've learned about the bad guys over the years is how uncanny they are. Eyes in the back of their head, eyes in the gut. Smell the law just like they smell trouble. Sometimes they just slip in between the covers."

Eileen said, "Don't talk like that. I want this thing over."

"You want satisfaction," Paul said. "You want it all wrapped up neat, the way we all do. The human heart craves resolution."

"I do," she said.

"It's a basic human need," Jane said. "We hate not knowing how something turns out. Makes the world seem too dangerous." She scanned the twilight with tireless eyes.

Jane was making perfect sense, as far as Roy was concerned. Before this, he'd always believed that human experience existed in a fairly narrow range, in which resolution was possible. But if they couldn't round up this killer?

Jane said, "At least we finally know who he is."

"Not exactly," Paul explained. "This guy is Jack the Ripper, Sweeney Todd, and Charlie Manson all rolled into one."

Jane said, "Tell me what you found. Don't leave anything out."

Paul puffed his cigarette and drank. "You want to know what we found out there today? You really want to know? Helter-fucking-skelter, ladies, that's what we found."

Slowly, deliberately, in a maddeningly methodical presentation, Paul recounted the story of the search, the books and tapes and tools of death, the instruments of dismemberment and torture, the over-sized animal cage—in which, Roy was certain, the killer had kept Cindy Callison. And how many others? And for how long each? What had she seen? What had she suffered? What had become of her? How had it ended?

Paul said, "It isn't just a hideout. That horror shop is a way of life, a vocation. He's dug in there. And why, after all this time, does he suddenly start shopping bodies around? I'll tell you why: he's coming to the end of it, that's why. Fed up. Wants it to end as bad as we do. Now, if he doesn't go back there, where's he going to go?"

"Got a point," Roy said.

"Sure I do. It's taken him years to collect all that stuff. And he must have had money, too. Plenty."

Roy said, "The books alone are worth a fortune."

"That was ten thousand dollars' worth of TVs, if it was a nickel."

Eileen said, "Who knows if that's the only place he lived. Think about it—where did he live before he lived there, huh? Where did he come from? Say he's thirty years old. So where was he for the first twenty? Was he out there all this time, living among us? In one of the offices I worked at? Waiting in line behind me at the market?" She rose and paced to the end of the porch and back. Zack followed her with his eyes, ready to go after her if she ventured off the porch.

Roy drank just often enough to keep a low-grade buzz, feeling his limbs unclench and settle into a heavy relaxation. He stared down the hill at Esmeralda's trailer. From time to time he heard a racket— things banging, voices arguing. The children were quiet. That unsettled him: the children were hardly ever quiet. He watched and waited for Paul's story to be done.

Lights were burning at both ends of the trailer, kitchen and bedroom. He heard Zapata's angry voice continuously now, but so far there was no sound of violence, no sound of any but routine trouble.

Jane said, "I bet nobody knows him. I bet everybody you talk to gives a completely different description."

Glass broke inside the trailer, and Zapata's voice grew louder, more belligerent. Zack perked up his ears and growled, trying to rise on stiff legs.

"Down, boy," Paul said. He slid the Colts into their twin holsters in an automatic gesture, then stood up.

"You going down there?" Roy said, standing up.

"I'm going down to get Jane's pots out of my trunk."

Jane laughed. "You mean you didn't drop them off in town yesterday like you promised?"

"Things got sort of busy. Probably all busted up by now. Give me a hand, Roy."

They walked down the hill to the T-bird and Paul popped the trunk. The two pots, nested in straw, seemed intact. Just then more glass shattered in the trailer. "Uncle Paul, we really ought to see if she's all right."

Paul sighed. Trunk lid still ajar, he said, "Come on, then." He hitched up his gunbelt. Roy followed him. When Esmeralda screamed, they started running.

Paul rapped on the flimsy door of the trailer.

"Zapata," he said. He rapped again and called her name. "You all right, Ezzy?" They heard Esmeralda say something fast in Spanish, then the sound of slapping, a struggle. Paul leaned his shoulder into the door and popped it open.

Quick enough to impress Roy, Paul hopped up the step and into the trailer. Roy followed. The trailer was narrow and cramped. The door swung closed on its own. Esmeralda was sitting on the couch, her face bruised, her lip cut, a smear of blood on her yellow blouse.

Through the little doorway Roy could see broken plates and glasses all over the kitchen floor. An empty Rojo mescal bottle lay among the debris. A plaster statue of the Virgin was shattered at the base of the wall. No sign of the kids. Standing next to Esmeralda, tightly clutching her forearm, stood Zapata. He was medium-sized but muscular in black chinos and a white snap-button shirt. He was raising his arm to hit her again.

"Zapata!" Paul said. "What's going on down here?"

He turned, holding onto her arm.

Esmeralda said, "It's all right, he's only drunk—"

"Let her go," Paul said without raising his voice.

Zapata stood uncertainly, breathing hard, his eyes darting back and forth between Roy and Paul. He yanked Esmeralda to her feet and stood behind her, bending back her wrist until she cried out in pain. Why didn't Paul do something? Roy wanted to tackle Zapata and then worry about Ezzy, but he waited to take his lead from Paul. Paul just stood there.

"Paul, what?" Roy said.

"Put down the blade, amigo, and we'll talk."

Roy saw it now, in Zapata's hidden hand. Paul, palms held out in front of him, stepped toward him. "There's no call for that," Paul said.

Where were the kids, Roy wondered. Back in the bedroom?

Zapata kept Esmeralda off her balance. Roy felt scared. There was no room to maneuver, no space to move. Paul advanced slowly on Zapata. "It's all right, Zapata," Paul said. "We all get carried away from time to time." Zapata let go of Esmeralda and shifted the knife to his left hand. He backed into the hallway leading to the rear of the trailer. Esmeralda stumbled out of the way.

"That's right," Paul said. "Now let's talk this out calmly." He stood at the head of the hallway, Roy right behind him.

Zapata's hand moved so quickly Roy never saw it. The next thing he knew Zapata was waggling one of Paul's Colts. Paul froze. "Amigo," he said quietly. Zapata cocked the hammer. "Amigo—" Paul said again.

Just then Eileen knocked on the door. "Paul?" she called. "You guys all right in there?"

As she yanked the trailer door open, Roy heard an incredibly loud explosion. Paul grunted and fell back into him, pinning him to the floor. The silence was stunning. Then the voices started. Names, at first—Ezzy, Paul, Roy, Eileen. Who was calling?

Levering on one arm, Roy struggled out from under Paul. He saw Zapata, still holding the pistol, backing down the narrow hallway toward the bedroom. Instinctively Roy reached for Paul's other Colt. He got to his knees, then his feet, facing down the hallway toward Zapata. Backing away, Zapata held up the gun, but it wasn't cocked. He looked terrified. Sober. His lips moved but no words came out. He turned and kicked out the rear window.

Roy went down the hall after him. When he got to the bedroom, Zapata was disappearing through the window. Roy held up the big Colt, cocked the hammer, aimed at Zapata's white shirt.

But he couldn't fire. He stood there, stupidly, holding the gun, while Zapata slipped out the window and disappeared. He heard the Pontiac start up, then the sound of tires on gravel. Only then did he uncock the gun, lay it down, and go back to help Paul.

Eileen was bending over Paul. "Help me here," she was saying.

"Help me here!" Roy leaned down and touched Paul's neck—he still had a pulse. He lay on his side. Roy opened the front of his shirt, and his hand came away bloody. Roy saw no exit wound on his back, so the bullet was still inside.

"Jesus, Paul," he said, then over and over, "Paul, Paul."

The hall floor was slick with Paul's blood. The bathroom door opened and there were the kids, scared past crying, whimpering like puppies. Gingerly, they stepped over Paul and clung to Esmeralda. Mother and children huddled on the couch in shock.

Eileen was already dialing for an ambulance. Jane came in, sized up the scene, and grabbed a dishtowel for a bandage.

Roy sat next to Paul in the hallway, holding his hand. Jane stanched the bleeding as best she could with the towel. Paul's breathing was shallow, but he wasn't bleeding from the mouth and he could still squeeze Roy's fingers.

Paul's eyes were open and he just lay there. They waited for the ambulance. Roy counted Paul's breaths, knowing now they came in a finite number. How many were left? Could the ambulance get to him in time?

"Hang on, hoss," Roy said. He said it again. Paul breathed and lay in his own blood. Was it really going to end like this, Paul gunned down in a domestic squabble? Paul lay on the floor, fading. Roy talked to him. He didn't say, "It'll be all right." He knew better. Instead he spoke names, Eileen and Jane and Esmeralda and Zack. "I'm here," Roy said, over and over. Repetition was prayer.

Esmeralda herded her kids outside. Roy could smell the blood now, sweet and thin. He hated being confined in this little boxy trailer. If Paul were going to die, he wanted him to do it in light and air, smelling the desert, letting his life go out on the evening breeze.

They heard cars outside. "They're coming," Eileen said. She kissed Paul's forehead.

They got out of the way to let the paramedics take over. Roy got to his feet and stumbled out into the darkness, lit now by the flashing red-and-blue lights of police cars and the ambulance. The lights made the rest of the desert dark as pitch. He stood and watched them carry his uncle out on a backboard. Gino and Billings were there, recalled from the stakeout, as were half a dozen uniforms, fanning out around the trailer. Everybody seemed to be talking at once, but Roy was dazed and could make no sense of it. Cops sat in cruisers, doors ajar, talking on the radio. Other cops fished in open trunks for shotguns and extra lights. The red-and-blue lights strobed across Paul's white T-bird, its trunk lid still ajar. He headed for the ambulance.

"I bet he's halfway to Mexico by now," one of the voices was saying.

At the ambulance Esmeralda took Paul's hand. "I'm sorry," she said, sobbing.

"He can't hear you," the paramedic said. "Shock." To Roy, he said, "You coming?"

Roy climbed into the ambulance and sat next to Paul, watching the lights and cops, the trailer and the house, recede into distance.

I sit protected in a ring of light—one flame for every season of heat.

Heat stirs in me, hot rush of something underneath, running deep as blood. The sun calls it out and in the cool dark it settles to a low murmur, it leaves me alone. The dark is where I come to be left alone.

There are fifteen tongues of fire in the rock.

Should have kept her, not given her to the train. All I did was put her on TV and now she's in my head. I'll never get her out now, over. Thought I whispered her dreams alive, but now she's breathed herself right into mine.

See my old man flying over that last jump, silks flashing green and gold, hear the thunder of hooves drumming the turf. Watch him fall, down and down, horse-crushed and spattered with mud, see the big ruined horse thrashing his broken legs—

Pretty cool.

When did I ever see that?

Was a bitch dragging her down, over. A pure bitch.

She's the first one I ever brought down here. Home. The hole in your pocket. Little black bubble. Infinite dimension in a finite volume. Absolute sanctuary, over?

Till he gets here. Now I want him. She wants him.

She's in love with the guy, man of words and stories. Right. He was in her eyes and in her mouth and on her wet tongue. Then her eyes went away and I felt my blood rise and push and swell till I felt I was tied with ropes under the skin.

Her eyes kept going away and only her hands talked to me.

All I wanted was to keep her.

Loved to take them apart, over.

Loved the clean blade. It was important that they be washed. Tidied them up, say again: Neatness counts.

His boots were spit-shined Moroccan leather, black as guns. There was brown foam around the horse's bit.

Quiet fills up the rock now. Up above, I can feel their heavy feet pressing it down tighter over my head, the stony sky. A hard sky, and no one can punch through, over.

Kind of sky you only find in stories. On her lips. On her wet tongue.

I slip in and out of here, copy. Invisible.

Foot of the rainbow. Where I found gold.

In certain locations in the American Southwest, gold is found mingled with copper, silver, malachite, turquoise, and many varieties of quartz. The veins are erratic and may yield one ton or one hundred tons of precious metal. The shallow deposits initially mined by the Spanish priests are long gone; remaining are rare deeper pockets accessible only by deep-shaft mining by large-scale operators who can afford the risk.

Can feel the blood going down. Can feel the cool dark stifling that urge to go out from it into light.

His name on her wet tongue. Never got off. Sky in his head. Words in his eyes. Fifteen bright tongues wag at the dark, over.

At us.

The path to my fixed purpose is laid with iron rails, on which my soul is grooved to run, over.

Of course there's no answer now, just habit.

Listen to the hum of sweet darkness, coming to carry me home.

End-o-track for grooved soul, over. You read me?

Signing off, amigos.

It's been real.

A goddam hoot.

Out.

Day Thirty-nine, Early Morning

At the hospital they rushed Paul into the emergency room. A nurse adroitly steered Roy into a waiting area and he watched them wheel the gurney down the hall, fast, attendants on either side, one of them holding up an IV bag. He sat and composed himself. Billings and a couple of uniforms came in presently and poured coffee from a pot in a corner stand. "Tough break," Billings said. "Why didn't Paul just draw his gun and whack that greaser?"

Roy had asked himself the same question, but he already knew the answer: Paul wasn't a hothead or a bully. He didn't go drawing his gun every time he got into an argument. He'd known Zapata for years. And it was Ezzy's house—he didn't want to make a fuss. He'd let his guard down. They rehashed the shooting and waited for word on Paul.

After some time, Jane Featherbead came in. "I spoke to the surgeon," she announced. "They're going to operate in a few minutes." It had taken almost an hour to stabilize Paul.

Roy nodded. "Where's Eileen? I figured she'd come in with you."

"I don't know—she was talking to the FBI guys when I left."

"I'd better call out there. I really want her here with me."

"I know." Jane squeezed his hand. "Going to be a long night." He tried Paul's number, but it was busy.

"The police are probably using the line," Jane said. "Relax." They settled in and waited as an hour passed, then another. Every fifteen minutes Roy called Paul's house, but all he got was a busy signal. He dialed the number of the cellular phone, but nobody answered.

Billings said, "Why did he pull a gun on Paul? Right in his own front yard! Jesus, I mean, it all seems so goddamned senseless."

"You just never know what people are capable of," Jane said, sounding just like Paul. "Maybe he felt cornered, threatened. Maybe it was all that tequila. Maybe he was jealous. Something stupid like that."

It was one more thing they'd probably never know the answer to, Roy thought. He wished Eileen would finish up whatever she was doing and get down here to the hospital.

Agent Hobbes came in, followed by Agent Carter. For once, Hobbes looked ruffled. His rep tie was loosened and he carried his sports jacket over his shoulder. His white shirt was all sweated through. Hobbes said to Roy, "Sorry about your uncle. Hate to see that happen to a cop. Any cop."

"Where's Eileen?" Roy asked. "My wife?"

Carter said, "I don't know. Took her statement, then she had something to do up at the house."

Billings said, "Fuck are you taking statements for?"

"Zapata's headed for Mexico. International flight to avoid felony prosecution. You figure it out. We'll get him at the border."

Roy said, "No, you won't. He knows the border." He flashed on that image of Zapata's white shirt disappearing out the window. Roy had had a clear shot, but he hadn't taken it. Even now, oddly, he didn't hate Zapata. He just wanted somehow to undo what had been done. And he wanted to ask him, why? He felt light-headed and sick to his stomach, as if his body were realizing what had happened.

Gino and two uniforms came in and talked to Billings, then the uniforms went out. Gino sat down next to Roy. "What the hell happened?" he said. "How'd he get the drop on Paul?"

Roy explained. "All happened so fast. Where's Eileen—didn't she come in with you?"

Gino shrugged and sipped coffee from a Styrofoam cup. "Last I saw her, she was talking to the Feds." He pointed toward Carter and Hobbes. "Isn't she here already?"

Hobbes said to Carter, "Now that Paul is out of commission, it's as good a time as any."

"We're taking over," Carter said. "Here on out, nobody goes near the mine without my authorization."

"You got paper?" Billings said. His temper was up.

"I got paper. I love paper. Signed and sealed from Washington."

"We think Paul's shooting is connected to the other stuff," Hobbes explained.

Roy said, "It's not connected." His stomach was boiling. The room seemed too crowded. Where was Eileen?

Carter said, "He's chasing the bogeyman and, just when he gets close, somebody puts a bullet in him? We don't buy that kind of coincidence." Under the fluorescent lights his orange hair looked unreal, like a costume wig.

Roy said, "I'm going to try Eileen again at the house." He went over to the pay phone on the far wall and dialed Paul's number. Still busy. He hung up, waited, and redialed. Busy. After a few minutes of this, he gave up. He stood for a moment breathing deliberately, then he joined the others.

"Get hold of Eileen?" Jane asked when he sat down on the vinyl couch next to her.

"Busy. Probably talking to her sister." He was trying to invent a plausible explanation. She should be here by now. His instinct said it was all wrong. She would have come immediately. He turned to Gino. "Can't you do something?"

"Sure. Let me call a radio car. See if any of our people are still out there."

"Thanks," Roy said.

"I'll see somebody gets out there to check on her."

Just then Esmeralda walked through the door. She came over to Roy and took his hand. She was crying softly. "I'm so sorry," she whispered. "I never meant for this to happen." Jane made space on the couch for her. She sat down between them.

"Ezzy," Roy said. "Is Eileen still at the house?"

"I left the children with my cousin," she said. "When I left, the house was dark. Everybody was gone." Jane held her while she prayed softly in Spanish.

Gino stood up. "I'll get somebody out there right away."

Incredibly, Paul hung on. Five hours of surgery later, the surgeon, a boyish fellow wearing bloody scrubs, confided to Roy, "Frankly, I'm baffled. But you just can't ever tell about the human body. Takes more to kill some people." He went prattling on about miracles. The bullet had blasted through his left lung, but Paul seemed bent on surviving.

Roy spent the night in the waiting area. He called his apartment. He tried Eileen's sister in Scottsdale. Gino reported that Eileen was not at Paul's house. "Where the hell is she?" Roy said, starting to panic. "You've got to find her," he told Gino. He and Billings promised. They got on the radio. They sent uniforms all over the city. They woke up her clients in the middle of the night. It seemed incredible to Roy that Eileen could have disappeared in the middle of all those cops and FBI and paramedics. Or maybe the confusion, the chaos of voices and lights and people coming and going, made it possible. He remembered how the flashing lights had ruined his night vision, turning the desert just beyond them into a black hole.

By the early hours of the morning, it was clear: Eileen was missing.

Roy sat on the couch between Esmeralda and Jane and wept, trying to get a grip on himself. He felt completely unraveled. Jane held him while he cried. Esmeralda was silent. At some point, exhausted, he fell asleep for a few minutes. Dreams cascaded through his imagination—confusing, troubling dreams. The young surgeon, now wearing clean scrubs, shook him gently by the shoulder and said, "Mr. Pope? You can see him now, if you want." Roy washed his face in the men's room. He was done crying. Now he must take charge of things. Paul would count on him. So would Eileen. He followed the surgeon into the intensive care unit.

Roy stood over Paul's bed. "I'm here, hoss," he said. Paul couldn't speak. He breathed shallowly. But he took Roy's hand and squeezed. He looked Roy in the eye. Roy kept his composure. "Keep fighting," Roy said. He didn't tell him about Eileen. He stood there a few moments, speaking quiet reassurance, holding Paul's hand. A few minutes of wakefulness were enough to exhaust Paul into comatose slumber.

In the corridor, Jane said, "Is he going to make it?"

Roy took her hand. "He's always been strong. I have to believe he will." Jane nodded. "Any word from the cops?" he asked her.

"Nothing," Jane said. "What now?"

"We've got to find Eileen, that's all there is to it."

"Where do we start looking?"

Roy shook his head. "I have no idea. But we have to start somewhere. All this waiting is making me crazy."

"The last place she was seen?"

"That's as good a bet as any. Ride with me out to Paul's. We'll start looking for her there."

She kept holding his hand. "Roy? You know the odds are against us."

"Don't tell me that," he said softly. "Just help me find her."

Day Forty-one, Afternoon

As for the murderer—the one they had been tracking for weeks across railroads and streets and dirt roads and the lined pages of Cindy Callison's notebook—that one had never returned to his lair in the hills, nor had he ever again called for his mail at the Tempe Post Office. After the designated seventy-two hours had elapsed with no sign of him, the coroner's team moved in with an army of cops and pulled up every floorboard in the place, crawled down every passage in the mine, and sifted through tons of rock and rubble in their search for the truth.

They impounded forty guns of various calibers and 3,800 rounds of ammo; eighteen knives, including a bayonet, two cavalry sabers, and a samurai sword; a steel crossbow and razor-tipped bolts. Also seized were a complete embalming laboratory; surgical instruments, syringes, and a minor pharmacopeia of anesthetics and sedatives; poisons in jars. Steel buckets, plastic aprons. Chemicals in bottles and jars, sacks and canisters, dry and in solution. Formaldehyde in jugs. Evidence.

Costumes. Complete uniforms for a mailman, a Pinkerton guard, a nurse, an Air Force major, a rodeo clown, a Big Burger Bunny, a railroad conductor, a baseball player, a fireman. Green surgical scrubs, a black cap and gown. Doctoral hoods from nine universities.

Two thousand six hundred and eleven books.

Four hundred nineteen videocassettes—mostly murder mysteries, war pictures, and Westerns. "The Faces of Death," parts one through three, and sixteen South American bootlegs—snuff films.

The remains of twelve more persons, some of them mummified,

some mere skeletons or parts of skeletons, all of them so far unidentified and many likely to remain so, were exhumed from walls, stopes, alcoves, shafts, holes, and shallow graves.

Two of the bodies had been quartered and stored in the deepfreeze. Others, reduced to bone by a method yet to be determined by the coroner, had been bundled in blankets and stuffed in the recesses of the mine—in blind passages, collapsed tunnels, rubbled stopes.

A rough track led from the pocket canyon cross-country to the boundary of Paul's property. The path was passable on horseback. Plenty of tracks were found, but no horse ever was, nor had any neighbors ever seen one.

The property, including the house and mine, were traced to an absentee owner in New York who had inherited it years ago and had never set foot on the place. He had no idea anybody was living on it.

Fingerprints were clear and plentiful, but a computer analysis yielded nothing: apparently the killer had never been arrested for a crime, nor been bonded, nor been in the military service.

He left no pictures of himself. Not one.

From the incredible assortment of clothes strewn about the place he—or she—was either short or tall, slender or stocky.

None of his neighbors had ever seen him up close enough to give a description.

It took the cops three days working around the clock to go through the place and be satisfied they had gotten it all. The search ended where the mine shaft had been blocked by a cave-in.

That's what Carter told Roy when he called. Gino and Billings were off the case. It was all federal from here on out.

While Paul lingered in intensive care, going in and out of critical, Roy went out of his mind with worry. Eileen had vanished. The last time she'd been seen was the night of Paul's shooting. Everybody saw her that night. Everybody talked to her. How could she have been taken right out from under the noses of all those cops?

*   *   *

Roy was exhausted. He'd spent one more day driving around to every place Eileen had ever been—the supermarket, the movie theater, the restaurants downtown, convenience stores on the highway, clients' offices. Nothing. Her sister hadn't heard from her. She hadn't called the hospital. Now he sat on Paul's veranda with Jane Featherbead. He kept coming back here. This was the last place she'd been seen.

Down below the veranda, beyond the white T-bird, the trailer looked abandoned. "How's Esmeralda?" Roy said.

"Gone, cleared out, near as I could tell." Jane touched his arm and offered him a glass of iced tea. "You look like hell, Roy. Let me get a doctor to prescribe some sleeping pills."

"Not till I find her." He leaned forward in his chair, hands clasped, ignoring the iced tea even though his throat was dry and raw. His eyes itched from fatigue. "Where is she? Where did he take her?"

Jane said, "There's only one place. And the FBI is crawling all over it."

"Carter says they're finished up out there. Found whatever they're going to find." Roy petted old Zack, who lay wary at his feet, from time to time fluting through his nose as with fright.

"Poor damn dog," Jane said. "Can't figure out where the old man has gone, eh, boy?"

Roy stood up and paced the narrow veranda. "So where do I look? How do I find her? Christ, how do I find her—"

"Take it easy. Let's go through it again. You and Paul went down to the trailer. Eileen went down behind you. When Zapata shot Paul, you went to the back of the trailer, chasing him. Eileen came in the door."

"Right. Then she dialed nine-one-one and the place was suddenly Grand Central Station."

Jane nodded, remembering. "Cops, Gino and Billings, FBI."

"Carter and Hobbes, they took her statement."

"And sometime between then and the time Esmeralda left the place for the hospital, she disappeared."

Roy stared into the desert and pictured the scene for the thousandth time: the paramedics in blue jackets wheeling Paul out on the collapsible stretcher. A dozen cops fanning out around the trailer. Other cops sitting in cruisers, talking on the radio, doors ajar. Trunk lids open to get at shotguns and police gear. It was dark, the mars lights strobing across the scene. Crazy shadows. Surreal, the way a crime scene at night is always surreal.

Jane stared out toward the White Tanks. "Then we're right back where we started, except for Paul. That maniac's still out there, and he's got Eileen."

The sun was still hanging over the hills and the desert was blotted by shadows. "But where did he take her?"

"He's got to go back to the mine."

"Why?

"Because he's got nowhere else to go."

"He can fit in anywhere, that's the whole problem."

"Yes, but that's only good in a temporary way. It takes tremendous energy to keep it up. Everybody has to come home. I don't care who you are—or what."

Roy stared down the hill at the empty trailer and the white T-bird, both closed up tight. He replayed the scene out loud: "Paul and I went down to get your pots out of the T-bird." He remembered standing there, next to the open trunk. It was closed now.

"Let's walk down to the car, just the way you and Paul did."

Roy ducked inside to fetch the spare keys from the hook by the sink. "Come on," he said. He didn't remember closing the trunk. He wondered who had—it could have been anybody. But it was an odd detail that stuck in his mind's eye.

Jane followed him. He inserted the key and sprang the trunk lid. On the felt liner of the trunk, among the brick-colored sherds of broken pots, lay a red ribbon.

Roy picked it up and held it to his lips. "Oh, Jesus, Jesus!" On the night Paul was shot, Eileen's ponytail had been tied by a red ribbon—with a big looping bow.

"I'll call Gino," Jane said, and sprinted up to the house.

Roy sat down in the driveway dust, dizzy.

Jane came back, out of breath. "They're on their way."

Roy nodded, too overwrought to speak. So she'd been confined in the trunk—alive, or dead? The killer had been watching the house, took advantage of the opportunity, the confusion. Disconnected words and images tumbled through his head. "For the love of God," he said, then he said it again. His mind was making crazy associations. The line came from that Poe story, the one in which the evil Montresor bricks up his enemy in the cellar. As Montresor is fitting in the last brick to bury him alive, Fortunato utters it.

Roy was still sitting in the dust when Gino, Billings, and Hoff arrived in a police cruiser.

Hoff poked around in the trunk and came up with a hypodermic needle, as if he'd been looking for it. "Drugged," he announced, holding it up with a handkerchief to preserve latent prints. "Like the others. No blood, though—that's a good sign."

Roy stood up. He had a grip now. The Poe story had triggered something. "We have to go down there," he said. "All the way to the bottom."

Billings said, "Makes you think that place has a bottom?"

"It's a dead end," Gino said. "We've been over this."

"No," Roy insisted, shaking his head, thinking of Montresor building a wall of bricks between him and his victim. "It's not. The tunnel goes beyond the cave-in. It has to."

"Carter will never let us go down there," Billings said.

"Fuck Carter."

Hoff said, "You're not making sense, Roy. How was he able to pile up rocks on this side of the passage if he took her to the part below the cave-in?"

"Maybe there's another way in," Roy said. "A trick. We've been thinking in straight lines."

"I ain't going down there," Billings said. "No fucking way."

Roy said, "You do whatever you want. I'm going to find my wife."

"I'm in," Hoff said.

Gino said, "Me, too."

Day Forty-one, Evening

As Roy drove the Jeep along the rugged track toward the mine, the purple clouds that had been billowing over the valley all day let loose.

"Going to be a big rain," Gino said as the breeze turned into a wind. "Monsoon."

Roy didn't bother to raise the top. That would mean stopping, losing precious time. Never had he felt more alive, more filled with passionate conviction, closer to the edge of panic. He would find Eileen. Or he would die trying. The rain pounded the hard desert floor and the wheel ruts quickly filled with muddy water. Even when landmarks were obliterated in the driving rain, he could tell by the dashboard compass that it was the right road.

"How we going to get in?" Billings asked from the backseat. He had agreed to come along, but would wait aboveground.

"Same way he does," Roy said. "He seems to come and go as he pleases. We'll just have to find it."

"Come on—the place has been staked out."

"Yeah," Roy said, "I remember how that worked with Loomis."

"This is different."

Billings said, "It don't figure. We got plenty of prints off the deep-freeze, the furniture, all over the place. But they don't match up with anything we've got on file. Psychopath like that, you figure he's got to have priors."

Hoff said, "All the prints the same?"

"Yeah. Same guy. Might as well be a space alien."

In the shotgun seat, Hoff looked as colorless as his dusty suntan, now darkening as the raindrops pelted him. "We laid out all the bodies," Hoff said.

From the back, Gino said, "Do we really need to hear this now? The man's wife, okay?"

Hoff said to Roy, "I'm sorry, but I want you to hear this before we go in. I want you to be ready."

Roy concentrated on the difficult road. The wipers made a muddy smear across the windshield. "Go on. I'm listening."

"We lined up the remains as best we could. Figured out dates. There's a pattern." As he talked the dark seams in his face moved, his eyes narrowed, his thin, dexterous fingers formed the words. "The early ones were simply killed. Apparent gunshot wounds, knife bruises. You can tell by the bones. Then later comes decapitation and post-mortem mutilation. At first, random stuff."

"At first?" Roy said, gripping the wheel hard, trying not to think about that stuff being done to Eileen. "What's your point?"

"Five of the bodies have been surgically tampered with."

"Surgically?" Roy said. "What the hell does that mean?"

"He killed them gently. If that word can be used."

"Christ."

"On the first two, he was doing his own autopsies. Trying things out."

Roy said, "Autopsies?'"

Hoff nodded. "Then he did something extraordinary."

As if the rest were ordinary. Roy squinted at the road. The rain stung his eyes but he would not slow down.

"He was mixing and matching parts. There are post-mortem electrode burns." He paused. "I think he tried to bring one of them back to life again. Swear to Christ."

Roy stopped the Jeep where he had parked that first time with Paul. From the hillock they peered through the rain into the pocket valley. There was the house, the shed. Billings scanned the hills with binoculars. "Don't see nobody," he reported. "I don't believe this— where are those guys?"

The FBI seemed to have vanished. Nobody was watching the house.

Roy started the Jeep. "Hey, where you going?" Billings said.

"Going right up to the front door," Roy said.

"They come back, they'll know you're in there."

"By then it won't matter. Let them come down after me."

They piled into the Jeep and Roy drove to the front door. Gino tried to push ahead. "I'm going first," Roy said. He had one of Paul's short-barreled shotguns and a length of nylon rope coiled over his shoulder.

Gino backed off. "Whatever you say. Nothing official about this. Just take it easy with that thing."

They crept through the house, now stripped for the evidence lockers. Leaving Billings upstairs, they entered the mine and followed it down to the cave-in. Each of them carried a flashlight. Roy had taped his to the barrel of the shotgun.

"Now what?" Gino said.

"This is as far as we went with the engineer," Hoff agreed, and stumbled, almost falling. He cursed.

Roy leaned the shotgun against the wall, then pulled at the rubble with his bare hands. "Help me here," he said. They pulled away boulders and scree for fifteen minutes, but it was no use.

"Tons of this stuff here," Hoff said. "It's an honest-to-goodness cave-in."

"Guess you were wrong," Gino observed, leaning on his knees to recover his wind.

Roy picked up the shotgun. "What direction have we been going in?"

Hoff said, "You're the sailor, you tell me."

"If the house is facing east, then the mine shaft must be about due north."

Hoff thought a minute. "I don't know—I'm all turned around."

Roy led them back out of the tunnel and into the house. Billings was gone. "Where the hell'd he go?" Hoff said, jerking his head this way and that, peering into corners.

Roy said, "Always disappearing. I don't like it."

"He always turns up," Gino said. "But just what have you got in mind?"

Roy didn't say anything. He went to the Jeep and consulted the little dashboard compass. In the rain and gathering darkness he paced north to the shed. He poked the door open with the barrel of his shotgun. Empty.

Inside, where the horse had been kept, still reeked faintly of ammonia and manure. Roy stamped back and forth across the dirt floor.

"We should have thought of this before," Hoff said. He, too, started stamping across the floor in a kind of weird dance.

Roy kept stamping, cocking his ear. "Everybody was looking in the house," he said. Then he heard it—an unmistakable hollow clomp. On hands and knees, he cleared away six inches of straw and manure, and there it was: a trapdoor. He reached for the ring in the center of the wooden trap. Gino drew his nine-millimeter. "I'll cover you."

Hoff said, "Afraid I didn't bring a gun." He laughed nervously.

"Never mind," Roy said, handing him the shotgun. Hoff fumbled it, nearly dropping it. "Wait a minute," Roy said, putting a hand on the gun. He flicked on the safety catch. Then he lifted the trapdoor and let it fall open onto the straw. A different smell came out of the dark hole in the floor—rank and musty. He took back the shotgun and shined his light into the hole. The passage dropped vertically for fifteen or twenty feet onto a hard floor. "There's a ladder. I'm going down." Shotgun clamped under his right arm, Roy descended and found himself standing in a mine shaft that sloped down into darkness. On the uphill side it was blocked by a cave-in. "Come on down," he called softly to Hoff and Gino.

Roy's waiting-room dream had begun this way. It came back to him now with the force of déjà vu. In the dream, they moved along dark, hard-rock corridors toward a yellow light deep in the heart of the mountain.

In the dream, the corridors descended, twisting and turning back on themselves. The passage narrowed and cooled as they approached the hollow core, their flashlights streaming ahead of them, dancing off the glitter of walls salted with real gold.

But this was no dream. Without hesitation, Roy descended.

Behind him and connected to him by a thick nylon rope, followed Gino, then Hoff, both wearing bulletproof vests. The floor was clean of rubble for a time, slick with a cold seep from the walls. A slight draft washed their faces and gave them fresh air to breathe. Then it got colder with the perpetual cold of deep rock. They were already drenched from the rain. Roy shivered.

Hoff said, his voice quivering with chill, "Pleasant down here. During the Depression, you know, folks lived in the abandoned mines under Tombstone and Bisbee." He went chattering on nervously. "Whole families, out of the sun. Constant temperature, out of the weather, safe from long John Law."

Roy was not in the mood for a guided tour. He didn't answer. What if he was waiting for them? How come the FBI had left the house unguarded? Where was Billings—prowling around the hills above, or had something happened to him?

Occasionally Roy halted to listen. Once he thought he heard the sound of a voice, another time human breathing, a third time footfalls on gravel. But he came to realize that the peculiar acoustics of the mine were throwing their own sounds back at him from different points of reflection. They were hearing themselves.

It was disorienting. All natural light and air were far behind them, and a quick exit in the shoulder-narrow passage would be impossible. Even turning around would be a tricky maneuver. A cornered man with a gun, hardly aiming, could get them all easily, vests or no vests. Like what happened to Paul.

But it had not ended that way in the dream. In the dream the dark cool shaft at last opened into a bright hollow whose ceiling was a sun-painted vault, a membrane between sunlight and the air of the hollow. Whose walls were mirrors that reflected you, not as you were now, but as you had been years ago, as you would be years from now, as you thought you were but were not, as you might have been or might be, according to what had befallen you, what choices you had made in your life, what you had or had not lived up to.

In those fickle mirrors, Roy saw himself as Paul. He saw himself too as a skinny, clumsy kid with a blank smile and doubt behind the eyes. He saw himself at his parents' funeral, dough-faced and red around the eyes. He saw a boy and an old man and nothing in between.

Now, in this dream of a dream that was realtime, they descended. At each halt Roy waited longer before going on. There seemed to be no end to the tunnel. Hoff, the last in line, played out a string marked at fifty-foot intervals to remind them how far they had gone.

Two hundred feet. Two hundred fifty. Four and a quarter. Six seventy-five. The seep turned the trail underfoot into a constant puddle flowing downhill.

"On my signal," Roy whispered, "everybody turn out your light."

"You're kidding."

"One, two, three," Roy said, and they were immediately plunged into a darkness more absolute than Roy had ever experienced. Darker than closed eyes at night. Dark as the center of a rock. Roy listened to their collective breathing and his own fast heartbeat. This was a place where daylight had never reached. He had hoped for a glimmer of light to guide them, a clue to the end of the passage. But this was not his dream and there was no yellow light luring them on.

All he heard was running water deep in the rock.

Something grabbed his arm. He cried out.

"Relax—it's me," Gino said.

"Jesus, don't do that to me again!"

One by one their flashlights lit the walls, once more throwing human shadows. Roy's heart slowed to normal. He took three deep breaths and led them on, deeper, farther, toward the answer.

He hoped for it. He dreaded it.

In the dream, in the hall of timeless reflection, the murderer lived in a mirror. His face was the face of whoever looked into the mirror, his eyes the flat dead eyes of a painting. The trick in the dream was that, as Roy stood in front of the mirror in which lived the murderer, his back faced a second mirror, so that his image was trapped in an infinite tunnel of regressing mirrors, each reflection farther and farther removed from himself, until he was just a diamond-bright sparkle at the very outer edge of perception. Then he disappeared altogether.

"Hey," Hoff called in a stage whisper. "Look at that. These walls weren't worked by modern drills. Must have been one of the old Spanish mines. One of the Seven Cities of Cíbola."

Roy inspected the rock illuminated by his light, but saw nothing out of the ordinary.

"Trust me," Hoff said. "I've read up on it. This is old diggings." He leaned toward the wall and ran his long fingers across the rock. "Worked with black powder and iron." He rambled on.

Roy couldn't get over how Hoff always had such a ready store of odd facts. He didn't trust people who knew more than they had a right to—such people had an aura of overlapping lives.

"No wonder it wasn't on any map," Gino said. "Are we going to do this or not? My tan is fading fast." His voice was a little higher pitched than normal. Fear, Roy guessed.

Roy led them onward. For a time they climbed slightly, then they descended through ankle-deep water. He could again hear running water.

"Watch out for booby traps," Gino said.

Immediately, Roy stepped into a hole. He floundered, wet to his armpits, for footing. Gino yanked the rope and pulled him out. His flashlight found a long heavy board, which he set in place to bridge the pool. It was a perfect fit, and Roy knew he was on the right track. "He's back in there, I know it," Roy said.

They crossed carefully, one by one.

"Out of string," Hoff called cheerfully. "One thousand feet."

"Fuck it," Roy said. "We're not stopping now." The air was heavy. He had trouble getting his breath.

"Oxygen is thinning out," Hoff said. "Take shallow breaths, you'll be all right."

In another hundred feet they came to a little vault from where three passages led in three distinct directions. "Lights out," Roy said, and they complied. They labored to breathe. This time he saw the merest crack of light down the passage at the far right. A sheen of water glided across the floor like quicksilver.

Roy took a deep breath and heard the coarse breathing of the other men in the dark.

The passage led, steeply, down.

Day Forty-one, Night

Soaked to the skin, Roy shivered constantly now. He fought down panic and claustrophobia. The passage led them down farther, deeper. They followed the water. Lights out, Roy poked the shotgun into the dark hole ahead of him, now lightening with just the promise of lantern glow. Gino followed, gun drawn. Hoff, rope coiled on his shoulder, nudged Gino's back.

Roy stepped carefully through the darkness, completely disoriented. He felt the rock closing in around him. He didn't like it that Billings had disappeared at a crucial moment. And where was Carter, the goddamned FBI? Paul didn't trust him—why should Roy? What was he up to? And Hoff was just like Stein—too infatuated with death. The images, the tools, the bloody results. Behind him, between him and daylight, were two men he hardly knew. Yet his life might depend on them. Ahead of him was probably the murderer. Going farther into that darkness went against every instinct he had, but Eileen was down there. She had to be. And with her, Cindy Callison.

"Watch your step from now on," he whispered back to the others. He said it mostly to make himself feel braver.

Gino said, "Remember, this guy may be waiting for you down below."

Hoff said, "Let's finish it." He was shaking. There was a tremor in his voice.

"Whatever happens—" Roy started to say.

"Whatever happens, happens," Gino said. "This ain't no fucking story."

Roy followed the light. But it was deceptive, dimming or brightening as they turned corner after corner, once seeming to go out altogether. An impossible beacon. Still, it lured him on. Minutes passed, a quarter of an hour, half an hour.

"We're close," Roy said. He couldn't keep the excitement, the fear, out of his voice. "I can feel it. I know we're close." He had to find Eileen. And if he found Eileen, he would also find Cindy Callison.

Gino said, "What do you know? You think you know this guy?"

"Take it easy," Hoff said. "We're all feeling the strain." They were all out of breath. The air was thick and damp and musty— ancient, Roy thought. The water trickled under their feet. They sucked in lungfuls of bad air.

The walls narrowed and the roof dropped until Roy was scuttling along sideways, head and shoulders stooped, back aching and neck stiff from the unnatural stance. He realized that if the passage closed up any more they could not go on—hell, they'd be lucky to be able to go back the way they had come.

Roy felt heavy in his limbs. All the strain, the fatigue, the shock were taking their toll. He wished he were anyplace but here—in this hole a quarter of a mile underground, stalking danger.

They passed a number of side passages. Roy investigated each with his light and shook his head. Not that he was so sure—wouldn't there be false passages, connecting tunnels, decoy shafts, deliberate obstacles in such a maze as this? Other ways in?

But they all saw the bones, planted like mileposts in the rubble. They were on the right track.

Roy was disoriented—north and south meant nothing down here. They were a good half an hour's hike from safety and light, all against gravity. He heard rumbling in the rock, the ticking of seep water into clay-murky puddles. He imagined the weight of the mountain shifting, bearing down on this unshored tunnel. He knew they couldn't go on very much farther. He was nearing the end of his tether, the outer limit of courage, physical stamina, oxygen, and luck. "It can't be much farther," he heard himself telling them.

"Don't be so sure," Gino answered. "When we hit China, you'll know—they'll all be wearing funny hats."

They arrived finally at a blank wall of rock. Roy stopped, fighting off a violent attack of claustrophobia. His wet clothes felt heavy, confining. He took several deep breaths, feeling dizzy, then examined the smooth rock face in front of him, the walls on either side, for a hinge, a crevice, a trick lever, trapped momentarily in the improbable world of tall tales and high-adventure movies. Nothing but solid rock, pitted and pocked from the labor of mining the last narrow vein of precious metal.

He breathed deeply for a few moments, then ordered, "Lights out." The others didn't comply right away. Roy heard sighing and the rasping of feet on wet rock. The passage was so close he could not move among them and flick their switches himself. He repeated the command quietly, and they obeyed.

The air crawled over Roy's clammy skin.

The blackness was perfect. He heard the water, tapping on stone, at a distance. He felt it puddling around his feet. He listened through dead rock.

They turned their lights on with no urging from him. Nobody said anything at first. Then Gino said, "So that's it, end of the line. I told you."

"Not so fast," Roy said. Where, then, had the light been coming from? Had he only imagined it? No, they had all seen it. Where was the light now? Why hadn't it shown from behind them, if indeed they had missed the passage that went deeper, all the way down? Did that particular light travel in only one direction? How could it . . . that was crazy. "Let me climb over you, Gino. Hunker down. Let me by."

"Careful with that scattergun."

"Take it and pass it back. Then I'm coming through." He handed the shotgun to Gino. "We're going to get to the bottom of this, even if it means going back the way we came."

"All right by me," Hoff said, as Roy climbed over their backs.

Gino handed back the shotgun and followed, and they automatically fell into the same order of march, backs hunched. Roy heard their ragged breathing over his shoulder.

"Must have passed it, gone too far," Roy said. He was still feeling dizzy, but it was a relief to be climbing. They would retrace their steps. He couldn't help thinking how Paul would appreciate this: too far was not far enough. To go down they had to first go up.

"All right," Roy said, "We must have passed the real passage somewhere along the line. My guess is not too far back. So from now on, no talking. When we come to a side tunnel, I'll raise the shotgun, like this." He demonstrated. "That means lights out. Follow me." At least he could talk like he knew what he was doing.

It was the third passage back. He could see easily why they'd missed it: the mouth of the tunnel was clogged with broken hunks of petrified timber, and when he shone a light into it the beam bounced right back at him. That was the main deception. The passage veered abruptly sideways—to see its depth he had to actually clamber over the timbers and go inside.

Roy hesitated: should he go in without the light, trusting to the faint glow beyond, or should they march ahead, lights blazing, and warn whoever might be in there they were coming?

Gino said, "What are you waiting for?"

Roy decided. "Lights out. Follow me. Quiet as you can." Sweat oiled his face and neck and hands.

"Maybe somebody ought to stand guard out here, make sure he doesn't trap us in," Gino whispered.

"Right," Hoff agreed. "I was just going to suggest the same thing. I volunteer."

Roy was struck with a moment of cold terror—he hadn't let himself think about what might happen. He could be trapped. Buried alive. No more investigation. The killer would go free. Eileen would turn up like the others, or never turn up at all.

"Better take this," Gino said, handing over his pistol.

Hoff smiled grimly and hefted the gun. "Don't worry, I won't let him get past me." His voice carried an odd note. Just nerves, maybe—or was it something else?

It felt wrong. Roy couldn't put his finger on it. Gino giving away his gun just when he'd need it most? It was like Paul letting Zapata steal a pistol out of his holster. Or Carter and Hobbes leaving the house unguarded. Billings vanishing.

But there was no turning back now. He untied the rope connecting them. "All right, Hoff—you stay. Gino, I'll go in first."

It turned out to be the tightest passage of all. Roy felt his way ahead with the barrel of the shotgun, and before long dropped to hands and knees and crawled.

The floor of the passage was smooth, as if from use, free of debris farther on. The water ran in slow shallow rivulets. The light was unmistakable now. He crawled carefully, praying the tunnel wouldn't close up any more. It remained constant and hardly turned at all now. He listened to the scrape of the shotgun's butt on the rock, the muffled rasp of his pants, his shoes. He made as little noise as possible, and still it was too much.

It was his dream, the descent toward solution. He came out of the tunnel and stood fully upright in a natural stope—a vaulted hollow big as Paul's living room.

Roy saw the source of the light: a ring of kerosene lanterns, only three of them still lit, ranged in a circle around the vault. He flicked on his flashlight and swept it around the circle, and there was the shape of a man. Panicked, he pulled the trigger, but nothing happened—he was too dumbfounded to release the safety.

He got his composure back and realized that the figure he'd tried to shoot was frozen in front of him.

The floor was a flat mirror of water, shallow enough to splash dry with a hard footstep. But it would fill right in again from the inexorable seep.

Roy crept forward into the ring of dying light. "Holy Mother of Christ," he said, and held his light on it. Roy felt now a strange calm, a slow-motion deliberateness to his actions. The danger was past. "Ecce homo," he said to himself—behold the man.

There he was, Roy was sure, the one they had been chasing, in their own active imaginations, across all the pages of confusing paperwork, between the lines of Cindy Callison's red notebook, among all the contradictory clues and evidence, down this twisting, long-abandoned miners' passage.

It must be the murderer.

At the center of the ring of lanterns, he was seated in a crude chair, upright, his face fixed in its death mask. The arms still hugged the torso, clamped firmly in the armpits. But what had killed him?

Roy moved closer. Beside the chair was a mound of ore—fist-sized rocks spangled with pure gold. Roy tucked the shotgun under his arm and picked up a chunk of ore, turned the rough weight in his hand. It was marvelous: he had never seen a lump of rock so rich in gold.

The chamber was strewn with trash—opened soup cans, empty cracker boxes, fast-food wrappers—and empty plastic water jugs. But there were no tools, no guns, no knives. "Hello?" he called into the darkness. "Hello?"

Against the far wall, a heavy shadow stirred: Eileen.

Her hands were cuffed and the handcuffs hung on an iron hook anchored in the rock. Arms raised over her head, she stared and moved her mouth and no words came out. Her eyes were filmy and dull. She was wrapped in an Indian blanket, gagged with a kerchief.

"You're alive!" Roy cried. He laid down the shotgun, and dropped the lump of gold ore in front of her, then knelt close and lifted her off the hook. "Gino!" he called. "Hoff!" But nobody answered. He untied the kerchief from her mouth.

Roy held her wrist in his hand. "Eileen," he said over and over and kissed her. He drew back and looked her in the eyes, searching for recognition. But her eyes were wide with terror. "Gino!" he called again. "Hoff!" But they didn't answer.

Her mouth was working. He leaned his ear close to her cracked lips. "Look out!" she rasped. "Look out!"

He grabbed the shotgun and stood up, half-turning, but too late. A blade slashed across his forearm and he dropped the shotgun. He cried out in pain. The flashlight taped to the barrel went out. An arm clamped across his throat. A shoe kicked the back of his knee, sprawling his legs out in front of him.

The last of the lanterns guttered out.

Roy couldn't get his breath. The blackness was absolute, smothering him. It seemed like a terrible stain seeping into his skin, wicking right into his bones. The arm was clasped across his windpipe. He couldn't even cry out. His ears buzzed and his head spun and he felt like he was being sucked down into the heart of a dizzying darkness. He was dying.

He struggled in the blackness. He had no idea who was at his throat. He had no time to think, only to struggle. He was fighting for his life in a black cave a thousand feet from sunlight with no hope of rescue. He felt only a last thrill of adrenaline spurting across his heart, and wild heedless sense of his body as the only thing between him and death.

Because he'd had a split-second of warning to stand and turn, the death grip wasn't absolute. Still, he couldn't get his balance—all his weight fell on his neck. His legs thrashed about uselessly. The darkness was splashed with stars. His head was going light. He was blacking out, and he knew the next sensation—the last he'd ever know— would be the quick burn of the knife blade gliding across his throat.

He would remain alive and half-conscious while the hand with the knife sawed his head clean off.

He felt the hot breath in his ear.

Eileen searched the floor in front of her for a weapon. Her hands found the lump of gold ore. She got to her feet, arms groping in front. She felt Roy's shoulder, felt the arm around his throat. Heard labored breathing from the man behind.

Roy heard a dull thump as she swung the lump of gold up behind his head, toward the breathing, and connected with bone. His assailant cried out and lost his grip and Roy spun around to face him in the dark, sucking in a long, painful breath.

He heard him fall and splash. He fell on top of him, hands around his throat. In the dark, Roy smashed the head against the rock floor till the neck went loose.

He sat down hard on the wet floor, fighting a blackout. His lungs and throat burned and his head was roaring. His arm was going numb. A ray of light cut the darkness and turned his arm bright red. Hoff's flashlight. Hoff stood in the doorway to the chamber, shining it on the floor. Roy crawled toward the body and the light followed, reflecting off the silver floor. Still handcuffed, Eileen clutched his hand and would not let go.

"Gino," he said. "Jesus Christ, Gino!" There before him in a red pool lay Gino, his head bashed in.

"Got too creepy waiting—what the hell?" Hoff played his light into Roy's face. He splashed into the chamber and knelt over Gino, fingering his carotid artery. "Christ! He's dead! You broke his fucking skull!"

In the thinning air, Roy heaved. "He's . . . he's the one," he blurted out.

Hoff picked up the knife and hefted it in his palm and Roy felt the thrill of terror all over again, but he was too weak to fight anymore. "Hoff!"

Hoff turned the blade in the flashlight, then tossed it away. "Take it easy," he said, as if dazed. "Sweet Jesus."

"Come here . . . with that light." Hoff obeyed. Roy's bad arm was numb from the shoulder down. Eileen held on tight. The blanket had fallen away and she was wearing nothing but panties. Roy carefully tucked the blanket around her. "Get the . . . key."

Gingerly, Hoff searched Gino's pockets until he came up with a handcuff key. He freed Eileen's hands and she immediately flung them around Roy's neck.

"My God," Hoff said. "Better get her out quick. She's pretty far gone."

"Eileen," Roy said gently, stroking her matted hair. "Where's Cindy? Do you know where Cindy is?"

Eileen shook her head. Hoff played his light around the chamber, but there was no sign of Cindy Callison. Just the sheen of rising water on the floor of the cavern.

"What happened to Cindy? Where is she?"

Eileen clutched Roy and shook her head. "Don't know," she said, her voice raspy. "Never saw her."

"We'd better get her out of here," Hoff said. "Fast." Hoff helped Roy to his feet in the circle of dead lanterns and they faced the thing in the chair. "And what do we do about him, whoever he is?"

Roy's arm was now a lump of pain, bleeding freely. "Fuck him."

Hoff tore a strip out of his own shirt and wrapped it around Roy's bloody arm. "That'll have to do," he said. Hoff turned his attention back to the dead man in the chair. He aimed the flashlight into the face and stared. "Who the hell are you?" he wondered out loud.

Roy found Gino's flashlight on the floor and flicked the switch. It worked. He held on tight to Eileen, whispering encouragement. Without the lanterns to guide them, they never would have found this place. Roy counted the lanterns—fifteen in all. She would have remained buried alive. All the days they'd waited, and another few minutes would have been too late. The lanterns would have gone out. There would have been no light to give the place away.

"She's about to pass out," Roy said. "Give me a hand." Roy wasn't even sure he could carry himself back up against all that gravity. Breathing came hard. His head wasn't clear. His ears buzzed. He stumbled, trying to get his balance and his bearings. The water splashed around his ankles.

Hoff said, "What about Gino? What about the other guy?" He sounded confused. "I need proof, something," Hoff insisted. "For Paul. An autopsy—"

"We've got the living to care for." Roy grabbed Hoff's arm. "Come on. We're running out of time. We'll send somebody back for them."

Roy saw the lump of gold ore in the puddle. With some difficulty, he picked it up and stuffed it into his jacket pocket. He left the shotgun behind and held the flashlight.

The hands-and-knees passage would take them back up to light and air. It would be as fast an ascent as they could make it. Roy shone his light once more at the wall above the seated dead man and the beam bounced back at him, reflected by the gold and silver in the rock. The wet floor held the glitter of gold.

The water was louder, deeper, rising.

"Come on now." Hoff led. Eileen crawled out after him. On hands and knees, bearing his gold, Roy left the dark chamber.

As they struggled up the main passage, Eileen propped between them, they were blinded by an explosion of light. Hoff dropped her arm and reached for the pistol.

"Take it easy!" a voice called down.

"Stein? Jesus Christ!" Hoff said.

Stein and Billings came down the tunnel toward them carrying flashlights. Stein had his flash camera looped around his neck.

"Heard somebody coming," Billings explained. "Went to check it out. It was only this joker."

"Couldn't pass up the chance," Stein said. "Here, let me give you a hand."

"Gently, gently," Roy said.

Day Fifty-one

A murder story ends when the killer is caught, brought to some kind of justice.

But people live on, each of them a story. By the time the murder story is finished, too many other stories have started. The characters hanging on to the edge of the story have been drawn to its center, and it's their turn now, one by one in the flickering light of the story lamp. Son et lumière, frame after bright frame, their faces etched in light and shadow, the frames reeling across before the flame, their faces and hands more shadow than light, fading off into the dark border of memory that is all the rest of the stories.

So the murderer is caught, and the story goes on, for a little while, without him.

A week after going into the mine, Roy sought out Esmeralda and found her at the Montezuma Hotel on the edge of the barrio in town. "Come back to Paul's place," he told her, as he stood on gritty linoleum in the blank hallway, dim as a cave even at midday, lit by a single forty-watt bulb.

"There is no going back from some things in this life," she said, refusing to meet his eye.

He took her gently by the shoulders. "Not for me—for Paul."

She hesitated, standing in the doorway, not leaning on the finger-soiled jamb. He watched her breathe and then lift her head, nodding. *"Bueno."*

They loaded her bags and kids in the Jeep and he delivered them to the trailer, then gave her a wad of clean twenties he had gotten from the autoteller on the way to find her. "Keep the pantry full," he said. "Yours and Paul's. Let me know when you need more."

She lingered at the door of her trailer.

"Go on in," he said. "It's a mess, and somebody has to clean it up."

She nodded and herded her kids through the door. Roy listened for the clatter of the swamp cooler starting up, then got back in his Jeep and drove to the hospital to meet Eileen. She'd been drugged, dehydrated, and scared out of her mind. She was suffering from exposure, cuts and bruises, and a bad cold.

But the killer hadn't done anything worse to her. He hadn't had time. He had bundled her into the trunk of Paul's Thunderbird and left her there, unconscious, for several hours. Then he had dragged her down into the tunnel and handcuffed her. He was too busy maintaining his identity aboveground even to visit her until he showed up with Roy.

The last mystery remained unsolved: what had he done with Cindy Callison? Roy accepted that she was dead. That was a certainty now. Her body would probably never be found—the only person who could have told them where it was hidden was dead and buried deep under rock. There were no more clues to be had. All alone at his apartment, Roy cried for her. He felt no relief in knowing she was dead—but grief did bring clarity. If Cindy was dead, then her pain was over. There was no justice in that fact, but there was some small peace.

A whole week of rest, a tetanus shot, and nutritious food gave Eileen back her color and vitality. Today she was being discharged. On the way out, they stopped in Paul's room.

They stood over Paul's bed, holding hands, Roy cautious of getting too close to Paul for fear of yanking out the tubes from his arms or otherwise disturbing the wires and monitors. Paul's chest was girded by a thick white dressing out of which ran the clear plastic tube that drained the wound. The blood trickled through the long thin tube in murky bubbles, slowly.

All the gadgetry of medicine kept him at arm's length from Paul.

Don't die in here, he found himself praying: Let him at least die outdoors. It had been touch and go all week. And he wasn't in terrific shape to be fighting it. "His lungs are a mess," the surgeon had confided. "All that smoking." He had been fighting off pneumonia and internal hemorrhage. It was a hard fight.

When Paul spoke, it was a relief. "Somebody's sitting on my chest."

Eileen rang for a nurse.

"Relax," Roy said. He let go of Eileen's hand, then drew closer to the bed. "How you doing?"

"I'm all shot up, that's how I'm doing. Kind of question is that."

The nurse arrived and without a word checked the tubes, changed the stoppered bottle at the end of the drain tube, and took Paul's temperature with an instrument she inserted briefly into his ear. She then scrubbed off a spot on his arm and injected a painkiller. "This will make you feel dopey,"

"Already dopey. Wasn't dopey, I wouldn't be here."

The nurse shook her head and left them alone with the machines.

"I'm doing better, that's the truth, but I don't want them slacking off."

"Glad to hear it, Paul." Eileen leaned over and bussed him loudly on the cheek.

His eyes brimmed with tears. He held her hand. "I'm glad, how it turned out," he said.

"I know," she said. She patted his hand.

"Your arm okay?" he said to Roy.

"Yeah, not bad." Twenty stitches, a bandage. Didn't even need a sling.

"Always wondered," Paul started to say and then faltered, and Roy could tell the drug was kicking in. "Wondered, you know. What it felt like, to be shot."

"Well, you got yourself blasted, all right," Roy said, trying to sound careless. "Barely missed the heart. You won't be breathing so good for a while."

"Hurts like a sonafabitch, you know. That's all it feels like." Roy could read the fear on Paul's pale face, in his tight smile, the narrowed eyes, the tense white lines around his mouth. "Worse thing is, they won't let me smoke."

On the way back to their apartment, as the car idled at the stoplight, the air conditioner spilling cold air into their faces, Eileen started crying. She made no attempt to dry her eyes and kept looking straight ahead. "I don't want him to die," she said.

"Shh. He's not going to die. Shh."

He put the car into gear on the green light, drove half a block, and pulled into the parking lot of a church. He left the motor running and the air on high.

Roy slid his arm around her shoulder.

"It's okay. I'm all right."

"We'll get through this. Paul's going to make it."

"No, he's not—didn't you see his eyes? Didn't you see how small he's gotten? He's just fading away."

Roy had noticed. "Don't fret. He's a fighter."

"But there's something wrong, besides the bullet wound. There's something wrong inside."

Roy petted her hair. He listened to the motor and stared at the dashboard gauges stupidly. He didn't want to go anywhere. "Come here," he said. He kissed Eileen softly on the mouth. He was tentative. He wasn't sure she was ready to be kissed. But she let the kiss linger. She started to cry again as they kissed, and the tears made her seem even more desirable. His tongue licked salt from her lips, and his right hand reached across and held her breast carefully, which caused her to quiver and deepen her kiss. "Oh, Roy," she said, "I want you to make love to me."

"Soon," he said, "soon."

"Don't ever leave me."

"Never."

"It was so horrible."

"It's over now," he said. "You're safe now." Now he, too, was crying. When they kissed again, their tears were in the kiss. They sat, holding each other. Roy stared at the temperature gauge steadily rising and listened to the hush of air pouring out of the plastic vents.

"Forgive me," he whispered into her ear, over and over again, kissing her eyes and mouth and neck and ears, tasting her salt.

"Don't ever leave me," she said, "not ever. Promise me."

"I promise," he said, "I promise. Shh, now. Shh."

"Not ever, no matter what."

"Not ever. No matter what."

A sudden thundershower poured down outside and lasted only minutes. The rain drummed on the roof and hood and quick rivulets streaked down the dusty windshield and left the asphalt of the parking lot and the boulevard shiny. Inside the car, the air was cool and wet and smelled of ozone. She stroked his hand with a silky touch.

After the cloudburst had passed, Roy drove them to the apartment and they made love in the living room. There was something sublime and innocent about their lovemaking, but Roy could not have put it into words. He didn't care about putting it into words. Lying on the thick white carpet afterward and drying their perspiration with a white towel, he was in a mild state of wonder.

Eileen said, "I want Paul to know us, the way we are now."

"We'll go back to see him later."

They snuggled on the rug, cooled by the humming air conditioner. As she slept, he held her in his arms, listening to her breathe.

Three days later, Roy was sitting in his office at the university with the door half-closed, working on his book. There was a tentative knocking. "Come in," he said, not bothering to look up.

"I didn't know if you'd be here," she said.

The voice startled him. He raised his eyes and stared. "My Lord," he said, half-standing. He dropped his pen and banged his knee on the underside of his desk. "You?"

In front of him, looking rested and fit, stood Cindy Callison.

"Sorry to shock you," she said, taking a seat. He leaned on his desk and stared at her, to be sure. There was no mistake. "I came as soon as I heard."

"But we thought—"

She settled into the chair and half-smiled. She clasped her hands tightly in front of her, as if she didn't know what to do with them. "I know what you thought. I saw the news—please, I'm sorry if I made you worry."

"Worry?" he said softly, sitting down. "Worry! My God, we thought you were dead. We thought—" He was getting choked up. He cleared his throat. His ears were buzzing so that he could hardly hear her when she spoke again.

She spoke quietly, her eyes looking away, slantwise, toward the ceiling. "I just got fed up, Professor Roy. I just split. You know?"

He nodded. He didn't have himself under control enough to answer.

"That last day in seminar, that Edgar Allan Poe story we were talking about—the one where the guy just walks away from his life?"

Roy kept nodding, dumbly.

"I made up my mind. I'd had enough of that place. I was tired of being ogled, tired of the creeps and the late hours and taking crap from everybody. Then I went outside and the car wouldn't start, that was the last straw. I walked away from my old life." She smiled and shook her head, as if she herself could not quite believe it.

"You walked away?" If he talked slowly, softly, he could keep his voice under control. "But your clothes—we found your clothes."

Cindy Callison cast her eyes to the ceiling again, the way she used to do when answering a hard question in class, then put a hand to her mouth. "I was feeling crazy that afternoon. I had two weeks' worth of tips stashed in my purse. I was going to stop at the bank to deposit it, but I didn't. Instead, I walked to the Greyhound station and got on a bus for L.A. Didn't even buy a ticket, just got on the bus. They never even checked."

"Why Los Angeles?"

She shrugged and tossed her hair out of her eyes. "Who knows. It was either east or west. I'd never been west. The bus was already full, getting ready to pull out. The driver was in the men's room or something. Then he came out, hopped into the driver's seat, and we pulled out. And I just thought, you know, here we go." She smiled again in that slightly embarrassed way she had. "I guess I expected they would throw me off. But since they didn't, well, I figured it was fate. Like I was meant to be on that bus. Like there was no turning back."

He was still getting used to the miracle of her being there, alive, in his office. He was ready to accept any logic she offered—almost. "But the clothes." Two changes of clothes, he thought: the cowgirl outfit the dead girl on the tracks was wearing, and the street clothes that were floating in the lake.

"Look, I wanted to escape from myself. From who I was. You probably can't understand that. But I was tired of being me—even in my working costume. Especially in that costume."

"It's all right," he said. "We all feel that way from time to time."

"You're just saying that."

"No, it's true. Believe me."

She nodded and went on with her story. "When I walked into the terminal, there was a girl getting off another bus, she looked pretty lost. I just gave her all my stuff. Then I gave her twenty bucks to trade clothes with me. We changed in the ladies' room. I rode to L.A. wearing a pair of ratty jeans and a Grateful Dead T-shirt."

"Just like that? You traded clothes?"

She shrugged, somewhat defensively. "Girls are always trying on each other's clothes. It's not a guy thing, I know, and usually it's just with friends. It felt a little weird, but it was also sort of thrilling. It made me feel, I don't know—dangerous. Incognito. I told you. I wanted to be somebody else."

Roy steepled his hands on his desktop. He was getting used to her again. He loved hearing her voice. It had a husky resonance to it. He stared at her, afraid that if he took his eyes off her even for a second she would vanish.

Cindy's eyes were tearing. She said, almost in a whisper. "I didn't know it would turn out that way for her."

"Hey, hey," Roy said. "Nobody could know a thing like that. You had nothing to do with it."

"Like I said," Cindy continued, dabbing at her eyes with a hanky, "I was in a crazy mood. I'd never done anything like that before."

"But my note."

"What note?"

"The one I wrote on your term paper—"

She put away the hanky and smiled, her eyes looking everywhere but at him. "Oh, I threw that paper away before I left the building. Never even looked at it. Just didn't seem you know, relevant anymore. You wrote me a note?"

"Never mind." Roy sighed, feeling small. "But all this time—it was all over the news."

"Well, it was all crazy," she said, leaning forward. He couldn't get over it that she was alive. "I get to L.A., where I know exactly nobody. I'm already starting to have second thoughts. I'm drinking coffee at this little place across from the bus station, and this guy comes in. A real-life Hollywood producer."

"That still doesn't explain—"

She leaned all the way across his desk now and took his hand. "Now don't get the wrong idea. He took me to Maui. You know— Hawaii? His ranch. I didn't come up for air until a few days ago. Just tuned out the world."

Maui. "So now you're back." He envisioned torrid romance, champagne in bed, servants, cocaine, gold jewelry. He was surprised—he actually felt jealous. And disappointed in her. He couldn't keep it out of his voice.

"Hey," she said, leaning toward him in her chair. Now she was looking him right in the eye. "Now listen to me: It was this really nice guy. He was a producer, that's true. But he also has a wife. They're happily married. They rescued me."

"They what?"

She didn't take her eyes off him. "Rescued me. We got to talking, and we hit it off. Next thing I know, I've got a place to hide out for a while. They always wanted a daughter, they said. They went back to L.A. after a couple of days and left me to house-sit the place."

"And tune out."

"It's what I needed. Sanctuary." She paused. "Don't you ever need that?"

Roy sat back in his chair and smiled. "Yes, we all need that from time to time." He was genuinely glad she'd found it. He was still smiling across the desk at her, but he realized his eyes were brimming with tears. "I'm so glad," he said. "So glad."

"Hey, don't," she said. "It's all right. It turned out okay."

He just nodded, too full to speak.

She brightened. "You going to finish your book now?"

He shrugged. "Who knows? I'm not much of a scholar. Not much of a teacher, for that matter."

She took his hand, the way she had done that other time. But now she only squeezed it. "Never think that."

"Thanks."

For half a minute they just sat in his office, not talking. Then Cindy let go of his hand and stood up. "I just came back to get some of my stuff. He's going to put me in a TV movie."

"I'm happy for you."

She said, "I'm sorry about everything. Those other girls. And your wife—"

"She's fine now. Wasn't your fault." Cindy didn't mention the boyfriend, Loomis, and Roy didn't bring it up. Anyway, it wasn't clear who had killed the poor guy. Maybe she didn't even know about that.

She hesitated, then said, "Sorry we never got to, you know."

"Oh, that. Yeah."

"I'd better go." She started out the door, then turned. "I only wish—"

"What?"

She smiled and put a hand to her mouth. "I used to write things about you in my notebook. I only wish you could have read it. But I lost it."

In the shock of seeing her, Roy had forgotten. Now he opened his top drawer and slid the red notebook out. The pages he had torn out were paperclipped to the inside cover. The cops had no more need for it. "Here," he said, trying to sound flip. "I've been holding on to this for you."

"Hey," she said, moving around behind his desk. She dabbed at his eyes with a handkerchief and took the notebook. "A good man is hard to find," she said. She hugged him hard and kissed him quickly on the cheek. Then she was gone.

Epilogue

The summer was over, and the sun was weakening its hold on the valley just enough to allow a deep breath and a brisk walk in early morning or at dusk. In this place the sun would never be low unless rising or setting, but it would be low enough to cast long shadows out from Paul's house and the air would cool quickly after dark.

The seasons changed subtly and the colors sharpened, but only a little and only at the right time of day. It was that time now. On the veranda facing the White Tanks sat Roy, Hoff, Esmeralda, Eileen, Jane, and Paul. Briefly, Roy and Hoff had been celebrities. The story made network TV and Roy had even been approached by an agent about doing a book. The agent didn't want his book on happy endings, though. He wanted the story of what went on down in that mine. Roy said he'd think about it.

Paul slumped heavily in a wheelchair. He coughed too much and with either hand could make only a weak fist. His eyes played tricks on him, he said, and he ate little and drank no liquor. For weeks now every afternoon he had come out here on the veranda to watch the sunset, one-eyed Zack sprawling at his feet.

"Christ, look at the two of us now," he said to no one in particular. He drank soda water but insisted the others drink all the liquor they wanted. "Drink up," he ordered. "I'm the one that got shot." Roy was drinking soda water, too, but Paul didn't seem to notice.

The sun was just hanging on the tip of the highest peak. Blue-and-gray shadows slanted toward them off the foothills, following the creases of arroyos and dry washes vertically down the bald high rock.

The air was clean, the light crisp. Roy watched the shadows come for the house and wanted this time to last as long as it could.

"I remember," Paul said, "first time I laid eyes on this damn place. January, cold as a well-digger's ass, wind howling along the flat full of that high-mountain cold. You get maybe five days a year like that— skin of frost on the windshield in the morning, your breath coming out in clouds. Saw four mule deer that day. Nine coyotes. Christ." He swigged from his glass. "This soda water shit is for the birds."

Paul was alive. Eileen was alive. Cindy Callison had gotten clean away. That counted for everything.

"At least we know where he got his money," Hoff said. "Gold, the real McCoy. Nuggets big as your fist."

"Maybe," Paul said. "But if he did no assayer in the county ever saw it. Must have pushed it through one of those crooked dealers downtown. Hot gold, wouldn't be the first time."

Roy still had his chunk of ore. "It was gold, all right."

Paul snorted and belched. "Glad you think so. I guess our man knew the ins and outs of the underworld. Hell, I taught him."

"How could you ever have known?" Roy said.

"My job to know," Paul said. "All that time, from the flower girls on, I'm a hell of a detective."

Hoff said, "Wish I could have had him on the slab. Love to have had a look at his brain. If only the FBI had gotten down there faster."

Carter and Hobbes had been off chasing Zapata in Nogales, where he'd been spotted crossing the border. By the time they returned and led a team down into the mine, the lower shaft was flooded, and the water kept rising with the monsoon. So Gino was still down there in the ring of dead lanterns. And so was the man he'd killed.

Floating on painkillers after the surgeon had stitched up his arm, Roy had wondered for days afterward whether it had happened at all. But then he would close his eyes and recall that sinewy arm across his throat, the burn of the blade in his arm. The weak lantern light that had led them to it.

"Why fifteen lanterns?" Eileen said. "Why not ten, or eight, or an even dozen?"

"You got me," Roy said. "Numerology, who knows."

"Maybe that was all the lanterns he had," Paul said.

"What gets me," Jane said, "is that we still don't know who he was, where he came from, why he did what he did."

"It was Gino," Roy said. "Leave it at that."

"But who was he?" Jane insisted. "Who the hell was he? That's the thing."

Hoff said, "I had an inkling. Remember, Roy, what I said about fingerprints? Paul and I had talked about that before Zapata—well before."

Paul said, "I told him about Gino leaning on the freezer. Yet there was only one set of prints on it—Gino's. Didn't give it a thought at the time. Prints don't always take."

Hoff said, "I pulled his prints out of the computer. Cross-matched them. Found something pretty odd."

Paul said, "Every cop gets fingerprinted when he's hired—routine. The prints they had on file for him in New Jersey were different from the ones in his departmental jacket out here."

Roy was astonished. "Nobody noticed?"

Paul shrugged. "Two different files, two different drawers, two different offices. We only went to computers last March."

"Why the hell didn't you tell me before we went down there?"

"Didn't prove anything. Could have been a routine foul-up."

Paul said, "I worked with the man for years, trusted him with my life."

Eileen said, "So he wasn't Gino at all."

"No, sweetie, he purely wasn't," Paul said. "An impostor all along, right from the get-go. He resembled the real Gino, enough to pass. He didn't have any family. Who'd ever know?"

Roy put it all together out loud: "So the real Gino is the other one buried in that cave. And the other guy, our desert killer, we don't know who in the hell he really was."

Paul added, "The odds are we'll never know."

Hoff nodded. "We think we know so much about this world."

"All that time," Paul said, still not quite believing it. "All that time. Right next to me. Right in my car. And at night he was going home to . . . that." Paul looked more lost than ever.

"How did he pick them?" Roy asked. "Why Eileen?"

Jane said, "The obsession is irrational. He saw her once and fixated on her. Something about her body type, or the way she held her head, or the sound of her voice triggered a reaction. Some kind of psychic template."

Hoff said, "What gets me is the Callison girl. Maui, Christ. Who'd have thought."

Paul said, "Yeah, we went wrong there. We assumed too much. Assumed she was connected. We should have gone by the facts—her clothes were connected."

"It was a reasonable mistake," Roy said. He still couldn't quite believe that, for some of them at least, this thing had had a happy ending. "She vanished."

"Maui," Hoff said, like he couldn't get over it.

Paul said, "The whole time we're looking for her, and she's not even part of the story."

Jane said, "But without her, Roy would never have been involved. Or Eileen."

Paul said, "We also might never have found the bottom of that mine."

"So who was he, really?" Eileen said.

Paul sighed, swiped a hand across his face. "Some poor damned lost soul."

"An impostor," Hoff said. "An absolute impostor. A man who didn't belong anywhere."

"A stranger comes to town," Roy said.

Paul added, "A certain kind of town—a place of ungodly heat and light, the Western frontier."

"A creature incapable of choice as we know it," Jane said. "Free will didn't operate as it should have. In simple terms, he was a moral idiot. He quite literally did not know right from wrong."

Eileen said, "You're saying he's not responsible—"

"He was all things to all people, nothing to himself," Jane said. "In his most private moments, it's fair to wonder if his mind actually operated at all—did he even have an interior life? Did he have what we so glibly define as a 'personality'? Or did he instead experience a sort of dial tone? Seems like he was a receiver, not a transmitter. He took in everything."

"The videos," Roy said. "You say nothing went on inside his head?"

"Don't you wonder? Christ, I do. Look—the brain learns. Physiologically. Repeated experience literally scores the tissue, mapping out responses. All that cinematic beating, slashing, shooting, stabbing."

"Movies didn't make him do what he did," Roy said. Zack stretched and then curled up at his feet.

"Listen: What would it be like to live in a world for which you had no clue?"

There was still light left in the sky. Roy listened, but the noises weren't coming up yet. No coyotes, no crickets or nightbirds. There were bobwhite quail downwind in the arroyo, though, their whistling muted by the dying breeze.

"He read books but didn't understand them. He was nearly a genius for memory and following instructions, but he had no judgment. None. That's the main point to keep in mind."

Hoff said, "If he was reading a book on human anatomy, then why not go out and hack open a body, compare it to the drawings? There's the spleen, all right. Look how easily the heart pops out, once we sever that aorta. Subcutaneous lesions, all right, looky there!"

Jane said, "He was an autodidact."

Roy said, "So was Abraham Lincoln. So were half the geniuses of Western civilization."

"But he had no judgment, and that's the difference," Jane insisted. "He was just taking in all this, this *stuff*—and it was all the same to him. He was bombarded with words, pictures, sensory impressions, all in a jumble. Nothing was better or worse, only different.

There was no right or wrong for him. For a mind like that, books are dangerous."

Roy thought of Cindy Callison's notebook.

"People used to believe that magic words could heal and kill. Many still believe it."

The desert sounds were coming up now. The first tentative coyote barked in the hills out west, calling to his mates. Things skittered among the creosote. An owl materialized in the branches of the sweet acacia down by the trailer. A javelina clacked its fangs in the arroyo, its several young chuffing along behind.

"For all the Gandhis who correctly read Thoreau, there are a hundred Hitlers who misread Nietszche."

"What about all the weapons? The other stuff? Knives, guns, costumes."

"Props. He projected himself into new roles every day."

"Surely he found right and wrong in some of those movies," Eileen said very quietly. "Surely in those books."

"How would he know? How do you extract a coherent ethical system from *Birth of a Nation*, *Taxi Driver*, *Ilsa, She-Wolf of the SS*, and *The Faces of Death*? Or from *Mein Kampf*, Plato's *Republic*, and *Dead Souls*. The great minds of our age can't do it."

Hoff said, "So his house was a blueprint of his mind. His library was a monstrosity."

Roy said, "When did he start the killing, and why?"

"Probably very early on. Somebody wandered by—lost. What was on his mind? Who knows. But he wanted to try out his new pistol on a human target—bang, bang."

Hoff said, "But in the end we got him—don't forget that. We read the clues and nailed the sonafabitch, just like we're supposed to. Just like we get paid for."

Paul sighed and looked out on the desert. "Took us long enough."

"Look," Hoff said, "what we've got here is a real-life monster. Frankenstein. The pure, perfect tabula rasa. Hitler in his head, B-westerns in his hands, Halloween in his heart."

"What did he want?" Roy asked softly. "That's what I'd like to know."

"Who was he?" Paul asked. "Can anybody tell me that?"

Down in the mine, Roy had seen the face of the man he had killed, livid in the glare of the flashlight. Now, in the wash of dusky shadow, the bleed of color off the mountains as the sun broke on the jagged edge of those corrugated iron peaks, Roy was sure he had recognized him.

He was a doomed Swede coming out of the blizzard to the company and light of the Blue Hotel.

He was Miss Emily Grierson feeding rat poison to her fickle lover, then sleeping beside him for forty years, a monstrosity in crinoline and lace.

He was the loser of the lottery, stoned to sainthood by well-meaning neighbors in the village square to assure, for another hard year, their own lives. And he was also the child who cast the first stone.

He was the Misfit on the road to Florida, the bad man who was not so hard to find.

He was Hawthorne's devil, bargaining for pure souls.

He was a very old man with enormous wings, a miracle gone awry, out of his time and place, if he had ever had a time and place outside of the skewed stories that were his mind.

He was the dark presence that had lain just beyond the ken of philosophers and priests and always would, because, Roy knew, things happen in this world. Not all the sums come out even. He was a remainder, a statistical error, a metaphysical conundrum. There was no accounting for him, exactly, and yet there was.

Down in the blackness, Roy had crushed his skull onto the rock.

Roy could not shake the eerie sense that all of them, together, had built him—not deliberately, but innocently, as a kind of byproduct of all their worst human instincts, all the dangerous ingredients of their culture. When it reached critical mass in a remote place, this monster was what came to life. Were they already building more like him somewhere, out in those burning desert hills, in all the hollow places where the light never reached?

Did he really mine pure gold out there?

Jane rose and walked to the edge of the veranda, where she stood, head cocked, silhouetted in the soft light.

"We don't know much in this life, not really," Paul said, staring out toward the pink mountains. Roy could tell he was brooding about something. Linda?

"The radio," Hoff said. "The goddamned radio. Who the hell was he talking to?"

Roy said, "It's a remarkable story. I'm not sure I believe it myself. And I was there."

Paul said, as if to someone not present. "How could I have been so close, every day, and never known what was in his heart?"

Roy addressed Paul. "So, did we solve it?"

Paul kept staring off into the dusk. He made a noise in his throat and chest. "Take a walk with me," he said.

"You're sure—"

Paul was already rising, with effort, and walking stiffly toward the edge of the veranda, leaning on a cane. Zack wheezed through his nose and didn't stop even when Paul reached down to pet his muzzle. Roy walked beside Paul but made no attempt to steady him. He didn't look as if he wanted any help.

They walked out into the blue shadows and Paul seemed to re-lax, though he didn't speak for several minutes. Roy heard his ragged breathing, and felt a knot forming on the back of his own tongue. In the late sunlight, fading to color, Paul looked to him diminished and frail, wobbling on atrophied legs. The muscles of his arms hung loose out of his shirt sleeves, round and soft, limp on the bone, as if someone had stuffed two small eggs under his pale skin.

His shoulders no longer rode high and straight. Roy understood at that moment that some strength, once lost, is simply irrecoverable.

"This is a man's place," Paul said, still looking off at the moun-tains. "Always has been."

They stood, Roy facing Paul's back. Paul straightened for a mo-ment and Roy glimpsed what Paul had been. He remembered the light glancing off the spangled rock in the dead man's chamber.

"Grief is a love story that's never quite finished. Some poet wrote that."

"Paul—"

"I'm going to tell you something, though I shouldn't. But it matters less than it once did. Some promises, I guess, like some men, just run out." He coughed dryly. "Has to do with your mother. With the end of that Mexican yarn."

"Go on."

"I won't spin it out. Haven't you figured it out by now? You're no orphan—never were."

"But how—"

"I already told you how I paid a debt to your old man. Now I've told you why. I think it should end here."

Roy watched Paul and took it all in, surprised he had lost the capacity for shock. "Just one thing. Did he know?"

"I knew your mother only briefly. Maybe, maybe not. It never came up between us. But who can say what's on someone's mind?"

What did it really matter now?

"I probably did wrong to tell you."

"No, don't think that," Roy said. "I just need a little time." Paul sounded so tired. "Are you all right? You're not bleeding again?"

Paul sighed long. "You're a good boy. Go on back and leave me be. I need time on my own."

Roy nodded and watched Paul's back. He looked all used up. Roy wanted to see his face, but could not bring himself to walk in front of him. "One of these days we'll ride out there on two good roans, just you wait."

"Thata boy," Paul said in a low calm voice. "You go finish your drink."

At full dusk when Roy went back for Paul, he found him lying face up to the new stars, hands straight by his sides, placid face already cooling in the sweet desert air.

About the Author

Philip Gerard holds an M.F.A. from the University of Arizona. A former newspaperman and free-lance journalist, he has published fiction and nonfiction in numerous magazines. His radio essays have been heard on National Public Radio's "All Things Considered." He is the author of two novels, *Hatteras Light* and *Cape Fear Rising*, and *Brilliant Passage . . . A Schooning Memoir*. He directs the professional and creative writing program at the University of North Carolina at Wilmington, where he lives with his wife, Kathleen Johnson.